Books by Robert Scott

Fiction
Mobile Home Heaven:
Trailer Court Hell (2003)

Guardabarranco (2009)

Poetry
Cyclops (2005)

Fiction and Poetry
A Scarlet Thread (2010)

Photo Essay
Los Perros del Pueblo (2008)

A SCARLET THREAD

ROBERT SCOTT

Anabasis Press
2010

Library of Congress Cataloging-In-Publication Data
Robert Scott
A Scarlet Thread: stories and poems of Robert Scott
ISBN 1-930259-52-2

Published by Anabasis Press
Oysterville, WA 98641-0216

This book is dedicated to the memory of
THOMAS LOWE TAYLOR,
publisher, editor, poet and friend. He was there
when I wasn't. He spoke up when I couldn't. He
was my brother.

Special thanks to **Mami Nomura** for help with
layout.

Graphic arts by **Cristina Martinez**

CONTENTS

Fiction

Things You'll Need to Save 1
Escalon 16
Hallows' Eve 33
Eighty Jaguars 46
Doing It Right 67
Silent Screen 75
Storage 89
Reservations at a Small Café 103
Sisters 115
A Scarlet Thread 130
A Nice View 147

Short Shorts

Hot Water 160
Red Red Lips 162
The Mail 164
Boys on the Side 166
Tow Job 167
A Wide Flat Pit 168
Christmas Choir 169

Mobile Home Heaven (concluded)

A Rush to Arrive 172
I'm Your Daughter 173
The Postwoman Always Thinks Twice 192
No Persons Under Fifty Five Allowed 194
Walking the Dog 204
Close of Escrow 205

<u>Poems</u>

Fall 223
Payphone 224
There's a Bomb in Starbucks 226
Zach 228
Cat in the Rain 229
Germany 1946 230
Two Women in a Bar 231
Sunday Drag Race 232
Blue Velvet 234
Expectation 235
Gunpowder 237
Leon Heads West 238
El Pilar 240
Forty Miles of Bad Road 241
Homeless 243
Photographs 1906 244

There is an old story of how the cathedral of Chartres was struck by lightening and burned to the ground. Then thousands of people came from all points of the compass, like a giant procession of ants, and together they began to rebuild the cathedral...I want to be one of the artists in the cathedral on the great plain. I want to make a dragon's head, an angel, a devil—or perhaps a saint—out of stone. Regardless of whether I believe or not, whether I am a Christian or not, I would play my part in the collective building of the cathedral.

(Work) for me begins with something vague—a chance remark or a bit of conversation… a few bars of music, a shaft of light across the street. Most of all it is a brightly colored thread sticking out of the dark sack of the unconscious…I begin to wind up this thread, and do it carefully.

Ingmar Bergman, Introduction to <u>Four Screenplays of Ingmar Bergman</u>, Simon and Shuster, 1960

A SCARLET THREAD

THINGS YOU'LL NEED TO SAVE

Everybody's saying it, I guess. Old Tom McCaw hasn't drilled a water well in years. But I got news for them, it ain't true at all. Drilled one a little over six weeks ago. Helped Bernie on it, anyway. But you can't do much about rumors that get around. So everyday I'm sitting here in my house next to the Catholic Church waiting for the phone to ring. I been watching people go in and out of that church for twenty years, maybe a few more. All dressed up, fit to kill, kids in shirts and ties, shiny cars. But I guess these folks don't much like the old broken down drill rigs I've got in my back yard. One of those junkers kind of hangs over the fence next to the church parking lot. Once I saw a guy park there, under it, then he looked up at the winch tower like it might fall down and crack his new BMW wide open. He moved his car. Those old rigs come in real handy though when you need spare parts. Anyway, it would be a shame to just haul them off to the dump after all the work they've done.

Yesterday I got this note stuck on my mailbox. It says: "Dear Mr. McCaw. Do you still drill wells? I'll call you on Sunday. Sincerely, John Kroll." Do I still drill wells? Well, I'll tell you something, Mr. Kroll, I've drilled more water wells than any man living in these mountains. And witched most of them, too. Anyway, I figure he'll call around noon, it being Sunday and all. And that's when the phone rings. I guess by the sound of it, kind of high pitched and anxious, that it's him.

"Tom McCaw?" Real loud. I look at the receiver, then hold it away from my ear a little bit.

"Yeah, this is Tom McCaw all right."

"Jack Kroll, here. I left a note the other day." I have his note in my left hand, I'm trying to unfold it.

"I thought it was John," I say, finally getting the note flat in my palm. I flip the piece of paper toward the kitchen table but it falls on the floor.

"Call me Jack," he says.

"Yeah, I got it, wife did anyways."

"So you drilling any wells around Scotts Valley? Bernie down at Freedom Pump said you might be starting up again. You know, he's got that shop down toward Watsonville."

"Well, I'll tell you Mr. Kroll, I drilled all over these mountains. You can't hardly find a road I ain't drilled on. That's the gospel truth, I'll tell you right now." I'm thinking Mr. Kroll might be going to ask for some kind of discount on account of knowing Bernie or something. But I don't care. What's money anyway? I'm looking out my window into the church parking lot and see a family open all four doors of their VW bus at once. The bus looks like one of those paper models unfolded on a table top. The VW hunkers down, then jerks, smokes a quick burst, and scoots off toward Glenwood Drive.

"So you got my note then?" I can see that conversations with Mr. Kroll will not always be quick ones.

"So that's what Bernie said, is it?" I taught Bernie everything he knows about drilling water wells. He was just another stinky kid living down the block a few years ago. "Well, I never stopped drilling wells. Not yet, anyways."

"Could you do some witching up on Weston Road next Saturday?"

"Where at?"

"I'll meet you down at the gate by the mailboxes at noon, if that's okay." Of course, that's just fine with me, it's only five minutes from my front door. I can tell that Jack Kroll is the kind of guy that doesn't like to give out much information.

"Where we witching at?"

"Well, it's up the road a couple miles." His voice tails off likes he's a real estate agent who doesn't want anyone to know what piece of land he's got a hot tip on. But I don't give up too easy.

"Past Gulick's place?"

"Look," he says, "I really don't know anybody up there. I just bought the land and I want to find out what I've got myself into."

"Okay," I say. At least I got a little bit of a rise out of him. "Noon is just fine." I hang up the receiver and look out my window. The church parking lot is empty. One abandoned car, an old Toyota, out back. Been there for weeks. Hell, I forgot to tell him my price for witching. Up a little bit from before, but not much compared to some of these youngsters around here who think they know how to find water. But you can't guarantee a thing, you know, some land's got water, some don't. Can't do nothing about that. Then I see my wife standing in the kitchen doorway, watching me, like she's been doing lately.

"Who was that?" she asks. A mighty pretty woman she was once, now mostly just pushy, a little too pushy for me. Always got to get her say in. Once in a while, though, she stands there like she used to, sort of loose and angular, ready for anything, like in the old days when we were younger and times were better.

"Some guy up on Weston Road, nothing much."

"What does he want?"

"Nothing much, just some witching, maybe a well later on." She looks at me real hard, like she's fixing to say something sharp, but then she just goes back in the kitchen and I can hear the fridge open and close a couple of times, water running in the sink. Then, real quick, she's back in the doorway.

"It's too soon, Tom, why don't you just go fishing or something? Why not get Bernie or one of the other guys to do it? Just go fishing for a couple days, Tom."

"Bernie's out drilling in Boulder Creek, Marge, he's real busy right now. I did plenty of fishing last week, didn't I?" I walk into the kitchen and sit down at the table. "What's for lunch?" I give Marge my best grin.

So I'm standing by my truck, looking out over Kroll's property. He called me back later and told me where it was. Guess he didn't want me hanging out around the mailboxes, after all. It's a pretty nice piece, all right, follows the road for a quarter mile or so, hilly but all usable, oak and madrone. Three acres is not that much, though, not when you're looking for water. No place to get a drill rig in down there. Just up here along the road. Suddenly this yellow Mercedes shoots around the corner down by the lower wash, disappears and I hear the diesel engine ratcheting, then he pops around the corner, gears down and parks a couple feet from my truck. John Kroll walks toward me. His face is open and amazed, sort of like a kid who has just opened a Christmas present he wasn't supposed to touch. But I can see he's no dummy, either. He watches what's going on.

"Jack," he says, sticking out his hand. It looks white, kind of like a marshmallow at the end of a short stick. "Jack Kroll." I take his hand limply. Guys who drive around in a Mercedes hate a limp handshake, so I give him a real fish and he looks at me in a knowing sort of way. Kind of a wink. "You Tom McCaw?" I nod my head but I don't say anything yet. I always think silence is the best opening. He steps back and shakes his foot like he's got gravel in his shoe. "Well, are we ready to witch this place?"

I know what I'm supposed to do all right, so I walk back over to my truck cab, open the door, and take out two plastic rods tied together at one end with twisted rows of white string. He doesn't miss a beat. Before I get back to where he's standing, his mouth is already moving.

"Plastic? I thought you guys used willow branches or hickory sticks, wood anyway." He's leaning toward the Mercedes, like he's wishing he could get in it and drive off. I guess he's scared he won't get his money's worth. So I give it to him.

"Some scientists up in Utah recently discovered a primal affinity between plastic and water," I say, "I saw it in the newspaper just the other day, the Sentinel." I watch his face and he's listening but unconvinced. Sort of like a guy I saw in a bar once who was taking a sip of non-alcoholic beer. "I've still got the article," I say and start to walk back to my truck as if I'm about to pull the newspaper out of my glove box .

"Okay, that's cool, no problem." He starts to walk down the slope, then looks back at me. "Where do you want to start?"

"Anywhere," I say, "how about up here on the road?" I scrape my feet on the surface, marking a spot in the gravel.

"Up here? Wouldn't water be somewhere down there in the wash or over there in the trees?" He motions toward a clump of redwoods beyond the oak and madrone. He scratches his head and climbs back up onto the road.

"Drill rig can't get down in there," I say, "too steep." He looks at me steadily.

"Water is only where drill rigs can go?" he asks. He's leaning toward his car again and now he has his car keys in his hand. But he doesn't run. He stands his ground. He's quite a guy, this Mister Jack! A tiny alligator on his t-shirt, Nike sneakers without a spot of dirt, razor cut hair job. Right now he has some burrs caught on his shoe laces and in his socks. I can see he feels them and really wants to pick them off. He doesn't though. Like I said, I know my job pretty well and so I quit talking and head down the hill with the plastic rods out in front of me like antenna sticking out of my belly button. I hear him behind me, padding over the dirt. The hunt for water has begun.

Sometimes the witching sticks can pull real hard. Of course those times come after I've taken in the lay of the land, the way the hills flow into the valleys, the types of trees and plants I see growing in various places. We're talking about underground lakes and rivers here, right? Anyway the witching sticks do what they have to do. I let Kroll hold the rods and set him to walking down a flat stretch between two trees.

"Is this how you hold them?" He looks like a little kid, walking with a bowl of soup, trying to keep it from spilling.

"Do you feel them moving?" I ask. "Do the ends of the sticks feel heavy?" He walks a ways toward the tree, then turns around.

"I think I felt something over there, by that bush." He walks quickly back to a manzanita bush.

"Slowly, slowly, you got to go slow, Mr. Kroll. And hold your wrists loose, so the sticks can move."

"Call me Jack, okay?"

We go on like this for about an hour, crossing the property back and forth. Big time well witching. I know from experience that, once you get the customer to hold the sticks, you've got them hooked. Finally, we settle on a drill site back up on the road about twenty feet from where the cars are parked. Nice spot for a water tank, too. Kroll pays me sixty bucks, three brand new twenties, and he hands them to me one at a time. For a minute I wonder if I'll ever see this guy again. He heads for his car and sits in the driver's seat, looking at me through his rolled up window. Then the window rolls down.

"Can you start drilling tomorrow?" Mr. Kroll has a flair for the dramatic.

"Sure enough." I say and I stick the twenties in my shirt pocket. Never bring out your wallet in public my dad always told me.

So the next day I scoot my best rig in real neat, right under the branches of a scrub oak. And there I am, drilling my own well again, just like in the old days. I get the first two lengths down in about an hour. That's how it always is, top soil the first few yards, then yellow crumbly sandstone. Even after that, it's pretty quick until you start hitting the blue sandstone which gets harder and harder, the deeper you get. Finally, you hit granite and then you know you're getting close. I'm just getting the first two rods pulled out, ready to put on the third, when I hear a car pull up behind me. I turn my head just enough to see a yellow fender, then I turn back and swing the chain grip up over the drill bit.

"Well, how's it going up here?"

"Right good, Mr. Kroll, right good. I'm forty feet down and drilling hard, yes I am." I yank the chain and get the bit started, then step forward to finish it by hand. That's when he sees my left hand for the first time, I guess, the missing thumb and finger. You can tell about things like that. He sort of steps backwards and does a double take. So I take a slow swipe at my hair with my bad hand, that way he can get a real good look. Now he's probably wondering why he hadn't seen it before. But it's no big problem for me, being looked at like that. You get used to it after a few months. Anyway, I'm almost seventy years old, so who cares?

"Forty feet, huh," he says, recovering, "how many feet do you think you'll have to go?" I look at him again, same Nike sneakers, clean white polo shirt. He looks like he wants to stick his foot up on the metal step of my truck. He wants to

lean back and talk like he's one of the guys. He has a little
boy with him, five or six years old, sharp eyes like his dad.
The kid tugs at his father's hand. Tugs hard, like he wants to
run. Kroll looks at him real sharp, as if reminding him of an
agreement they had made earlier. Then he looks back at me.

"I guess it might go pretty deep up here on a hill like this,
maybe two hundred feet or so," he says. He looks at the
stack of twenty foot drill rods piled against the trunk of the
scrub oak—twenty in all.

"Well, Mr. Kroll," I start out.

"Call me Jack, okay?"

"Okay, Jack, well, I'll tell you, I'll stop this rig the minute
I hit good water, you'll want at least 10 gallons a minute, I
think. I'll save you every dollar I can, that's just how I
work." I've got the new rod on and I reach to attach the bit.

"Pretty hot out today," he says. The kid has broken loose
and is running up the road toward a clump of trees. Kroll
pretends it's no big deal but you can see he doesn't like it at
all. This is a guy who would never yell or spank a kid in
public. The kid knows it, too. I'm ready to rev up the engine
and get to drilling, but Kroll is still standing there, looking at
me, like he's waiting for something.

"Yeah, hot it is, I know that, I know that. Well, it takes a
while to drill a water well, Jack, a few days, probably more.
Gets real hot standing out here like this, that's for sure." I'm
waiting for him to head for his car, go find the kid, do
something. I get the feeling he might want to tell me some
kind of story, maybe about his life or a problem he has. But
he doesn't say anything.

"Okay, well Jack, it's back to work for me, I guess." I
shove the throttle and the bit channel turns with a clunk and
starts grinding in slow turns. I feel him standing there,
watching, and my neck feels tight under my shirt. The shaft
grinds and spits, the rig shakes. It's sinking pretty good and I

know I'll have to change again in twenty minutes or so. Finally, after the rod is halfway down, I look up and I see him up the road, holding the kid up in the air by one arm, speaking low and hard and mean. Then he drops him and the kid lands on his feet but he doesn't run anymore. I turn back to the rig. I can imagine the bit, down in the bottom of the hole, cutting, shredding rock, hot and brittle. It turns cleanly, clipping stone the same way a sharp wood chipper can turn the branches of a huge tree into a small pile of wood chips. The bit is relentless and unforgiving, but somehow beautiful, too, giving new shape to raw earth. Sort of like the machines in the hospital, the clocks that keep ticking in silence, the fluids that drip endlessly through circles of plastic tubing.

In the hospital bed I could feel my arm, my hand where the bit had caught it and snatched the thumb and finger away. You can still feel the thumb but, when you look, you know it isn't there anymore. Just a white bandage and dizziness and the white walls and the blank television screen. The doctor comes in and looks around the room.

"Looks like you're doing okay in here, Mr. McCaw." He is looking at me over the top of his clipboard. He begins to move the pencil. "How do you feel today?"

"Feel?" I say. I wonder how the doctor would feel with no thumb and forefinger and a fistful of white gauze. But I don't say anything more.

"Well, anyway, you're doing great. I talked to your wife a few minutes ago. You can go home in a day or so." The doctor's white smock turns slightly toward the door. He is ready to leave.

"Yes, home," I say and the room tilts. Sharp surfaces slide together and the tubes and wires climb toward the ceiling like spider webs. I can see the bit, deep in the ground, slicing the rock, turning in a red hot circle, shredding, grinding matter to dust.

When I stop the engine to pull the rods, I turn around. The yellow Mercedes is gone. It goes on like this for days. I drill deeper and deeper, the stock of rods against the tree gets smaller. Kroll shows up, it turns out, at regular intervals, sometimes at noon, usually around five thirty.

He's an engineer at one of those new buildings over by the freeway. Over where Lost World used to be. Back then I'd take my kids there to see the ten acres of plaster dinosaurs carefully tucked in among the redwood trees. The Tyrannosaurus Rex was painted bright purple, claws as big as truck tires. It was so tall you could see it from the freeway, its neck craning up over the tree branches, like some monstrous vegetable grown wild and curious in the rich, hidden soil of Scotts Valley. Of course, all that was good for business. Just not good enough.

To get into Lost World, you walked through a magic forest of miniature trees, trained and twisted into incredible shapes, the snake tree, the double heart tree, the tree of a thousand dances. The owners drove around town in a station wagon with a baby dinosaur perched on the roof. Of course, in the end, they sold the land to one of the computer companies sprouting up on both sides of the freeway. Now we have Mr. John Kroll, the software engineer, checking on his well driller twice a day. He's a hands on sort of guy, anyone can see that.

After a week or so, we reach a turning point and I begin to get that empty feeling and realize I might have a problem on my hands. I'm standing on the rig, looking at the scrub oak—only three rods left. We're over three hundred feet down and no solid bedrock. A little water, at under a hundred feet, just surface stuff, then nothing. Decomposed granite but nothing hard enough to stop the water, make it flow in one place. So I'm waiting to hit the hard stuff, the solid blue granite and I know that, around here, if you don't hit it at around three hundred feet or so, you probably aren't going to. You might be digging through some sort of deep valley full of loose rock and dirt but no river or lake.

I can close my eyes and see clear, clean water pouring out of a white pipe. My first well, fifty years ago. Just before the war when nobody had any money to drill anything. But there was this movie director guy over on Sandhill Road in Scotts Valley and he wanted a well. The driller I worked for got sick, so there I was, drilling my first hole. A hundred and fifty feet, that's all you had to drill to find good water back in those days. It gushed out at twenty gallons a minute, too, pure and tasty. We pumped out for over an hour and I stuck my head in there and let the water soak me good. I remember touching the water, wondering, really, where it came from. What was down there? Underground caves, rivers, another world? Or maybe just solid rock and dirt, something hard you have to drill through.

I'm wondering how Jack Kroll will look when I tell him we might have a dry hole. Maybe we should have drilled down by the redwoods like he wanted to. Maybe we could have got bulldozers in there and made a road and got the rig in that way. Maybe I should have called Bernie out here, he's got better equipment. But Kroll doesn't need to hear any of that, I'm sure. Sometimes no amount of good plans or good equipment can find water.

So, on the last day, I've got all my rods pulled and I'm waiting for Kroll to show up. I'd talked to him on the phone the night before. So he knows something isn't going right. Everything's out of the hole and stacked back under the scrub oak. I've been sitting here, looking out over the trees down by Bean Creek Road. They say one old lady owns all that land, that she won't sell and she won't build anything either. She just wants people to leave her and her land alone.

Which is just fine with most folks around these parts, we sure don't want any strip malls or apartments popping up.

After a while the yellow Mercedes pulls up behind my truck and right away I can see things are pretty grim. He has his wife with him, no kids, and they don't get out of the car for a while. They sit inside, talking. I can see their mouths move, once in a while they make hand motions in my direction. They look a little like two teenagers in the middle of a love spat at a drive-in movie. Finally, they reach some kind of agreement, maybe. They both look steadily out the windshield toward me. I'm sitting up on the drill rig, I figure it's safer that way. They get out and walk toward me.

"Well, how's it going today?" Kroll asks. The wife is blonde and thin and is standing straight up like she just had in injection of iron in her backside. I watch his eyes and I see he has just noticed the pile of rods over by the tree. I look down at him.

"Not much different than the other days, I guess," I say. I would like to be civil and diplomatic, of course, but things don't look like they're going to be easy.

"Okay, McCaw, what's the bottom line here?" Kroll says. There's a bit of wind and his sport coat puffs out and flaps like a seagull. I figure he has to show his wife he's tough.

"The bottom line?"

"About the water?"

"There isn't any, Jack, it's a dry hole."

"A dry hole?" He seems to muse over the words, as if looking for some secret meaning between the syllables.

"I should warn you, McCaw, I have spoken with my attorney. He thinks we have legal recourse here." Kroll looks at his wife for confirmation. She is staring at the drill rig. "Rest assured that we will take all possible legal steps."

I look at him for a moment and wonder what sort of legal steps might help a dry hole develop water. "Dynamite might help," I say after a short silence. "I heard about this one guy down in Watsonville who dropped a stick of dynamite down a dry hole and, sure enough, he got water right away." Of course, I feel bad about the whole mess and want to help them out.

"Dynamite?" he says, rolling the word around on his tongue, getting the feel of it. "Dynamite." He turns to his wife. "What do you think about that, Kimberly?"

"Think about what? What is there to think about?" Her voice is shrill and she is furious at the unfortunate turn the conversation has taken. "What on earth is there to think about? Dynamite? That's what it would take to get you to do anything in this world. Dynamite, my ass."

"Wait just a minute," he says, stepping back from her.

"I will talk to the lawyer myself, even if you don't have the balls to do it," she says.

"Who said I wouldn't?" he begins, then stops. He has just remembered I'm sitting on the drill rig. He puts his hands out in front of his body, turns them flat, as if feeling for rain. Very theatrical. But I'm getting a little edgy myself, since it looks like the Krolls might not be real happy about paying their bill.

"I'm sure you've read the contract you signed, Jack." I can imagine myself in a courtroom, in front of a jury. My mother always said I should be a lawyer. They make big money even in the worst of times. "Page four, paragraph two. Dry holes are compensated at fifty percent of contract or the down payment, whichever is greater." I'm getting ready to jump to the ground. It's time to start loading pipe onto the rig. So I conclude my case. "That would be about four grand. Which is what you already paid."

"What?" Silence. I see that he is about to make some sort of move, some gesture to placate the wife. Maybe something desperate. "What did you just say?" He squeezes the words out between dry lips. I figure in situations like this it's better not to fan the flames. So I stay put and keep quiet. But I'm watching the wife, not him. She's got keys in her hand and she is quietly walking backwards toward the Mercedes. He is staring at me as if he might climb up and throw me off the drill rig. His face glows in the afternoon sun.

She fires up the engine and has the car turned around before he even knows what's happening. The Mercedes jerks forward, almost stalls, then spits gravel and blasts down the road. She's hitting almost fifty before the first turn. The engine whines, spins, whines, then you can't really hear it anymore. It's gone around too many bends. Jack Kroll is standing still, sort of, but it's more like someone has pulled the strings out of a puppet and left the parts hanging in midair. But, hey, give the guy some credit. He doesn't turn around, he doesn't look at me at all. He straightens up a little, kind of touches his shoes with one hand, then starts walking down the road. I watch him until he turns the first corner and is out of sight. Then I jump off the rig and start loading pipe.

Monks used to live in these mountains. If you follow an old trail, past a deserted boy scout camp, then go through the old lady's land, you'll see an open space, then walk down a wash a half mile or so, you'll find it—the old shrine. I found it when I was a kid living down on Bean Creek Road. All the kids knew about it. You're pushing through reeds and branches and suddenly you notice something, a colored bench covered with green vines. Red and blue and green tiles and a mosaic of the Virgin Mary standing right on the head of the Baby Jesus. Then you see an archway with stone lions guarding it and a brick path leading to a baptismal font. The font has this incredible painting in blue and gray tile, a conquistador on a black horse at full gallop and another rider, on another horse, white like a ghost, racing alongside the conquistador, beckoning to him. The white rider motions with his hand but the man on the black horse won't stop or even look at his fellow rider.

This image is like a negative stored in the cold locker of my brain, the racing white figure, the grimace of speed, the reaching hand. When I was a kid, I'd hike up there and stare at this baptismal font for what seemed like hours. I could feel monks in the air, almost hear them whispering on the hard path under the archway. The red bricks were scuffed with the simple sounds of devotion. Then a dog would bark up on a hill overlooking the shrine. Other dogs would starts barking and I'd walk slowly back down the path toward home.

One day I saw that someone, some stupid kid probably, had been hitting one of the stone lions with a hammer. Anyway, part of a foot was broken off. Stone dust was scattered over the bricks. Small pieces were missing but the toes, mysteriously, were still sitting there, intact. I picked the toes up and they were heavy in my hand. I thought about gluing them back on, somehow, but I knew it wouldn't work. They didn't fit anymore. So I took the lion's toes home with me. That made me a criminal too, I know, but it was better I had them than someone else. That's what I told myself. Now, sixty years later, those stone toes are still on my desk, pressing bills and notices against a brown lamp. Doctor's bills, equipment rentals, taxes, old letters, all pushed tight by the foot of a guardian lion. The note John Kroll left on my mailbox. All the things I need to save.

ESCALON

Isabelle is haggling with a Portuguese man over a brass cross engraved with a Virgin on one side and a matador with a red cape on the other. She is holding the cross flat on her palm, balancing it, tapping her feet rapidly, as if she were a kid jumping rope. The man has a thick accent and Isabelle doesn't understand what he's saying. Then a younger man walks up behind her. He is looking at Isabelle's reddish black hair.

"I speak Portuguese," he says. Isabelle does not turn around at first. She has been searching the flea market for bullfight posters, used books about bulls, calendars featuring bullfighters, even the bullfight postcards that are sold to tourists in places like Pamplona and Barcelona. Isabelle spends a lot of time walking around flea markets. Finally, she spins on one foot and takes a look at the man behind her.

"Okay, then, get me a good price on this cross," she says. "I really want it but you don't need to mention that." The young man speaks quickly in Portuguese and the old man nods solemnly, then holds up five fingers. Isabelle looks at the fingers and yanks at the zipper on her purse. She pulls out a five dollar bill and hands it over.

The young man starts talking. "I know this old man, you know. He's from the Valley, a Portuguese, like me."

"What valley?" Isabelle has stuffed the brass cross into her purse but it's a little too long and it's wedged at an awkward angle, pushing against the leather as if it's trying to escape. She is looking around for Hank.

"The San Joaquin valley, over by Stockton. A little town called Escalon. Ever hear of it?" Isabelle is not listening to this guy and he knows it. "Okay, okay, it looks like maybe you're interested in bullfights."

"And why not?" Isabelle pats the bump in the side of her purse. She takes a closer look at the man she's talking to. He's thin, angular, black curly hair. His movements are smooth, like those of a dancer. She pulls out her keys and rattles them.

"I am Orlando, the seventh American matador." He is watching Isabelle's eyes as he says this.

"Sure, and I'm Madonna, look I have to find somebody. Thanks for your help though." Isabelle starts walking toward the parking lot. Hank is probably out by the car.

"Okay, okay, it doesn't matter, anyway. Who cares? But I know where to find lots of stuff like the cross you just bought." Isabelle turns around and looks at him again. He seems honest enough, even innocent.

"Where?"

"All the old grandmothers in Escalon have things like that hidden away in their attics. Like my own grandmother who just happens to be here today." Orlando gestures over the crowd toward a long row of vendors selling fruits and vegetables. Isabelle follows his arm with her eyes. She pulls a hamburger wrapper out of her purse and scribbles down a phone number. Orlando opens his wallet slowly and places the piece of paper with great care next to the dollar bills.

"Call me if you find something good. I might buy it," Isabelle says, then she turns and walks away.

After that the phone calls start coming and then, a few days later, the postcards. Isabelle is in the kitchen with her seven year old daughter, Amanda. She is roasting an ear of corn over the open flame of the gas stove when the phone rings. Amanda answers it and yells out.

"It's for you Mommy. It's a boy." Amanda picks up a raw ear of corn and turns the husk down like a banana peel.

Isabelle picks up the phone. "Bueno." She looks into the front room to see if her father is nearby. She can't hear any music.

"Who?" Isabelle switches the phone from one ear to the other, waves at Amanda, pushing her hand down through the air.

"What? Who? Oh yeah, I remember. Of course, I remember. Listen, that's great but I have to cook dinner for my daughter and my dad." Isabelle is working her mouth at Amanda but the little girl isn't watching. She's holding a corn cob with a partial husk over the flame and now the husk is on fire and she drops it on the stove top. It rolls, teeters, then drops onto the linoleum floor.

"Yeah, that sounds great. I wish I had one of those." Pause. "No, I really do." Isabelle's voice has softened. Amanda dumps a glass of water on the blackened cob. She stands there holding the empty glass.

"Well, sure I would but I really don't have time for stuff like that. I work every day. I go to school. I have a daughter and a father to take care of." Silence. "And I have a boyfriend." Isabelle takes the phone away from her head, as if her ear hurts. Amanda has the broom and is running it through the spilled water, pushing the burnt cob across the floor. Isabelle puts the receiver back on the hook silently. She picks up the burnt ear of corn. Then her father walks in.

"Who was that? Hank?" The father is looking around the kitchen for something to eat. He stands in front of the refrigerator.

"No, a guy from Portugal. A bullfighter, maybe." Isabelle holds the burned cob out in the air and her dad takes it by one end, touches it tentatively, as if it might still be hot.

"Well, marry him then. I can raise bulls in my old age. Why not?" He turns and walks back into the front room. In a minute Mexican music is blasting from two large speakers near the kitchen door. It's a ranchera from Chihuahua. He sticks his head back in the kitchen door.

"I married your mom, didn't I?" Isabelle's mother is from Germany and she divorced the father ten years ago. It was all a big mistake, she had said as she walked out the front door pulling two huge suitcases behind her. The grandmother had been waiting in a taxicab out front at the end of a long driveway. Now Isabelle and her mother talk on the phone every couple of weeks. The mother asks if the father is getting enough to eat. She wants to know if the house is warm enough in the winter. If the father is taking his pills. Isabelle tells her that everything is just fine.

Isabelle has been getting postcards for the last couple of weeks, sometimes one a day. She's thinking maybe she shouldn't have given the matador her address. The cards are stacking up on her dresser, piled on an old wooden platter. Isabelle has seen Hank looking at them. Once he picked one up, held it from his fingertips like a caught mouse, then dropped it back on the platter. These postcards feature bulls and bullfights. The words are in Spanish or Portuguese. The Spanish is often clever. Isabelle does not really understand the Portuguese. She does not respond to these postcards. She just looks at them and tosses them on the platter.

Isabelle is sitting in front of her bedroom shrine. A statue of the Virgin Mary sits quietly in the center, surrounded by photographs of bullfighters and bulls. Colored candles flicker and drip wax. She has said a few "Hail Marys" and is getting ready to light a bright blue candle when she hears the doorknob turn and sees Hank in the mirror behind the Virgin. She does not turn around. He stands there with one hand hidden behind his back. He is flexing his shoulder and neck muscles. Then he pulls out his hand with a sweeping motion and tosses a postcard toward the wood platter but it misses and clicks on the hard top of the dresser.

"What?" Isabelle says.

"What nothing. Are you ready to go?"

"What do you mean? What was that?" Isabelle still has not turned around. She is staring into the eye of the blue candle, watching the new wax flow.

"You know!" Hank is red in the face now, moving his feet in circles on the carpet. "Let's just go, okay."

"Let's not." She turns finally, moving her head but not her body. "Look, so I met this guy, okay, you know that already. He keeps sending cards. Is that my fault? I didn't ask him to, you know."

"Where? Where did you find this guy for hell's sake?" Hank steps forward into the room, then stops. "Where do all these guys come from, I wonder?"

"At a flea market, of course, where else do I ever get to go? Anyway, you were there, weren't you? I saw you looking over my way." Isabelle blows out the candles, one by one.

"Great! Just great! I suppose he likes bulls or some bullshit like that. You know what, who cares? Let's just go before I get really pissed off." Hank turns toward the doorway, his keys rattling in his hand.

"Well, he's a bullfighter, if you really want to know. One of the only ones in the United States." Isabelle stands up. "At least that's what he told me. His dad raises the bulls." Isabelle stops and waits for Hank to turn around. He does.

"We're invited to a bullfight on Sunday next week, by the way." Isabelle walks over to her closet, crosses her arms and pulls off her t-shirt. Hank watches her thumb along the hangers. She steps out of her shorts and glances over her bare shoulder at Hank and smiles. Then she puts on a black and white Mexican dress.

"Now we can go to the flea market," she says and stands up straight. Hank says nothing for a moment. He is thinking.

"Since when do we even have bullfights in this country? Aren't they from Spain or Mexico?"

"Well, they have them here, too, only this one is Portuguese." Isabelle looks at Hank and pushes her hands out into the air. "Hey, that's what he told me. The difference is they just don't kill the bull."

Hank is holding his car keys like a baseball in his right hand. He watches Isabelle in front of her mirror for another moment, then walks out of the room. Isabelle hears the front door slam and, a minute later, the car radio blaring. She buttons up her dress slowly and looks one more time in the mirror.

Isabelle is a serious student of the bulls. She has read the books of Hemingway and Barnaby Conrad. She knows the names of the old Spanish bullfighters. Tears come to her eyes when she thinks of Joselito's final moments in Talavera de la Reina. On the backs of her eyes she can see the muleta skip high in the quick wind, the horn veer to the bundle, the bright red blood leech into the hard packed sand.

Isabelle has a map of Spain that highlights the major bullfight cities and the typical dates of the ferias. Sevilla and Ronda, Bilbao, Santander, Valencia and, of course, Madrid. She would give anything to be in Pamplona during the running of the bulls. Isabelle runs her fingers over the map. She can almost feel the dust in her mouth from the long ride between bullrings, the taste of strong brandy in the back of her throat. The Virgin de la Soledad, the patron saint of bulls and bullfighters, is imprinted on the top of the map. This is the Virgin that appears on the brass cross she bought at the flea market. Isabelle has read that this Virgin hovers on the ceiling of the chapel at the bullring in Madrid.

More postcards arrive. Hank is moody and impatient. The father is invited to the bullfight in Escalon but he would rather work in his basement workshop. He makes his own water skis with saws and drills and layers of glue and lamination. He sells these skis at flea markets. Hank is invited, too, but he would rather walk stiff legged through the clandestine rooms of Isabelle's house and skulk in the bushes by her mailbox. Isabelle has asked him once but she will not ask again. Now something new has appeared on the wooden tray—a clean white envelope with no return address, postmarked in Manteca, California. Hank picks it up but the letter is missing. He drops it back on the pile. Isabelle starts putting things into an overnight bag, a pair of shorts, some socks, a toothbrush. Just in case she needs them.

Amanda is standing in her mother's room, looking at the overnight bag.

"Will I be going with you to the bullfight, Mommy?" Amanda is almost eight years old and she has grown accustomed to talk about bulls and matadors.

"What bullfight?"

"The one you and Hank are fighting over." Amanda is standing in the middle of her mother's room with her hands on her hips.

"Amanda, we are absolutely not fighting about any bullfight. Anyway you can stay home and have fun with your Grandpa. What do you think of that idea?"

"It stinks." Amanda says this and walks quickly out of the room.

Isabelle gets up early on the morning of the anticipated Sunday. She wants no arguments or scenes with Hank or Amanda. She grabs a banana and her bag and heads out the door. She has not answered any of Orlando's cards and letters. He does not know she's coming. She doesn't want him to know. Isabelle just wants to see with her own eyes what goes on at a Portuguese bullfight in the San Joaquin Valley.

The red Volkswagen beetle skips down Interstate 580, then shoots over toward Stockton. Isabelle figures that Hank is probably following her. He's somewhere out there hiding under a concrete overpass. Isabelle can feel him, the dark black of his car, the gravel spitting under his tires, the stubbornness of his grip on the steering wheel. She is watching her rearview mirror and misses the turn on Highway 120 at Manteca. She has to double back at Farmington. Well, that clever maneuver should help confuse Hank anyway.

The little red bug passes the farm houses, the long brown fields, the John Deere tractors squatting in front of broken down barns. Finally, she swerves right and stops in front of a sign with faded letters—CAMPO BRAVO, PRACA DE TOUROS. The bullring is made of tubular steel and is not nearly as big as Isabelle had imagined it might be. It's not like the Spanish bullrings she has seen in books, the stucco arches, the pillars and ornate brocades of brick.

The Portuguese bullring is surrounded by open pasture. Cows and calves linger by the fences, chewing grass, taking their time. There is a special field nearby for the bulls. It is noon and already six bulls occupy the concrete pens that partially surround the bullring. Half a dozen men have climbed the side of the bullring to a horizontal perch and are watching the bulls from above.

Isabelle parks her car on a dirt road that parallels the bullring, then dead ends in a cow pasture. She knows she is early, the bullfight doesn't start until four in the afternoon. She sits in her red VW and waits. Isabelle sticks in a cassette and Mexican corridos drift out through her open windows. Several of the men who are studying the bulls turn toward her for a moment, then turn back to the bulls. Isabelle knows what is happening here. It is the apartado, the time when the bullfighters observe each bull's idiosyncrasies. They will take note of the tilt of the eye, the placement of hooves, the length and shape of horn. Will the bull veer to the right or to the left? How well does he see? Maybe Orlando is one of the men watching the bulls. Isabelle is too far away to tell.

Isabelle hears a tap on her window and a face pushes up close to the glass. It's a kid with black hair, a long thin face, a funny sort of grin. Isabelle opens her door quickly and the kid jumps back. He's wearing a shirt embroidered with flowers and the sleeves are too long. He watches Isabelle and his grin gets wider like he's laughing at some inner joke. Isabelle gets out and stands by the door of the red bug.

"All right, what's so funny, muchacho?" Isabelle says. The boy kicks his feet and dust rises around his knees. He is silent and looks like he might run away.

"Are you from the city?" the boy asks, finally.

"So you can talk, can you?" Isabelle says. The boy moves closer. He speaks confidentially.

"These bulls are nothing, no better than cows." He stops talking and watches Isabelle. "My grandfather told me last night."

Isabelle does not know what to say. She takes a step toward the boy and he turns and runs in the direction of an empty lot where men are stretching an awning over some aluminum poles. He yells over his shoulder, "my brother is a bullfighter." Then he disappears behind a tent full of silver beer kegs. Portuguese women are beginning to prepare food under the awning.

Isabelle slams her car door, then opens it again and turns off the stereo. She starts to walk toward the bulls, her red leather skirt rubbing against her knees, her black purse swinging loose on her shoulder.

Hank is following Isabelle. He hadn't thought he would do it, he had told himself that he wouldn't do it. He had waited for her to invite him. She had invited him, sort of, but not really. Anyway, it was obvious she didn't want him along, or her dad or her daughter either. Then she had started using the word "I" when she talked about driving to Escalon. The postcards reclined like a nest of thorns on her dresser. These cards were full of bulls and bullfighters. Where do you buy postcards like that? Hank had wondered. He had certainly not seen any at Payless or Thrifty.

Hank really had not planned on following Isabelle but then he saw she was packing an overnight bag. Each day she would put some new item in the bag. At first there had been some shorts and a toothbrush, then a white plastic egg, containing nylons, a hair dryer, a hairbrush and fingernail polish, a bottle of aspirin and, on the last day, a pair of canvas tennis shoes. Then the bag was full and zipped.

It is the day of the bullfight and Hank has driven out on the freeway where he knows Isabelle will have to pass. He is plenty early, eight o'clock, and he's hiding behind some oleander bushes on an on-ramp. He's afraid he will blink and miss her. The cars are moving faster than he had thought they would. He follows each dot of red until it gets big enough to see whether it's a Volkswagen beetle. Then suddenly he cranks the starter, slams the black Dodge into gear and shoots twenty feet up the on-ramp. But it's not her. It's a red Fiesta with two screaming kids in the back seat.

The cars get bigger, smaller, change colors, disappear. Limousines and cops and trucks and motorcycles. Fat cars, long cars, all the wrong cars. Hank feels like going back to Gilroy. He could find a dark bar somewhere and order a beer, a big one, a Foster's maybe. Then, suddenly, there she is, cruising cool as a breeze, the red VW rolling on the big highway. Hank sees her lean a bit, as if looking in the rearview mirror, and so he waits, then pulls out neatly into the traffic, just behind a big pickup truck. No problem.

Things go smoothly for the next hour or so. Hank turns on the radio, not too loud, and listens to some old favorites on KABL. Isabelle calls it elevator music but Hank doesn't think elevators even have music, not the ones he's been in anyway. Where does she get ideas like that? Hank slips over to the left once in a while to make sure she's still there. Isabelle is no speed queen, she's always right there in front of the pickup. Then somewhere around Tracy, out on 580, the pickup turns off suddenly and he's right behind her, not fifty feet away. Hank hits the brakes, lets up quick so the tires won't squeal, then runs off on the shoulder. A cloud of dust follows the black Dodge, then he stops, kills the engine. He tries to start it and it just grinds. It's flooded. He tries again and the engine spins and grinds uselessly. Hank shouts at the windshield, kicks the firewall under the dashboard. He will have to wait for the carburetor to calm down.

Hank is parked in front of the only restaurant in Escalon. There's a large sign that says "EAT" and a Coors neon shades yellow and blue through the front window. He will have to ask for directions to the bullring. To tell the truth, Hank does remember the flea market where Isabelle met the stranger. He had looked up from examining a rusty pipe wrench to see Isabelle talking to a man. This guy held his body like a foreigner, one arm behind his back, almost as if he were going to bow. Isabelle was holding something, a small statue maybe, in front of her stomach. Hank did not like the looks of it. He thought the dude was probably talking about his fast car or his high paying job. That's what guys do. He'd probably drop a few names, famous people he knows, lawyers, movie stars, bullfighters. Of course, he'd know all about bullfighters and bulls and bullshit. Hank had seen Isabelle fumble with her purse and write something on a piece of paper and the man put the paper in his wallet. This is what Hank remembers, how long it took the guy to put the damn phone number into his wallet.

Hank gets out of his car and walks into the restaurant. The room is crowded with Portuguese, talking rapidly, gesturing with their hands and arms. Everyone knows everyone. Hank knows a little Spanish but this is impossible. He can't understand a word. A young man with very black hair walks up to a table and everyone stands up. Their voices rise in pitch. Is this the guy he had seen at the flea market? He is thin and confident, straddling a backwards chair. Every man looks the same to Hank now.

Isabelle is standing in the bleacher seats of Campo Bravo. She would like to look for Orlando but she doesn't know where to start. She thinks bullfighters probably have a special room where they go to get dressed. It would be very quiet in such a room. There are mental preparations, too, she knows that. But she doesn't know where to look or even where to sit down. The wood seats are dirty. Hay and dung have blown in from the fields and bird droppings speckle white over the faded redwood stain. Along the back row, directly opposite the gate where the bulls will enter the ring, sits a tiny chapel. Two narrow doors stand wide open. The seating in front of the chapel is painted green and is positioned under a narrow roof. These seats appear to be clean and so Isabelle goes there, peeks into the chapel and sees paintings of saints, an alter and an open Bible set out on a pulpit. Two chairs sit by the open doors. Isabelle is beginning to feel more comfortable and so she sits down in the middle of the green seats.

It is still early but now cars are turning off the narrow highway into the dusty field next to the bullring. People congregate in the parking area and around the food booths. A few people walk up the ramp into the bullring. At first nobody at all is sitting in the green seats. Just Isabelle. Then a man walks up.

"I guess you're from out of town," he says. He has a friendly smile and looks Isabelle up and down.

"I know, I know, I'm probably not supposed to be sitting here, am I?" Isabelle holds her jacket close to chest, she stands up, ready to move.

"Well, it's no big deal, really, but it's customary for the mayor to sit here and the mothers and family of the bullfighters." The man holds his palms out in front of his large stomach.

"The mayor? Okay, I'm leaving, right now." Isabelle edges along the row of seats.

"It's okay, I'm the mayor." Isabelle has gotten a few paces away, she turns and walks slowly back. She sits down near the mayor. She looks up at him. Old ladies and a few younger women are starting to fill the green seats.

"You're really the mayor?" She smoothes the leather skirt over her knees. The mayor watches her hands. He is considering what to say next.

"Have you tried our Portuguese food?" He waves a hand toward the booths in the parking lot. Isabelle gives the mayor a smile and takes off her jacket, folds it neatly on her lap. "Sardines and onions, now that would be a good start." The mayor looks at Isabelle, then signals to a young girl sitting nearby, whispers in her ear. In a few minutes a plate of sardines appears in front of Isabelle. She turns around and sees a priest sitting in one of the chapel chairs. The priest smiles at the pretty girl in the red leather skirt..

"You know," Isabelle says, "I'm really glad I came to this bullfight. It's really nice here. I guess I always thought bulls were a Spanish or Mexican thing." She is waiting for that magic moment when Orlando will appear in his suit of a thousand lights.

Hank drinks a few beers at the Portuguese restaurant and arrives late at the bull ring. The field next to the ring is full of cars. Hank hears the martial music the minute he opens the car door and, as he walks past the food booths, he can see shapes flashing through the gaps in the bleacher seats. Hank pays his fifteen dollars and walks up the narrow ramp between two holding pens. The bulls he sees here have their horns cut off and some of them wear bells around their necks. Hank knows these are the steers. He has read a magazine article on Mexican bullfighting.

Hank sees immediately that the bullfighter is on a horse. This is no farm yard animal, it is more like a circus horse, a dancing horse. The bull scrambles, charges, seems to have the horse cornered, then, at the last minute, the horse spins, spurts forward, the man leans out and jabs a feathered stick at the bull's heaving back. It sticks and the bull bounds up into the air in a quick cataclysm of fury. After a while, the bull pauses in the middle of the ring, watching the man and the horse, his mouth a froth of saliva. His tongue hangs out.

The bull ring is full of people, not an empty seat anywhere. A thousand bodies, Hank thinks, maybe more. Then he sees the tiny chapel with the open doors up along the top rows of green seats and he knows that is where Isabelle will be. The chapel is on his left but that route is blocked by a locked gate and so Hank has to walk around the entire ring.

The bull is slowing down, his back is festooned with feathered sticks. There is no blood and there is a black patch tied to the bull's back. Velcro. That's technology for you, Hank thinks. Even here in the middle of nowhere. Hank sees Isabelle long before he gets to the green seats. The long black hair, the black sweater, the red skirt. So he climbs to the top row and squeezes by in front of a hundred legs. Finally, he reaches the chapel and stands by the open doors.

Isabelle is just below him sitting by the mayor. The priest sitting in the chapel doorway casts a watchful eye in Hank's direction.

The horseman and horse approach the near side of the ring and the mayor stands up. The horseman bows over the front of the horse. The mayor tips his hat and waves a white handkerchief.

A gate opens and the steers with the cropped horns run in, bells clanging around their necks. They flow in one direction, then something changes and they swerve right, then left. The bull looks at these newcomers. He seems tempted. Then he looks around for the horseman. He paws his feet in the dust. The steers run in a half circle in front of the bull. The bull is watching the horseman, getting ready for another charge. Then, suddenly, the air seems to go out of the bull's chest, he turns toward the herd, joins the steers. They all run together, half way around the ring, then out the gate, bells jangling.

Hank and Isabelle are positioned like opposing ends of a bookshelf, she sitting by the mayor, he standing above next to the chapel. Another bull comes in like a tornado, crashes around the ring, chases the horseman, stands exhausted in the middle of the ring, then leaves meekly with the steers. Hank is watching Isabelle carefully, watching her talk to the man sitting next to her. He wants to know what he's getting himself into. Nothing much, he decides after a while.

Now Hank is standing right behind Isabelle. He waits for a moment, then taps her on the shoulder. She turns quickly, sees him, turns sharply back to face the ring. He taps her shoulder again. She turns.

"I knew it. I knew you'd be here. You didn't fool me at all." She says this in a low whisper.

"Well, did you find him? Where is he?" Hank is not comfortable, the mayor is beginning to notice the whispers.

"Who?"

"You know. The guy you came all the way here to meet. The bullfighter or whatever he is." Isabelle turns back to face the ring. She tries to ignore Hank but now the mayor is looking back at Hank, then he looks at Isabelle. He wants to know what's going on. Isabelle faces forward and will not turn her head in either direction. Then she does.

"Hank, I didn't find anybody. I came here, talked to a little kid. Now I'm sitting by the mayor and he was nice enough to get me something to eat." Isabelle speaks in a rush of breath. "Does that make you happy?" Hank and the mayor look at each other. The mayor recognizes the shape of familiarity in their gestures. He shakes his head and turns his attention back to the bull ring.

A new bull has entered the ring. His horns are covered with leather. Men with capes attract the bull, he charges the capes. A horse enters, the bull charges the horse. The horse teases the bull, allowing him to come close, then evades the horn at the last moment. The bull tires and froths at the mouth. Eight men enter the ring.

"It's the Forcados, the bull grabbers," the mayor says. "The one in front is my nephew." Hank squeezes onto the row next to Isabelle. She pushes against him but says nothing.

The eight bull grabbers line up vertically in front of the bull. The bull charges, catches the lead man in midair, he flies back, seemingly stuck to the bull's head, between the horns. The others scatter like ten pins, then jump back in, grabbing the bull's neck, his legs, the hair on his back. The men are like ants on a giant grasshopper. They have stopped him. He does not move. Finally, the bull kneels to the ground.

Hank is standing next to Isabelle. He has her hand in his. Suddenly the bull grabbers run in all directions, hiding quickly behind wooden shelters along the sides of the bull ring.

One man is left holding the bull's tail.

"That's him. That's Orlando," Isabelle cries out. "He's got the bull by the tail."

Orlando twists the bull's tail sharply and the bull hurtles blindly forward. Then the gate opens and the steers run in. Bells jangle around their necks.

HALLOWS' EVE

Maryanne is standing at the kitchen table reading a newsletter when the phone rings. It is a Christian newsletter but it's printed over in Phoenix, so the names and phone numbers and pictures don't seem familiar. She would like to know who these people are, maybe go to their meetings. But Phoenix is more than two hours away from Sedona. These do seem like happy faces though, understanding faces, next door faces. Maryanne knows that Jesus can be found in faces like these. Of course, she also knows that Jesus can be found almost anywhere. She reaches for the phone.

"Really? What's going on with you?" Maryanne says. Pause. She twists the phone cord around her left wrist. "Great, okay. Listen, haven't I always said you were welcome anytime?" Maryanne's lips move as if she is repeating the words she is hearing. "Of course, why not?" A pause. "Okay, we'll be there." She looks toward the door leading to the front room. "You know we'll both be happy to see you." Maryanne has pulled the phone slightly away from her ear. "Okay, love you, bye." She holds the phone in front of her chest, hears the distant burr of the dial tone and pulls it tighter toward her body. Then she lays the phone on the kitchen table. It starts to beep.

"She's coming!"

"Who's coming?" Ted is in the front room, sitting at his light table, looking at negatives. Some prints are hanging from clips on a thin wire in back of his chair. He has a magnifying glass in his hand.

"You were listening. Don't say you weren't."

"Maybe I was, but I still don't know who's coming." Ted sits up straight and holds a negative out in the air in front of his nose.

"My mom, that's who. She's coming for Halloween."

"Oh." Ted picks up another negative.

"Oh?" Maryanne runs her hands on the inside of the doorway, presses hard on the wood. "Oh? Is that all you have to say? Now what's going to happen?" She walks toward Ted. Her knees touch the back of his light table.

"Well, it's your mom, right? What's the big deal, anyway? She'll be fine. You can take her down to your health spa for a workout. You can go shopping for costumes." Ted stands up slowly, as if doing a deep knee bend. His legs pop straight. He puts his hands on Maryanne's shoulders and pulls her toward him.

"Ted, don't do that. How many times do I have to tell you? It throws off my balance." Maryanne pushes Ted back, his arms fall to his sides. She looks at him and feels sorry. "It's just that I need my own space, Ted, I need to be balanced." She holds one hand out in the air for a moment, then walks back into the kitchen.

Maryanne is nearly naked and she is massaging a fat lady's back. This woman's backside is huge and waves of flesh roll loose under Maryanne's hands. Kneed slowly toward the extremities, let the tiredness, the bad energy, flow out through the fingers and toes. This tight spot here, rub it deep, push it out, let the pain go free. All this energy must flow. Maryanne's hands move down the spine, down the arms and legs, bringing the warmth, the chi, finding the center. The true balance. Maryanne feels something holy flowing through these rolls of fat, like the layers of heaven maybe, the many mansions. The fat lady is named Rose and she has her head hidden in her folded arms. Her voice is muffled.

"I hope you don't mind," Rose says. Maryanne likes working in this female only health club. Ted had teased her at first, he said the place was probably full of lesbians. But, as far as she can see, the customers are just women who want to lose weight and get a massage. And to not have a gaggle of nosy and noisy males watching every move they make. Besides this spa owner encourages the girls working here to wear as little clothing as they feel comfortable with and Maryanne likes to be naked. Somehow she feels closer to God when she leaves her clothes behind.

"Mind what?" Maryanne is not thinking, just rolling her hands, letting power pull through her arms and hands.

"You know. The way I am. I'm sorry. No, actually I'm not but.... whatever." Rose lapses into silence. The only sound is flesh rubbing flesh. "I mean, you're really very good at this, aren't you?" Maryanne just keeps working.

"I like your body," Maryanne says finally, "I feel love and joy in all this flesh. Like cotton candy or big, big pillows. It's beautiful." Maryanne sometimes thinks she could crawl inside fat like this, be covered, protected and shaded from the sun. It would be soft and safe and smell like sweat on the inside of a t-shirt. She doesn't talk like this to Rose, of course, people wouldn't understand.

Maryanne happens to glance in the mirror and sees Ted standing in the doorway with his camera. Surprise pulls at her face. She makes pushing motions toward the door, mouths words into the mirror. But he doesn't leave. He is snapping photos. Maryanne is not happy. Her hands grab the fat and squeeze, then soften. Rose pushes up with her hands.

"Are we finished?"

"Sorry, was that too rough?" Maryanne turns and looks back at the empty doorway.

"Oh no, I just thought you seemed finished. It's way over my hour, you know, not that I wouldn't stay all day if your boss would let me." Rose's clothes are draped neatly over a straight wood chair. Rose looks toward the chair but does not get up. She is embarrassed.

"Okay," Maryanne says. She wants to look around for Ted anyway.

"I'm just nervous, you know. You girls all have such fine bodies, such lovely bodies," Rose says, "especially you." Maryanne does not have any answer for this. She is not so young anymore. She has fine white hairs on her face that glow in the light and she has faint lines beginning around her down turned, petulant mouth. Maryanne touches Rose's back one more time.

"Just a minute," Maryanne says, then turns and walks toward the doorway. In the corner of her eye she sees Rose raise up, lower her feet to the floor. Maryanne grabs her robe from the towel rack and walks quickly by the drink machine, out past the first fountain where you can begin to see the desert through a window. The fantastic desert that they had traveled halfway around the world to live in.

But, of course, Ted is not anywhere. How can he get away with that? Doesn't anyone ever watch the doors? He's probably back in his darkroom by now. When Maryanne gets back to her massage cubicle, Rose is dressed and ready to leave.

"Sorry I rushed off. See you next Thursday," Maryanne says. Rose waves her hand back and forth quickly as she walks out the door. She stops and looks around before she walks into the parking lot. As if someone might be waiting for her.

Ted's name is really Takahashi, but people call him Ted. He's Japanese and he's a photographer. His photographs line the walls of their rooms, fill the kitchen drawers. They poke from the bottoms of cupboards and stack deep on the bookshelves. Sometimes Maryanne forgets that he's also a very good photographer and his photos appear regularly in local newspapers and magazines, even down in Phoenix. But it's a wonder he can even find anything in this blizzard of photo paper. He develops them in the darkroom and studies them for awhile. Then he deposits them in a damp stack somewhere, anywhere. Or they hang on endless kite strings, between windows, down hallways, over the kitchen sink.

"I know exactly where each photo is. I really do," he says. Maryanne has dish soap on her hands and she has decided to keep quiet, for the moment, about Ted's intrusive photo session at the New Age Health Spa. She is making circular motions with her wrists over three photos lined up by the kitchen sink, next to the dish drainer. She bends over, looks closer, then stands up straight.

"What's this? Now what are you up to? Isn't that Mr. Patel, our neighbor?"

"So?"

"He's right next door. Over the side fence."

"Right, again."

Maryanne turns back to the sink and spats a pan lid under the faucet, then slaps it into the drainer with a loud clack. Ted picks up the three photographs, makes a shuffling motion like with a deck of cards. Maryanne folds the dish towel into a neat square, lays it on the sink, pats it twice.

"So why spy on him? He's not bothering us or anything is he?" Lately Ted has been taking pictures of people who don't necessarily want their pictures taken. Like in the supermarket, old ladies in the vegetable section, squeezing the tomatoes. Or the pale white woman packing persimmons into a plastic bag—she screamed and pushed her cart into the watermelons which tumbled like bowling balls down the liquor aisle. The manager walked over but Ted and Maryanne just kept on strolling toward the cereal and crackers. This is the sort of thing that Ted has been getting into. Now he shows up during massage time at the health spa. Maryanne doesn't need anymore stress. Not with her mother on the way.

"Well, he's always there in his back yard. He's kind of interesting, you know, the way he walks, the way he stands in one spot, looking at nothing."

"So? He's from another county, Ted, they have different ways, right? Why bother with him? He's our next door neighbor." Maryanne walks by the fridge, almost opens it, then walks out to the front room. Then she walks back in before Ted can move. He is holding a photograph up to the light.

"It's all right, Ted, you can take pictures of whatever you want, okay. It's okay." They look at each other. "Just help me out with my mom, okay?" Ted nods his head. Maryanne fidgets like she has something more to say. "Listen, let's get a couple of pumpkins this year. You can carve big teeth like you used to do."

"That's cool," Ted says, slipping the three photographs into his shirt pocket. "Does that deal include the fat lady?" Maryanne turns to says something but Ted is not there. He's probably back in his darkroom already. A place where, for some reason, Maryanne has never gone. There is a red light, she knows, and the sharp smell of chemicals. She imagines that it is dirty, full of cockroaches and spiders. It's not like he doesn't want her in there, not like he's said anything. She just never goes into Ted's darkroom.

Rose and Maryanne are in the sauna. They are naked and Rose's body fills the bench on her side of the tiny room, her arms flow from her shoulders like balloons.

"You ought to go, really, Maryanne," Rose says, "You're good, I'm not kidding, you're the best this place has ever had."

Maryanne is sitting up straight in front of the fake rocks that hide the heating element. Her chest is pushed forward, her eyes closed. She is flicking water behind the rocks and steam billows up around her legs.

Rose says, "what I mean is that it's a dead end here. Rubbing old lady's backs. Right? In the middle of a nowhere desert, at that." Maryanne is trying to picture Jesus on the cross but the image keeps shifting and she sees a fat male Buddha, laughing, with one flat hand held out toward her. Maryanne opens her eyes.

"We can go to the massage table now, if you're ready," Maryanne says. She stands up. Her body really is beautiful, long pale legs, light yellow hair, not a thread of extra flesh. Rose has not moved an inch.

"Like I said, I know the couple that runs the place. It's like a dream, a real resort by the sea. I've even got postcards." Rose reaches with her hand as if she might pluck a post card out of a shirt pocket. Maryanne bends over and reaches down, offering her hand for Rose to grab.

"In Hawaii?" Maryanne asks, she pulls hard. Rose is up.

"Kauai, actually, the garden island."

"I haven't mentioned this, I guess, Rose but that's where we came from, before Sedona I mean. Ted has relatives over there. We lived on Oahu on the other side of the mountains." Maryanne and Rose stop talking and look at each other—it's almost like they are seeing each other for the first time. There is a long silence.

"I've never told anyone this, Rose, but sometimes I fly during my sleep at night, you know, like lift up out of my body and fly. Those mountains in Oahu are the mountains I fly over." The two naked women are standing in the doorway to the sauna. They haven't moved. "So it was really hard to leave Hawaii. But it was time. I needed to fly somewhere else."

Maryanne reaches out and touches Rose on the shoulder, looks into her eyes. "I really like Sedona. I like being in the middle of nowhere. These red mountains, the almost human shapes, you know, there really is something going on here.

You can feel it in the air." Maryanne likes the cactus and the parched thorns reaching out for water. The desert is clean and simple. Just the right kind of place for something really important to happen.

Rose holds onto Maryanne's hand and they bend through the short door, around the towel rack, and walk toward the massage table. Heat follows them, flows through them. Rose stops suddenly.

"I forgot my clothes." She goes back to the bench by the sauna door. She holds up a pair of purple shorts and a yellow shirt a big as a beach umbrella.

"Can you believe that? I forgot my clothes."

The futon is lumped and curves toward the center of the bed. Maryanne rolls softly toward Ted and dreams. She dreams that she has awakened in the night and Ted is not in the bed. She pats the sheets, pats in widening circles but no one is there. Maryanne walks to the front door and looks out at the deserted streets. It's like in a 1930s black and white movie where long shadows cross over people's faces and naked street lamps stand in painful circles of light. These are the movies where evil is palpable, a kind of dark light that floods over the streets and houses. Maryanne has always had dreams like this, especially when she was younger and used to stay up late watching midnight movies on TV. Her mother would burst heavily into the living room, look at the TV as if she had seen a ghost, then chase Maryanne off to bed.

"It's Satan's work, I tell you, TV is the devil's workshop, just like preacher said, and I'm getting rid of it tomorrow," the mother would say. She never did though. She liked to eat potato chips and watch soap operas too much. She watched exercise programs, too, that cute Simmons guy with the curly hair. But she decided it was no use trying to exercise. It just wouldn't work. The Lord had made her a woman with big bones and lots of meat on those bones. One day, on a whim, she had bought a bathing at a thrift shop and she kept it for awhile on the top shelf of her closet. In the end, she gave it Maryanne. It was a one piece suit of thick material with sleeves, like something from a beach scene in a 1920s photograph.

Maryanne, however, did not go swimming in those days. But even then she had wanted to be naked, believing that Jesus was more likely found between her cool sheets than in a church packed with sweating bodies. Her mother's church, for example. Of course, these were not sentiments she could share with her mother.

Maryanne starts suddenly and wakes up. Ted is there in bed with her. She feels an inexplicable desire to wake him up, to touch him, to talk. She stands up and walks toward the kitchen, then veers off and finds herself in front of the darkroom door. She stops and waits. She listens. Nothing. She opens the door and walks in.

The darkroom is dark, of course, but her sleeping eyes are used to darkness. And the red light is still on. She can see pretty well and she picks up a small penlight that she knows Ted uses. She stares at photos, pulls them off the drying lines and hooks. She searches through drawers and pulls out a Playboy magazine from behind a stack of photography manuals. It falls open in Maryanne's hands and the centerfold flops out. An Asian girl, perfect skin, long black hair. Maryanne feels dizzy. She doesn't know what she's looking for.

Then she sees the photographs from the New Age Health Spa. They are pretty good, actually, almost flattering. But that's just the beginning—now she finds a short clothesline of photos of Rose. Rose walking in the street, Rose in her car, Rose opening her front door. Shots of Rose inside her house, opening the refrigerator in the kitchen, drinking from a bottle.

Maryanne stops. She arranges all the photos she has looked at face down on the light board. She takes her time and makes a straight line. Maryanne can feel something taking flight in her mind, like a large heavy bird flapping hard over still water. She lays the penlight where she found it and closes the darkroom door softly behind her. Maryanne lies on her side of the bed, holding her breath, then letting the air out slowly, silently. She is breathing, finding her balance. She is waiting for night to finish.

Ted is frying four eggs in a pan when Maryanne comes up behind him. The eggs sizzle and sputter as Ted shakes salt and pepper into the pan. He hears her coming but he doesn't turn around.

"Well, I might as well say it right out, I guess. Last night I found all those photos you've taken of Rose." Ted keeps on moving the eggs in the pan.

"So?"

"So? You followed her in the street. You filmed through her windows. You have no right to do any of that. What do you mean, "so"? Who do you think you are?" Ted flips the eggs over in one easy splat.

"I'm a photographer. I photograph whatever interests me. You said that was okay, didn't you? Rose is pretty interesting." Ted shuts off the flame under the pan and turns around to face Maryanne.

"I didn't know what you were really up to when I said that." The color is rising on Maryanne's cheeks, her throat is red where she's been rubbing it with the palm of her hand. "What you're doing is not okay. Not okay at all."

"Not okay? Fine." Ted flops the eggs onto a plate and sets the plate on the kitchen table. "Maybe some of what you're doing isn't so okay, either. How about that?"

"Like what?"

"Like your whole holier than thou business about Jesus landing here in Sedona. What about that? What's he landing in—a spaceship? What bullshit!" Ted forks a piece of egg into his mouth.

"What? Bullshit? What? I never said any such thing. When did I say that? When?"

"Well, you think it though, just admit it. You think that might happen, that's why you wanted to move here to begin with. Just admit it." Ted adds a touch more pepper to the eggs.

"You're the one full of bullshit. Right up to here." Maryanne holds a flat hand up to her neck. "Right up to your chin."

"Yeah, well your porked out family couldn't even fit into a spaceship. Your fat Uncle Jack, your fat Aunt Fanny. It'd crash with all those fatsos in there." Ted sets his empty plate on the counter. "Is that why your mom's coming over here? To get an early reservation on the judgment day express?"

"My mom? Now you're dragging her into it." Maryanne is holding her head in both hands and staring at Ted's empty plate. It is flecked with pepper and stripes of moist yellow egg. She collapses into a chair. "I give up. You've made fun of everything. You don't love me. So fuck you, Takahashi."

Ted comes up behind her chair. He puts his hand on her head, pats her hair. She bats once at his hand. He's expecting her to say don't touch me. Isn't that what angry women always say? But she doesn't. She puts her hand on top of his hand. They don't speak. They both rub the side and back of Maryanne's head. They smooth down her hair. Two hands rubbing together.

Ted has a plan. He wants more photographs of Rose. He wants Halloween photographs and he wants Maryanne to help him get them. He thinks he can sell them to a big time photo magazine. Maryanne doesn't like it but she wants to protect Rose and so she agrees to go along with Ted's scenario. Ted wants to trick or treat at Rose's house. He will dress as the devil and Maryanne will be an angel. It will be perfect. It will be fun. And, of course, there will be lots of photographs.

Maryanne and Ted are standing in front of Rose's house. Maryanne hadn't even known how to find it but Ted knew the way. Why not? He had followed her home. Ted is not a very convincing devil, his red suit is too tight and the claws on his feet keep coming off. The tail is pretty good though. Maryanne is a perfect angel, her halo follows her head when she turns and her short white skirt is as innocent as it is provocative. They knock on Rose's door.

Rose opens the door immediately, she has been waiting for kids to trick or treat. She is dressed as a pumpkin and has a large bucket of mini candy bars in her hand.

"It's you, Maryanne, what an angel you are!"

"And what a pumpkin you are!" Maryanne says as she and Ted walk in the door. Ted is snapping photos but nobody pays any attention. A troop of little gremlins has arrived and they stand in an orderly line to receive their candy. A red Buick trails along the street curb, keeping an eye on the children. Rose is popping mini bars into the sacks. Maryanne thinks how light Rose is on her feet, such heavy arms and legs, yet she is like a cat, almost, a quick dance from light to dark. They close the door and, almost at once, the door bell rings again and the air is alive with giggles and Snickers bars. Rose gets out another large sack—Three Musketeers. They are throwing candy at the children's plastic bags, two points, a ringer, bull's eye. It's like throwing popcorn to the ducks when there are hundreds of them flying from all parts of a pond. They quack and laugh and scream and the door slams, then rings again.

Finally the action tails off. A few stragglers ring the bell, then nothing. It is too late for children to be out on the streets. Rose shuts the door and turns out the porch light.

"I have a surprise. I had a feeling someone might be here tonight." She leads the way to a dining table with a huge bowl in the center. She gets a large container out of her freezer and starts tossing colored balls into the bowl. Nine flavors of ice cream floating in a soup of cold seven-up.

"Bouillabaisse, Sedona style," Rose says. Ted and Maryanne look at her.

Maryanne chips in, "it's beautiful, look, mango, chocolate chip, coffee crunch, chocolate raspberry truffle, pistachio, everything I've always wanted." Rose tosses in one last scoop.

"Oreo cookie." Rose says. She hands out miniature buckets with ropes attached. You're supposed to throw in the bucket and see what you can catch. Ted is getting a few good angles with his camera. That's when the telephone rings. Rose says, "forget it, let it ring. It'll stop."

But it doesn't stop. Rose doesn't have an answering machine. It just rings and rings and rings. Just when you think it will stop, it doesn't. It just keeps on ringing.

"It's probably my mother," Maryanne says, finally. She speaks with grave assurance and resignation. "My mother has landed in Phoenix and is headed our way."

EIGHTY JAGUARS

I first saw Melissa and the red Jaguar on one of those AAA jobs, you know, the kind where you can only tow them three miles and you don't even get a tip. How much do you make out of that? Twenty bucks, if you're lucky. Anyway, I'd rather stay in bed. They got me out of the sack at one in the morning and the dispatcher lady said the job was already stale. Which means it was called in over an hour before and by now the customer had probably disappeared.

Donna probably didn't even hear the phone ring. She sure didn't move in bed or say anything. Of course, this kind of rude awakening happens pretty often. So I blew out of there and busted ass down highway 580 until I saw the Shell station the car was supposed to be at. I saw the guy the minute I hit the exit, perched on the hood of his red Jaguar, like some sort of Buddha, arms folded, pissed off. Well, that's how it is in the towing business, you don't exactly meet people in the happiest circumstances. They are either angry or depressed or both. He saw me coming, all right, and jumped down to the pavement, but I guess he was a little dizzy because he landed and tipped forward and almost fell into a gas pump. I pulled up behind the Jaguar. It had personalized plates, YOUFISH, figure that one out for me. So I stopped quick and started writing on my ledger pad. That's what we're supposed to do, document time of arrival, license plate, and so on. But this guy was anxious, naturally, and he came up to the door of my cab. He looked up at me.

"Can you see the mess from here?" he asked. He looked like he wanted to rest against the tow truck but he just leaned slightly in my direction.

"See what?" I asked. You can't see much of anything from inside the cab of a tow truck.

"The oil under there, look, what do you think it is?" I opened the door and he moved back. I jumped down beside him. Sure enough, a pool of oil spread out under the Jaguar, then narrowed behind the car for fifty feet and became a thin trail which disappeared onto the freeway access road.

"What happened?" I asked. He looked at me, then over at his car. That's when I saw the woman. A major splash of red hair huddled down in the shotgun seat.

"What happened is I lost all my oil out on the freeway and the oil gauge went flat. So I turned off the engine and coasted in here. I added four quarts and drove a few yards and the oil came right out." He bent over at the waist and stuck his head under the Jaguar, then popped up straight with one hand pushing on the small of his back. I could see he was hurting. His eyes had a kind of an irrational sheen, like he wanted to scoop up all the oil and put it back in his engine. The gas station attendant was watching us through the glass window. She could easily see the splash of oil on the white concrete. She was probably the one who would have to clean up the mess.

"What do you think?" He spoke in a low voice, almost a whisper. These fat cats never want their women to be in on conversations with guys like me. You know, workers. They want to handle issues man to man. Then, just like that, the woman was out of the car, looking at the pool of oil. She was sexy all right, tight body, high heels, red hair down to her waist, a real looker, that one. She was wearing one of those wide black belts that make a woman's waist look as trim as a flower stem. She started to walk toward us and, right away, his voice got more authoritative, like a Sunday school teacher who sees his subjects sneaking out under a curtain. So I tried to help him out.

"Where do you want to go?" I was leaning back against my truck. "There's a garage two exits down, in San Lorenzo."

"They open tomorrow?"

"Tomorrow's Sunday, right?" I said this and looked back at the girl and the Jaguar. She was standing there, watching us. "Probably not."

"How far is it to a BART station?" I could see he was getting desperate, his lips tightened, his hands fluttered in front of his belt. The night was a lost cause, anyway, so I decided to break the log jam.

"Look, I'll tow you home, or wherever, just give me fifty bucks and sign the AAA book." He looked at me.

"Doesn't it have to be under three miles?"

"That's what the fifty bucks is for. It's a good deal. I'd grab it if I were you." But I knew he would agree to just about anything, I had known that the minute I saw the woman. He nodded his head slowly and patted the back of his pants to check if his wallet was still there. The girl hadn't said a word but she was watching and listening. I could see she was the type that didn't miss much.

So I set up the clamps on the bumper and took the car out of gear, put a lock on the steering wheel. I've got one of those old fashioned rigs, the kind where you lift the front of the car and pull it along on its rear wheels. Other guys have trucks where you pick up the whole car. Now that would be sweet, wouldn't it? But who can afford the payments on a truck like that?

"I'll stay in the car," he said. I looked at him.

"That's against the rules," I said and then paused for effect. "It's an insurance thing." That's what we always say, no matter what the customer wants to do. But this guy wasn't buying it, I guess, because he walked right up to his car door just as I was raising the front end.

"I'll ride in here," he said, as if he hadn't heard me at all. I looked at the woman, his wife I supposed, but she looked away, down at her feet. She was standing by the truck cab, so I guessed she wasn't planning to join in her hubby's big adventure. Then he got in. I hit the lever, the belts squealed and the Jaguar climbed up with a jerk. I looked up at him.

"Don't mess with the wheel lock, okay?" He sat there with his face down on the steering wheel for a second, then his head jerked up when he heard my voice. I locked the car into towing position. He was tilted back at a crazy angle like one of those mannequins you see in a department store window.

So were sitting in the cab rolling down the freeway when I really started to notice the wife. How could I help it? She was sitting over by the window, I was shifting gears and looking in the rear view mirror. I couldn't quite see the husband, the rig and the front end of the Jaguar blocked my view. But I could see his arm sticking out the window in my side mirror. She was a classy one, this wife, tiny sharp features, freckles. Her eyes were wide, as if she had just seen something she didn't quite understand, the ghost of a question resting gently on her lips. The red hair was an explosion, like those burgundy fuchsias that hang from the ceilings of flower shops.

I reached for the radio. "Any station you want to hear?" No reply. She was looking in the side mirror. Of course, she couldn't see anything, it was adjusted for me, not for her. "Any type of music you like?" I asked. She looked at me, finally.

"Whatever." For a minute I thought she was going to roll the window down and try to adjust the side mirror. She didn't. Then she said, "we need to take 238, then go north on 880 to Marina, okay?" So I tuned in a country station and pretty soon we were listening to good old Hank Snow. She stared at the radio.

"I like this old style country music myself," I said. "You know, Charley Pride, Patsy Kline, Merle Haggard, those kind of folks." I was trying to loosen up the conversation a little. Might as well be friendly, I always say. She looked at me again, then reached out and snapped off the radio.

"What's your name?" she said. I was looking at my radio, wondering if she broke it.

"Jack," I said. "Jackson, actually, Jack for short."

"Okay, Jackson, don't pay any attention to Charlie back there." She looked back at the Jaguar. "He's a little upset."

"Okay, lady, that's fine, it all pays the same."

"Exactly!" She fished around in her purse, then handed me a card. "Call me," she said. I held the card out in the air over the dashboard. "It's about another tow job." We got off the freeway and headed down a side street. She popped open her seat belt. After a minute or two, she pointed out the window and I hit the brakes and pulled over to the curb by a large house set back from the road. I didn't look at the card, really, until I was back out on the freeway again. A fancy drawing of a flower and a woman's name. On top of the card it said THE TEMPLE OF HEART CONSCIOUSNESS. Now what in the hell kind of church is that, I wondered? I put the card in the ashtray but I never called her. I didn't need that kind of trouble.

I was lying in bed at eight o'clock in the morning when the phone rang. My phone never rings when I want it to. Dead cars are catastrophes, life stoppers. They never come at a good time for anybody. I had been holding my hands over my head, spreading my fingers, letting the light through, then closing them. A type of morning hypnosis. I listened to the phone ring for a while, then picked it up.

"Jackson Towing?" someone said in my ear. It was a statement more than a question. I knew her voice.

"That's right, I'm Jackson."

"You're the one who towed our car at the Shell, right?" I could feel a lot of distance in her voice, the length of space from me to the gourmet kitchen where she was probably sitting, munching slivers of watermelon and granola muffin.

"I'm the guy. What's up?" I was sitting up in bed by then, alert. Donna was waking up, too, but she was used to phone calls at all hours.

"I've got a tow job for you." She stopped, waited for me to ask questions.

"That's good. I could use the work." I didn't bite. I can wait. I guessed she'd got my phone number off the side of the truck. Like I said, she's pretty quick.

"It's a little far from here though," she said.

"How far? Where is it? Gas costs a lot and my rig gets about eight miles a gallon."

"North."

"Where north?" Donna was sitting up, listening. I put my hand over the mouthpiece. "It's a tow job."

"Oh really? What a surprise!" Donna said and climbed out of bed. She looked pretty good, too, naked that is, reaching for her purple robe. She turned around. "What else could it possibly be?" I turned back to the phone.

"Okay, lady, where is this car, anyway? This could get pretty expensive, you know." I wanted to go downstairs and eat. Donna throws together some great bacon and eggs and hash browns.

"Just meet me a ways down from that Shell station around ten in the morning tomorrow, okay?" I wasn't used to this cloak and dagger stuff. Tow jobs are usually pretty boring.

"Okay, I'll be there." I put the phone down and looked around for Donna. She was downstairs and I could smell bacon and sausages sizzling in a greasy pan. Well, ain't that great, I thought, a tow job and no address.

The next morning I could see her and the car almost a mile away. Another red Jaguar, this time a vintage 1959.

"Didn't you say it was up north somewhere?" I had ignored some other calls, supposing I'd be all day on this one. This lady could be big money, I'd been thinking.

She ignored my question. I reached out to touch the fender. A tow job on a cherry model like this? It was a classic beauty. So I gave her a hard, questioning look. She read my mind.

"It doesn't run. It's dead." She walked up to the driver's door and waved her arms over the windshield. "It's been like this for months." The Jaguar sat comfortable by the curb.

"Here on this corner?" We were standing in front of a Seven-Eleven store and I could see a liquor store bordering the back parking lot. Not the best neighborhood to be hanging out with a dead Jaguar-.

"No, bright guy, somewhere else. But now it's here. Lucky you. You don't have to drive so far." She was standing in back of the Jaguar, arms crossed over her black sweater. Her mouth was set in a no nonsense frown. I gave up.

"Okay, where to then?" I looked over at my rig. "Where are we headed?" She let some air out of her mouth, then pressed her hands down on a front fender.

"A junk yard!" She tucked her hands in close to her waist. "Maybe I can sell it."

"What?" I looked at the car again, walked over to the front window. Real wood interior, original red seat leather, clean as a whistle, a real beauty. "What junk yard?"

"I have a choice?" She looked more surprised than usual, a little less demanding. So I told her what I thought.

"Look, this is ridiculous. Just sell it through an ad or take it to a used car lot. Put a for-sale sign in the window. Anything. It's worth good money, running or not." My dad had owned an old Jaguar just like this. Same year. Then he got old and sold it for peanuts. "Hell, I'd give you way more for it than you'd get at a junk yard."

"Right now?" She held a hand flat out in the air between us. She wasn't kidding.

"What? Hey, I'm a little short on cash right now." I reached back and felt my empty wallet with my left hand. Then I got angry. "Look, I don't have all day here, what do you want to do with this vehicle?"

"I want a tow job," she said slowly, as if spelling out the words. "To a junk yard where I can sell this car. Is that going to work for you?" She had the keys in her hand and she walked up close to me, opened her hand into mine. That's when I smelled her perfume and I knew right then that I was out of my depth. But, to tell the truth, I had known that ever since she punched out my radio.

"Listen, lady."

"I have a name, Mr. Jackson!" I knew that, of course, I had her card in my ashtray.

"Oh, what is it?"

"Melissa Larsen."

"Okay Melissa." That wasn't the name I remembered from the card but who cared, anyway. "We can tow it over to FIFTIES if you want. It's back up in Berkeley, though, it'll cost a little." I turned around to walk back to my truck. She came up fast behind me and I smelled her again, sort of like flowers or that potpourri that comes in little pots.

"Don't worry, Jack," she said softly. "We'll do okay. I have a good feeling about it." Fine, just fine, I said to myself and I spun my truck around, lined it up, then I was out there, hooking up the chains. I hit the lever and up it went. The red

Jaguar sat there, kind of helpless, nose in the air, rear tires dragging behind. You might say raising a car is like putting someone into traction in a hospital, like taking control of something. Then I turned to her and laid it on the line. Or tried to anyway.

"What's this all about, Melissa?" But she didn't say a word, just climbed up into my truck and sat by the window with her arms folded. Pretty much like the last time she'd been sitting there. I looked over at her and flipped on the radio. Cowboy music filled the air between us. She watched the bugs hit the windshield. That's springtime for you, bugs and butterflies and a splattered windshield after five minutes on the freeway. There was a big orange and black splotch right in front of Melissa's nose. A Monarch, I guess. Finally, she started up.

"Charley's not my husband, by the way. Or my boyfriend even." She reached up and bent the sun visor down. She was looking for a mirror, probably.

"Who?" I knew who she meant, of course, but it doesn't hurt to play the dummy game once in a while.

"You know, the guy at the Shell who insisted on riding in back while you towed the Jaguar—that's Charley."

"Oh, that guy, he seemed pretty nervous about something or other." I shifted gears.

"Well, he had good reason to be. Anyway it's not what you think." She was looking directly at me now, I could feel it, but I didn't turn my head. I stuck to my business, driving. I've been driving these tow trucks for twenty years now and I've seen just about everything.

"It's not what I think?" I stuck the truck in a lower gear, we were going down the hill just before the junk yard, under the freeway by the train tracks. "What I think is that you stole this car somewhere, that's what I really think."

"What? What do you mean?" The wind blew in the window and her hair spun red and wild around her head. I figured it would be best to keep quiet. "Well, I didn't steal it and I wouldn't, Mr. Jackson. I couldn't, even if I wanted to. It was more of a gift, really, anyway it's mine, that's for sure, all mine." She zipped the window shut, biting off the wind.

"Right, sure," I said. "And I suppose that Charley guy was on the up and up with that other Jaguar." I had decided that Melissa was not going to fool me with theatrics.

"Oh, he's just another peon like me." Then she looked at me funny and clammed up. Like she had said way more than she had wanted to say.

"Whatever," I said and pulled the truck over into the FIFTIES parking lot. The rusted body of a 1957 Chevrolet was mounted on a two story roof, a streaked turquoise relic, cracked and chipped from wind and rain. The funny thing was that the gas cap cover, which is hidden in the tail light on a '57, was sticking up in the air, stuck open. I had worked in a gas station as a kid and leaving a fill cover open like that could get you fired. Of course, that was all probably part of a junkyard joke. It had to be.

"Okay, so it's your Jaguar then. That's good because you're about to sell it," I said. "Got the pink?"

"The what?"

"The pink slip. The ownership certificate."

"What's that?" Her face was round like she had just bit down on a hard walnut. "You mean the registration? It's in the glove box."

"No. It's pink. It's what you need to sell it," I said and I looked at her real hard. But it didn't do any good, she just sat there. "Okay, okay, I'll talk to the guy, we'll see, I've done business with him before." So I jumped down and left her up in the truck. I started to walk off, then turned back.

"Just stay there, okay?" She didn't move. "Is that okay?" She nodded and I got the idea that maybe she was sleepy. Maybe she had been up all night, who knows? Getting this Jaguar to where I found it had probably been no picnic. Maybe she's going to fall asleep in the tow truck. Wouldn't that be something? A babe like that sacked out in my tow truck. I turned and walked toward the office door.

FIFTIES was more than just a junk yard. They rebuilt old cars from the ground up, especially old Corvettes and Thunderbirds. Wrecked cars were stacked up three, sometimes five high, along the fences. The cars below were partly sheltered from the weather but the ones on top were caked and rusted. The yard was littered with hubcaps, fan belts, radiator hoses and pieces of plastic tail light. I walked past labeled bins filled with generators, alternators, drive shafts, engine blocks, transmissions. A German Shepherd watched me with lazy eyes.

I hit the buzzer and a man in a white tee shirt walked out of a back room. He had a pack of Marlboro cigarettes rolled into the sleeve of his left arm. His hair was combed into a greasy ducktail. He was a fifties sort of guy. All of the men working here looked that way. I'd seen this guy before but he was not the one I usually dealt with.

"Yeah," he said, "what'ya need, bud?"

"I've got a good one out there on my rig. Want to have a look?"

"One what?" He looked out the window and saw my tow truck and the Jaguar. "What year is that?" he asked and he was already half way out the door. I followed him. "Well, these aren't worth so much no more, you know, not nowadays." He had his hand on a red rear fender. I kept quiet. He walked around to the front of the car and looked up at the bumper hooks. I hadn't lowered the car yet.

"Won't run?" he said and turned to face me.

"Nope," I said. Silence.

"What's wrong with it?" he said.

"What's it worth?" I said.

"Depends." He stood with his legs straddling a pool of oil on the hard packed dirt. His shoes were shiny and bright. He had a comb tucked in his belt and he looked like he might take it out.

"Head gasket," I said. "That's all."

"Right, right, they all say that. No cracked head, no cracked block, no cam shaft, just a head gasket." He unrolled his sleeve and took out a cigarette, then rolled the sleeve back up. He put the Marlboro in his mouth but didn't light it.

"How much can you give me for it?" I was making ready to get back in my truck. I figured that would get his attention. He picked up a distributor cap with three spark plug wires hanging from its head, held it by the coil wire, then started swinging it in small circles.

"I'll give you seven fifty, as is," he said and he swung the cap harder. The cap popped off the wire and flew against the tin wall of the parts shed with a loud clatter. He stood there holding the drooping coil wire. I took a step toward my truck, reached for the door. I turned around quick.

"Sold," I said. "Pink's in the glove box." I hit the down lever and the Jaguar creaked to the ground, the tires sat hard on the oily dirt. I didn't look at him, I knew better. He was thinking he could have gotten it cheaper. That's when he saw Melissa sitting in the cab.

"Wait a second!" He stepped back, then came forward quickly. "Lemme see it." He stuck out his hand. "The pink slip, lemme see it." I walked over to the passenger side door and jerked it open, popped the glove box. I stood up straight.

"Don't have it."

"Three hundred," he said. He pulled out the comb, ran his finger down the teeth. "Take it or leave it." The sound of the comb was like strange background music in a scary movie, something to mark a turning point. He stepped back, leaned against a wall, ran the comb through his hair, then stuck it back on his belt.

"Okay," I said. He had me.

Melissa opened up the top two buttons of her shirt and stuck the money in her bra, three one hundred dollar bills. Can you believe it? I'd seen that happen in movies but never in real life. Then she looked at me with a kind of secretive smile and all the little lines perked out around her eyes and mouth. She wasn't that young, sort of a years later hippie, I was starting to think. The hair, the old fashioned dresses, her way of touching you on the arm when she talked.

"Melissa," I said, "why'd you do it?"

"Do what?" She was looking out the window.

"Come on, you know, steal that car. I know you stole it from somewhere, somehow." I felt like I was getting to know her pretty well by then, like I could be straight about certain things.

"Well, I didn't really steal it. It really didn't run, hasn't for quite a while." She was putting out her hand, touching my arm every once in a while, as I ran through the gears. "He'll never miss it anyhow." Now we'd gotten down to it, the real business.

"Who's the he?" I asked. She didn't answer but she left her hand on my arm for a quick minute. We drove down the freeway, high up in the air in my old tow truck. I turned the radio a little louder.

Things got a little more complicated after that but not very complicated. We'd get together in a coffee shop or a deli and talk about another tow job that might or might not happen. I figured it was just small talk. One time we went down by the railroad tracks and watched the trains go by.

Like I used to do when I was a kid in Sylmar. In those days the trains seemed like wild buffalo rushing along the rows of olive and orange trees and, sometimes, I would see a hobo jumping from one car to another. It was usually real quiet between me and Melissa, like we were afraid to say much. It was like we were waiting for something to happen, maybe something bad.

I'd talk about Sylmar and she'd talk about men she'd known but nothing recent for either of us. There was this guy who'd bought her a fancy ring, then disappeared. Then one day she saw his face in a newspaper, shot dead in a liquor store robbery. I talked about a couple of women I'd known, too, but nothing about Donna. Why complicate things? It was like that and then I wouldn't hear from her for a week or two, maybe a month, I figured she was out of town or something. Then I'd get a phone call.

One morning the kitchen phone rang pretty early. Donna was already up and she was sitting on the downstairs john, so she could hear me talking just fine.

"It's Melissa," she said.

"I know." I was standing in the kitchen, holding a banana, scratching my nose with one end of it.

"Is she listening? Can she hear us?"

"Yes, I do tow jobs," I answered cleverly.

"Well, this really is about a tow job, okay?" Melissa was all business, but then she always was on the telephone. She was nicer in person.

"Where's it located?" I sat down on a kitchen chair.

"Up north," she said. I could hear Melissa breathing. The toilet flushed. Up north? Hadn't I heard that one before.

"Up north? Up Highway 101. Okay, let's see, just outside where? Myers Flat, yeah, before Richardson Grove. Yeah, I know the spot. A white Cadillac Cimarron, okay. License number?" I was writing quick notes on a bumpy paper towel and the pen kept tearing the paper.

"That's just great," Melissa said, "you're a natural talent. Just come over here, okay? I'm serious. There really is a car to tow this time."

I put the phone down and looked for Donna. She wasn't in the bathroom. She was standing in front of the TV, staring at the screen. An eighteen wheeler had flipped on the 980 freeway and it had been full of cantaloupes. The cameras got there right away and cantaloupes were everywhere, crushed on the pavement, huddled by the hundreds alongside the asphalt. A highway patrol car drove through a pool of cantaloupes and they leaped and splattered in all directions. The news lady was standing by the side of the freeway with a cantaloupe in one hand and a microphone in the other.

"Look at that!" Donna pointed at the screen. A cop was pushing a shop broom into a wave of broken rinds, guts and stringy seeds. "Look what's happening out there," she said. She had her hands on her hips and her face was flushed. Maybe she'd heard something in my voice when I was on the phone, maybe she'd heard Melissa.

"It's a truck accident. Happens everyday." I didn't want to get drawn into some political discussion. "Not much anyone can do about it."

"Do about what?" Donna's face was getting redder.

"About whatever. Hey, you're the one watching TV, not me." But Donna had me in her sights and she was bearing down. So I kept on talking. "Listen, Donna, I've got a   big tow job. Up North on 101. It'll be all day, I think, maybe more." Donna jabbed the TV button. The picture shrank and died. She walked into the kitchen and pulled some pans out of the cupboard. They clanged on the counter top. I followed her, walking softly.

"Hey, you okay?" I said, then I walked over and put a hand on her shoulder.

"Sure, I'm okay, why wouldn't I be?" she said. "Want some eggs?" She cracked two big ones on the side of the skillet. The eggs spat fat and skittered sideways under the spatula. Donna turned them carefully, touching the speckled skin with a little finger, spinning them out onto a dish.

"Sit down," she said, "eat."

So I picked up Melissa and we headed north on 880 and I figured to cross the Bay Bridge and get over to the Golden Gate and Highway 101 or maybe take the Richmond Bridge to San Rafael. She said up north, right? But no, she wanted to take Highway 80 East and head for Napa. So that's what we did.

"Hey, if I'd known we were going wine tasting, we could take a cheaper car, you know. This truck only gets eight miles a gallon." I didn't know what else to say. Actually, I was pretty happy to be going anywhere with Melissa Larsen. She seemed different that day, anyway, like she had decided something. More sexy, sort of. More focused.

She gave me a serious stare. "I know how many miles a gallon you get, Jackson, you've told me often enough. The car we're towing is off the road up above Calistoga. This is about a tow job, remember?"

Melissa seemed to relax as we drove through the miles and miles of grape vines. "They look so peaceful growing out there," she said, "so orderly, look at the little tubes of water leading to each vine." Bobby Bare was on the radio singing about a mermaid that got away. He's swimming after her and she has the head of a fish and legs of a girl. I listen to the words of cowboy songs. You never know what you might learn.

Finally, she turned to me. "Okay, Jack, listen to me now. I do want to steal a car." She said this easy enough. Big surprise. "Well, he's got eighty of them, can you believe that? Eighty Jaguars and all of them are red. Eighty!" Melissa had her knees pulled up under her chin and her words came in a rush.

"I guess he's got two less right now, doesn't he?" I said. Melissa gave me a curious look.

"Charley got that first one and it needed a new engine. The last one didn't even count—three hundred bucks, are you kidding?" Melissa was more excited right then than I had ever seen her. "I even had to pay someone to pull it down there."

"Some guy, right?"

"Of course." She spat the words out of the corner of her mouth. "Do you think a woman would help me haul a broken down car for three hours and through rush hour traffic to Oakland?"

"Why not?"

"Look, don't be stupid, it doesn't help. Anyway, I want to get a good one this time and I know how to do it. It's worth eighty grand and I can get the keys. The pink slip will be in the glove box and it'll be signed off." I could see Melissa had been learning quite a bit about cars lately.

"What do you need me for then?" The tow truck was hitting over sixty on the straightaways and the front end was vibrating, so I slowed down to fifty five.

"It's less suspicious, right?"

"Less suspicious?" Now how would a tow truck pulling a red Jaguar be less suspicious than a red haired girl driving one? That was a philosophical question, if I'd ever heard one.

"Okay, then, who is this guy, the guy that owns all the Jaguars?"

"That doesn't matter," she said and we were silent for a few miles. The grape vines flowed by in a green blur. Then, finally: "A swami, you know, a religious leader. Whatever. I gave massages up there for a while, over a year, actually. It was a great job, if you want to know the truth, a beautiful place." Melissa stopped and took a deep breath. "Hot tubs, live geysers, saunas, even a movie theater."

"And lots of old farts with money who want a massage, right?" I shouldn't have said that, of course, but I did. No response. "Okay, then, if the place is so great, why steal the swami's cars?"

"Because I need the money, why else?" Right about then Melissa decided to change tactics. She moved over closer to me, she even snuggled up a little bit and put her head on my shoulder. That was real nice, for sure. Still, it was hard to believe that I was about ready to help her steal a car. It was too far fetched.

We passed St. Helena and Calistoga and then took a side road off into the mountains. It was just getting dark and the moon was coming up, a full moon, bright between the trees and down the narrow road. Nothing seemed real. Just the moonlight, the brake pedal, the gear shift, the dashboard with the fuel gauge drifting low. Melissa's breath by my side.

"How much farther is this place?" It had been more than three hours on the road and we'd stopped for gas three times.

"Just a little further," she said.

Then we were there. I parked on what seemed like a large plateau, trails led down in most directions. I turned off the headlights. The full moon was all Melissa needed, she obviously knew exactly where we were and where she was going. She was whispering in my ear.

"The cars are in a corral over that way. You just stay here until I come back. I have to talk to someone first." I was standing by my tow truck, wondering when some guy with a shotgun was going to pop out of the bushes. My lips felt like they were stuck to my teeth. Melissa was about to start walking down a path which ran under a giant fig tree. She turned around and looked at me. Then she walked back.

"Jackson, look, this is not a scary place. It's dark. There are all kinds of overnight guests here. Most of them are sleeping on wood decks or hanging out in gazebos. There are hot tubs everywhere you turn." Melissa waved her arms toward the trees as if to envelop the whole enterprise in a benediction. "Nobody knows anybody, really, so you're just as good here as anybody else. Look around a little. Just be back here at your truck in half an hour, okay?" She looked at me one more time, then turned around and walked down the trail.

I stood by the safety of my truck for a few minutes. Then I thought what the hell, I started walking down a gravel path. Very smooth, no roots or rocks to trip on. The moon was bright enough. I saw a bigger light through the trees and so I walked toward it. Then I stopped. What I saw was like falling to the Earth from the moon. Wood decks surrounded an emerald pool, other decks descended in terraces along a hillside, between pathways of trees and flowering shrubs. Beautiful women, naked women, were massaging old bodies on flat wood tables. Naked men and women, even children, were relaxing on the decks, talking in low voices. There were people in bathing suits, too, even people partially dressed. I saw a small hut with a Pete's Coffee sign on one side.

Then I realized I was very near the edge of a darkened pool from which steam billowed. I stepped back behind a tree. Stone steps led down into the pool, a man and several women stood silently in the chest deep water. A fat Buddha sat at the opposite end and a white pipe extended from under this statue over the edge of the pool—hot water from the pipe poured into the pool, pushing up clouds of steam.

One of the women moved under the pipe and looked up at the Buddha. She raised her arms, as if in prayer, then turned onto her back, pushing her breasts up into the air. Steaming water poured out onto her belly. Then a gust of wind must have blown some chimes in a tree somewhere. The music was like something from another universe. Like when an angel calls with a lyre for peace in a world of suffering and pain. And the hot water just kept on flowing up from the center of the Earth.

Jaguars were lined up along the inside of a tall wire fence, along all four sides, an acre or more of dark red fenders, almost black in the shallow light. I was outside the fence, looking in. A couple of Jaguars sat in the middle of the space but they didn't appear to be any different than the others. The moon light skimmed over the shining hoods. It was like nothing you could have imagined—all that blood dark red under the hot moon. There was no gate, only a long dark concrete building on one side in place of the fence. A large overhead door in the building appeared to be the only way in or out of the compound. I stood there, looking down one of the rows, each rear bumper in a perfect line. The Jaguars were of different years, some chubbier, some sleeker, all in apparently perfect condition. I was waiting for something to happen.

The moon was bright, the trees threw flickers and shadows. Then a grinding noise. The door in the concrete building was rising. It jerked, then ran up to the roof line. Melissa was small in the doorway, standing next to a Jaguar. She walked forward, stopped, then looked over my way, waving her arms. She pointed silently toward where my tow truck was hidden behind some trees. Her arm moved, her wrist flicked. Then she was in the car, the engine purring, just a tiny buzz like a fly in the vast forest of watchful pines. She drove through the doorway and the door dropped, slowly, slowly, behind her, clicking to the concrete pad. It sounded like a dish falling on a tile floor. That was all I could see. All I would ever remember hearing.

DOING IT RIGHT

Sal had just finished dialing Stella's number when he saw the door to the phone booth move, a squeak and a ripple of cold air. Sal looked under his arms and saw white tennis shoes with orange stripes. A kid was inside the booth. Short with wild, curly hair and a huge grin. Sal could hear Stella's phone ringing, ringing. He looked at the kid, maybe he was playing some kind of game, maybe some other kids were chasing him.

"What's up, kid?" No answer, just the grin. Nice teeth, Sal thought. He's not homeless. Stella answered the phone.

"Where are you? You were supposed to be here hours ago. What am I supposed to do all day? Just wait for you? Where are you?" Stella's voice was high pitched, desperate, but controlled in a familiar but still odd sort of way. After all these years.

"I'm in a phone booth near the San Mateo bridge. Traffic's been stopped for over an hour. It's like a parking lot out here." The kid was drawing what looked like a naked woman on the wall of the phone booth. A bright red magic marker pushed like a finger through his fist. His curled yellow hair looked like it was ready to lift off from his skull.

"Fine, just fine. Look, all I ever hear from you is excuses. Just get your lying ass over here, okay? I've got a lot of work to do." Then her voice changed. "I've got a surprise for you, too." Sal stood on one foot, then the other, the free foot rubbing the back of the other leg.

"I'll be there, Stella." Sal hung up the phone and looked at the wall. The kid's drawing was pretty good, actually, better than what you'd see in most restrooms. The boy grinned, then applied the finishing touches: a belly button, nipples, a curly wisp of hair.

"Okay, what do you want, kid?" Sal was reaching in his pocket for change as he pushed through the folding doors. He stopped halfway and looked back at the kid. His belt was tight and too long, the end sticking out from his side like a misplaced tail. No answer. Sal walked out and he could hear the coin return flip loudly, angrily. He turned around and walked back in and laid a dollar bill flat on the ledge under the phone.

Sal walked into Stella's house without knocking. He was carrying tools and a box of joint compound. "I'm here," he yelled. Stella came down the stairs and Sal could tell by the angle of her head, the shyness of her feet, that she wanted to revise the tone of the phone call. She wanted to be loved, to be touched.

"I guess I'd better get these cracks patched up," he said, brushing past her. There was a long crack in the kitchen ceiling, splayed into three forks, like lightening, from wall to wall. Sal squeezed the joint compound into the cracks with a large, flat trowel. The correct tool for the job, he thought with a smile. Stella was emptying the dish drainer. She grabbed each glass, as if by the neck, gave it a firm wipe with a white towel, then placed it soundlessly into the cupboard.

First you fill the crack and let it dry. That might take a day or so when the crack is wide. Or you could use a hair dryer to speed things up. Then you cover the entire area with a light layer of compound, smooth it out, let that dry. Finally, you get some compound on your trowel and tap it lightly into irregular rows on the dry surface and wait about twenty minutes for it to partially dry. Then you flatten the peaks and match the surface of the surrounding wall. Skip trowel, they call it. Not an easy job in old houses like this one. "Stella, this is as far as I can get today. You want to see?" No answer. Sal closed the lid to the joint compound and wiped the trowel with a paper towel. It's not good to wash this stuff down the sink, it clogs drains. "Stella, can you hear me?"

Sal knew what was coming next but he had no power to resist. He did not want to be working on this house, he did not even want to be in Berkeley. He felt coerced at every turn. Sal was angry but to stay angry he had to stay away from Stella. If he touched her or smelled her, his resolve would collapse into a rubble of old hurts and stolen books. And lack of appreciation, that was the worst part, being taken for granted all the time. But the whole careful construction of his anger would dissolve as he fell into her arms, enveloped, her firm, lustrous body beneath him, around him.

Standing outside her bedroom door, he could already hear her sniffling. He pushed open the door and saw Stella, naked and crying on the bed. Her tears dripped onto her breasts, a soft streak by the brown nipples, the solitary and familiar hairs. Sal took off his clothes and sat by her. They lay down together. And then, for that moment, Sal was content. He hung there, like a drowning man, one hand on her right breast, his nose in her left armpit, his legs entwined around her legs. He could see Stella's ribcage rising lightly and falling, her breasts pushing up into the soft light, the descent to her stomach, the legs resting quietly on the quilt. These legs that had just the right open space at the top of the thigh. You could see daylight through there when she stood against a light or in front of a window. Her skin was almost orange now in the early evening light, the slats of the Venetian blind cutting her toes into thin slices of shadow. Stella was looking up at the ceiling, perhaps watching the sway of the lamp or the skittering outline of a tree. The tears were dry on her skin. The thump of reggae rumbled up from the apartment below.

Sal spoke into Stella's ear. "When I was a kid, I tried to shave my head once." This was the sort of revelation that

Stella felt good hearing. She moved slightly against his leg, encouraging him to continue. "I had been playing doctor with the little girls who visited a family down the street and we got caught naked under a blanket." Stella sat up a little. "So I got spanked with my dad's old razor strap. Funny how you never forget stuff like that." Stella stood by the side of the bed for a moment, then walked over to the stereo.

"A little music maybe..." She stuffed a Malvina Reynolds tape into the stereo.

"That's when I took my Dad's straight razor and tried to cut my hair off. It looked pretty funny, I guess. They took a picture of my hair cut up like that." Stella lay on the bed and rubbed her hand over Sal's head.

"Where is that picture? Can I see it?"

"Where is the surprise you mentioned on the phone?" Sal felt a kind of glow, bordering on carelessness. The room floated along. It was dark now outside the window.

The next day Stella carried her usual stack of books and papers into the Berkeley coffee house. People everywhere, no place to sit. Sal stood in line and Stella stood with her arms folded across her chest by a couple of Asian girls who looked as if they might be leaving. A mocha with three shots of espresso, that's what she always wanted. Sal could feel her arranging her books and flipping through her flyers as he balanced the tray toward the condiment ledge. Brown sugar, a shake of cinnamon, a squirt of honey, a flurry of chocolate powder. All these, Sal knew, would combine to make her happy. He applied them to the brimming cup with studied abandon. Then he brought the tray over to the window table and set it down. Stella sipped her mocha, her forehead wrinkling.

"Shall we talk?" she asked. "Everybody else here is talking, let's talk, Sal."

"Okay, let's talk." But Sal did not want to talk. He did not want to be in this coffee house with Stella or to be in Berkeley repairing cracks in Stella's house. To tell the truth, he no longer even liked her pile of books or the assorted flyers she was always collecting. Sal had come to perceive Stella as a pack rat and he was tired of her excesses. When Stella drank coffee, the corners of her mouth collected a tiny spot of brown. It was one of the little things Sal had loved about her at first. Now he did not like to look at the brown specks in the corners of her mouth. And Sal could no longer think of interesting things to say.

"Well?" Stella had drained the last drop from her cup. Sal was watching people, a woman leafing through a book titled "Silent Scream," a couple holding hands, whispering into each other's hair, a guy with long fingers tracing the lines on a page of the East Bay Express. Sal thought that everyone here seemed to know what they were doing, why they were sitting in this café.

"Well, let's go to a movie, then, or that party over in San Francisco we were talking about," Sal said. A skinny guy with a bald head and an umbrella had just sat down next to two girls. He began talking rapidly and making broad hand gestures. The girls were not pleased. The guy had a pasty white face, almost like a clown, and he leaned forward over the table, talking into their faces.

"Okay, let's go," Stella said and she stood up just as the guy with the white face jumped to his feet. He was talking loud, almost shouting, waving his wild hands, and he backed right into Stella. She gave him a hard shove and he tipped to one side, almost fell, then spun around. He looked ready to swing his umbrella. That would be big trouble. But he didn't and suddenly he was out on the sidewalk, still talking to himself, dodging a car, then shooting across the street onto the campus grass. He started shouting again. His umbrella stuck out behind his long black coat like an outrageous appendage.

Sal looked at Stella and he could see that she was frightened. The two girls were acting as if nothing had happened. Maybe nothing had. Certainly, nothing had changed. Sal would like to have been walking down a narrow sidewalk in Mexico somewhere, looking for a restaurant, the comfortable shift of pesos in the bottom of his pants pocket.

Sal and Stella drove quietly across the Bay Bridge. The sun had broken up the clouds and hung large and yellow between the sweeping bridge cables. Sal could see the waves, chopping under a stiff wind, and he was glad he wasn't down there in the water, struggling to swim against an unseen current. He felt the safe vibration of the car engine, the smooth roll of rubber tires.

"I've been wanting to see this film for weeks," Stella offered. "Those early party members were really brave people. It sort of makes our problems seem trivial, don't you think, Sal?" Stella adjusted the sun visor mirror and touched her hair.

"Yes, it's true. They were. 'Seeing Red,' that's the name of it?" This is what Sal had always loved about Stella, her politics, her commitment to something larger than herself. But just now it irritated him somehow.

"What exit do we take?" Sal asked.

"I don't know, you've been there before, Civic Center maybe?" Stella was spinning the radio dial, trying to get KPFA.

Sal swung to the off ramp, got off on Mission and drove halfway down the first block, then pulled over and stopped. "Where do I turn now?"

"Keep going straight," Stella said, her voice rising. Sal's shoulders started to hurt, his thumb was drumming on the steering wheel. "Sal, why do you always insist on getting lost, can't you even look at a map or ask someone for directions?"

"Why don't you look at a map, Stella? Is this where I turn?"

"Probably, it looks familiar." Sal shot down a side street and started to turn left.

"It's one way," Stella screamed.

"Shit." Sal cranked the wheel, jammed the brakes and spun to a stop. A black Cadillac with wire rims swerved and missed his front bumper by inches.

"Now what?" Sal said.

"Why does this always have to happen?" Stella's voice was shrill, puncturing the air in Sal's ears.

"Look Stella, why don't you take some responsibility for directions sometimes? You never take responsibility for anything." Sal edged back into the traffic but his whole body was vibrating. Objects rushed by the car window, alien and hostile objects. His eyes hurt somewhere down deep.

"I do."

"The fuck you do."

Stella sat still in the car seat, her face stretched, her lips ready to crack. Sal slammed up to a stoplight. Stella looked at him quickly and then popped open her door and jumped out, dodged a blue van, half tripped on the curb, then walked, erect as a tree branch, under the awning of an office building and disappeared.

"Here we go again." Sal made a moaning sound deep in his throat. Here he was, over in the big city, a million cars, and now he had to park and chase after her. He was responsible for her. It would take hours just to park and then where would she be? He looked over at the building with the awning—Mercantile Center. "Great! Just Great!"

Sal parked in a handicapped space and lurched down the sidewalk. Columns of concrete beneath high rise office buildings. Tiny offices with an elevator on the ground floor. These buildings looked like spaceships ready to blast off for another universe. Sal walked beneath the columns. Where is she? Sal knew she would be crying in some alcove somewhere and it was his job to find her. He walked down a row of pillars which diminished toward a distant street. A little gray man, hair fluffed with wind, sat eating a thin sandwich on a concrete bench.

Maybe this guy saw her go by. Just one more damned impossible situation to get through. A stop light across the street blinked red and a rush of cars roared into the darkening light. Sal sat down on the bench with the little gray man. He gave Sal a startled look and pulled a paper sack closer to his body. It occurred to Sal at that particular moment that he might have a rather long time to wait. He sat perfectly still and pretty soon he could hear the faint beating of his heart.

SILENT SCREEN

Madge Bellamy's body is partially hidden by a tree which splits the movie frame into two parts. The patient pine needles are in soft focus. The young man has his hand on the rough bark, near hers, his neck inclined in a loving circle toward her radiant, upturned face. Madge looks up into his eyes and seems about to move her hand, slightly, toward his. The air falls away all around them and the moment stretches like a thin luminous wire through Jonathan's silent inner world,

Jonathan who is now sitting as close as possible to a sparsely decorated theater stage. Last week was Halloween and the little rats had had little brooms tied under their bellies. He had watched them drag the brooms across a tiny enclosure, making thin furrows in the dust in front of the hidden stage lights. Jonathan looks at the dull red curtain and wonders what costumes the rats will be wearing tonight. He is early and almost alone in the old fashioned vaudeville theater. Jonathan's mother is sitting by herself in the middle of a back row. He looks back toward the lobby, past his mother, and sees the two girls who sell popcorn and candy looking his way. They turn toward each other, whisper, then disappear around the corner of the swinging doors. Jonathan picks up the program from his lap and runs his finger over the writing on the pink page. *Samantha Martin, Professional Hypnotist and Animal Trainer,* and her **wild** act with genuine **wild** animals. Maybe she'll have something new tonight.

Jonathan has seen this show quite a few times. The most important part comes at the end of the hour long performance when spectators can line up and touch the animals. The line is always long and overwhelmed with noisy little kids and their pushy mothers. So usually he hangs back until most of them have gone home. He is planning someday to wait for Samantha out back as she packs up to leave.

Madge is lying on a huge white and fluffy bed, one hand holding a dainty cigarette holder, her right leg stretching over the sheets toward an ancient phonograph. Her big toe almost touches a large "78" record and her lips pucker in anticipation of the new song she will soon hear. The metal speaker rises like a listening flower in the foreground of the frame, opening toward the bed and the quiver of whiteness

that runs along Jonathan's arm as he feels people entering the theater behind him, hears the chatter, feels he warmth. He can guess how many people there are without looking, the echo of furtive movements bounces off the walls into his eager inner ear. Jonathan is keeping busy with the pink paper of the program, feeling the texture, rubbing the ink to see if the colors will smudge. He scratches with his fingernail at the letters. He holds the paper up to the ceiling light and sees the mottled flow of intertwined fibers. It reminds Jonathan of snake dens he has seen in science magazines. Of all the animals in the show, Jonathan likes the snakes and the rats best and he wonders what these animals do when they're not acting for the stage. At home in their cages, for example, at their leisure. His palm itches when he thinks about touching the scaly shale of a snake's long back, the sleek gray fur of the largest rat, the thin hard tail.

Jonathan is no kid. He has two degrees and is a published author. Silent film actresses—that's his specialty. He spent a few years at a local college, but he did not make too many friends there. His name was Michael then. One problem for Michael had been his smell. When he got nervous, he would sweat and the odor was quite unusual in its pungency and staying power. And colleges made Michael pretty nervous.

However, he convinced a friendly teacher to sponsor showings of 1920s silent movies. He would show the films on a spindly "regular 8" film projector to small groups of indifferent students whose teachers had required them to attend for extra credit. Michael would punctuate these showings with verbal outbursts. During *"October"* he had yelled, "down with Capitalism" and "long live the revolution." Then he looked around the room and saw that there was no reaction at all. This was a response he had not anticipated. So he summoned up his deepest voice and shouted "down with the teachers." A number of students stood up and walked out of the room. After that Michael did not show films at the community college.

Michael was driven to school by his mother and father who were greatly concerned about Michael's future. They wanted him to turn out okay. Usually the father would drive back home and the mother would walk around campus and wait for Michael to finish his classes. That could take all day. Sometimes she would follow behind him as he walked from one classroom to another. At a discrete distance, of course.

Michael did not spend a lot of time talking to his fellow students. He was rather odd looking and felt out of place. Anyway, he much preferred the company of teachers, at least they knew something. What he wanted, really, was to talk about movies, old movies, silent film stars, actresses. He haunted the crowded collegiate corridors, buttonholing harried professors, pointing out specific pages in academic film journals. He was, actually, a remarkable student, possessed of a prodigious memory and an effective writing style. "Amazing," the teachers would say when they read his term papers. But then came the visits to their tiny offices and the pungent smell. All this did not bode well for Michael's future.

Once Michael managed to arrange a free showing of D.W. Griffith's *"Intolerance"* at an off campus theater. He hired an organist and rented an organ. He spent months rehearsing his introductory remarks. But only ten people showed up and the organ was damaged coming down the steep steps into the theater. The projectionist got the reels mixed up and Michael tripped over an extension cord and fell with a thud onto the stage floor. All but two people left after the first reel. Eventually the organist played the final note and the lights came on. His mother was fidgeting in her seat and his father was pacing up and down on the sidewalk outside the theater doors. Michael sat down on the organ bench with his notes. He circled certain passages that he wanted to give more emphasis in the future.

Today papers are laid out carefully on Jonathan's bed, pages of a manuscript he is working on. He is standing over his pages, reaching high up to a bulletin board. He pins photographs and clipped newspaper articles in straight lines. Michael is holding a still of Madge Bellamy posing on top of a reclining elephant. The photo is from "*Soul of the Beast.*" Madge has an open make-up kit on her lap and is powdering her nose while looking into a mirror. Her very white face is dazzling against the corrugated skin of the elephant. The serpentine trunk curls in adoration toward Madge's head.

Jonathan's mother appears in his doorway. She is small with heavy bones, the carpet is pushed flat under her feet. The mother is shaped like a pear and stands at a tired angle, as if she has been doing everything she does much too long. To tell the truth, she has been. She watches Jonathan stand on his bed as he stretches to pin yet another photo on the wall.

"Have you called them, Michael?" Her thick voice puffs up the air of Jonathan's room. He does not turn to look at his mother.

"Called whom?"

"You know very well who I mean, the school, of course, who else?"

"Not yet, Mom. Anyway I don't need to. We have an arrangement." The mother takes three quick steps into the room.

"What arrangement would that be?" The mother's voice is shrill. Jonathan steps clumsily down from his bed, stumbling on a bump in the carpet. He stands up straight, a publicity still of Lon Chaney hanging from his fingers.

"It's a special arrangement." Jonathan turns toward his desk.

"Doing what, for heaven's sake? Don't I have a right to know? After all the work I've done for you?" The mother's eyes hang like flattened bulbs in the depressed surface of her forehead.

"It's a book signing, that's all, just a book signing for Ladies of the Silent Screen." Jonathan has a hand pressed flat on his forehead. He feels a sharp pain deep inside his skull.

Jonathan turns to face his mother. "Why do you have to make such a big deal out of everything anyway?"

"Oh, that's good, Michael. That's very good. Why do you hide things from me?" The mother is moving backward toward the doorway.

"My name is Jonathan now? Can't you call me that once in a while?" Jonathan is climbing back up on his bed.

"Oh, fine, you've been Michael O'Connell all your life and now, all of a sudden, you're Jonathan Drewman. Just because you published a couple of books. Books, by the way, that cost your father a pretty penny and don't make a dime." She goes silent for a moment, passing a hand across her forehead as if chasing a thought.

"Of course, your new name is just fine. It will help you get along in the real world out there, won't it? Yes, that's just fine." The mother is out in the hallway now. Her voice

A Scarlet Thread

trails weakly in the air. "It's the real world that matter, after all, isn't it? Just look at your father…"

Jonathan is standing by a large concrete pillar. He is waiting at the theater's back entrance for Samantha Martin to come out. His mother is somewhere in the background, nervous, tapping her feet on hard concrete. His father is running the car engine around the corner, listening to Tchaikovsky's "The Sleeping Beauty" on the car stereo. The theater door opens and Samantha Martin walks out. At first, Jonathan doesn't recognize her, she is dressed plainly—no tights, no tower of hair, no colored lights reflected on her sleek white skin. Three men follow her, they carry boxes. Then comes a long cart with more boxes and cages. Samantha stops to watch the men who carry the boxes toward a waiting truck. Jonathan walks toward her.

"I saw your show," he says. Samantha Martin looks at Jonathan quickly.

"It's you again. Why don't you just get in line with everyone else after the show?" Samantha is standing with her hand on a large box with many air holes drilled along the side. Jonathan's face is tight, his eye muscles are like rubber bands, but his voice begins quietly.

"I wasn't fast enough. There were too many people." He stops and touches his forehead with a quick finger. "I had so much to say, you were in a big hurry." His words end in a low pitched whisper. Everyone stops work and looks at Jonathan. Animals scratch in their cages. The boxes rattle. Samantha Martin's body sags slightly, as if each breath she takes requires special energy. She must be tired.

"Well, I guess you're my biggest fan around these parts. You're in the same seat every time I come here." Her hand caresses the old wood of the box she is leaning against. "So you really like these animals, do you?"

"Yes. Yes, I do. I was hoping that I could still…"

Samantha moves nearer to Jonathan, gives him a close look. It's almost as if she might reach out and touch his chin. Her hand falls to her side.

"Look, we have a mailing list, you know, dates and places we perform. There is a special night for hypnosis. Why not just sign up and come back another day?" Samantha looks as if she might pick up the wooden box and take it to the truck herself.

"Can I then?'

"What?"

"Touch an animal."

Samantha Martin bends at the waist for a moment, like a tree in a stiff wind, then straightens up and pats the wooden cage.

"Okay, why not? How about a rabbit?"

"No! A snake or the biggest rat!"

Samantha walks over to a small box. "Rat it is, then." She opens a small door and the biggest white rat is suddenly out in her hand, sniffing the air. Jonathan walks forward into the sunlight

which radiates from Blanche Sweet's pearl shoulders as her hand curls around Warner Baxter's neck. He is looking off into space and doesn't really see her but she is perfect, anyway, a tiny brown mole placed like magic on her chin. Two black armbands clinch the firm flesh of her upper right arm. She only has eyes for him.

Jonathan waits outside the pet shop until he is pretty sure that no other customers are inside. Mr. and Mrs. O'Connell are in the family car, waiting a few blocks away. Jonathan imagines he has given them the slip. He is wearing a large coat with bulky pockets, his hands are in the pockets and he looks as if he has just walked outdoors during a snowstorm. His hair sticks out in electric circles, his fat pasty face is moist and sincere. Standing by the door, he feels an exciting hum of energy coming from inside the pet shop—bird chirpings, claws scratching, rustlings of paper and a mysterious swishing of air. Then a phone rings somewhere in the near distance and Jonathan pushes quickly through the doorway.

"Well, my good man, what can I do for you today?" The store owner stands with his hands on his hips, an old fashioned fountain pen sticking between thumb and forefinger of one large paw. Jonathan does not speak at first. Then he does, rapidly.

"A rat please, a white rat with a pink face." Jonathan takes his hands out of his pockets as if to demonstrate the space available to house a rodent. The store owner looks at Jonathan, then sticks the fountain pen in his shirt pocket.

"Do you have a cage at home?"

"I really wanted a snake but I guess a rat is more practical."

"More practical? Yes, a rat is practical enough. But do you have a cage at home? You can't just keep a rat in your pocket, you know."

"Yes, of course, I used to have a guinea pig." The store owner walks quickly down the fish aisle, turns past the birds, stops in front of some low cages. He walks back with a white rat on his arm.

"How much is it?"

"Twenty bucks. Comes with a How-To-Care-For-Mice manual." A loud clatter, then a howl from the back of the store. Tiny feet chatter over the tile floor. Jonathan looks at the store owner.

"Just a troublesome bird."

Jonathan picks up the white rat and slowly strokes its head and feels the tiny pricks of the rat's feet on his wrist, *and suddenly it is Colleen Moore and she is pulling Jonathan slowly toward her, toward the grass and twigs of a green field, away from the open door of the small airplane behind them, his duty, the reason for everything he has done during his whole life. Her mouth is a petulant black line and the scarf on her head twinkles with the bright stars of invitation. Jonathan knows this is one of those opportunities which come only once in a lifetime.*

Jonathan is sitting at the kitchen table. He has put a slice of bread into the toaster and is waiting for it to pop up. He can feel the white rat breathing in his sock drawer back in his room.

"Michael, Michael, have you been using the phone? Michael, where is the phone?" Jonathan's mother is in the doorway and her body is like a whistling triangle, pointed at the top, as if her voice were pushed upward through a tiny hole. The toaster pings and Jonathan reaches out his arm.

'You haven't called the school, have you Michael? Well, I'll do it myself. Someone has to do things around here." She puts her hands on her hips. "That's what I'll do all right." The mother walks toward the stairs and Jonathan watches her take each heavy step, knowing that she will stop just before she is out of view, knowing she has one more thing to say. "Someday you'll thank me for all this, someday you will."

Jonathan thinks she's probably right. In fact, he is thanking her already. He has a newspaper spread out on the kitchen table and is circling items in the want ads. You never know when you might see an old movie for sale. Jonathan buys old videotapes now, they are definitely more convenient than the 8 millimeter films he used to collect. And they are cheap. He makes careful red circles with his magic marker. He sees an ad for a snake charmer who is coming to town. And a silent film showing at the Atlantic Film Archive: a hitherto lost film from Japan called "*Page of Madness*." Jonathan would really like to see that film but the theater is so far away. One thing's for sure, though, he will go to Samantha Martin's final show the next Wednesday, the day before his book signing. Once or twice a year she performs hypnosis. People talk about their other lives, sometimes she finds animals in people's hats. Jonathan has seen photos of Samantha Martin pulling a pigeon from a man's vest.

Jonathan picks up his newspaper and walks down the hallway. He hears his mother on the telephone.

"But isn't there some special class he could teach? Something to do with films or actresses or something?" Jonathan knows he shouldn't listen, that he should walk on to his room. But he doesn't.

"Something where he has a lot of supervision, of course." Silence. "Yes, of course I remember. Well, that won't happen again, I'm sure." Silence.

"You've been kind and patient but, you know, he's not getting any younger. Neither are we. He just has to find something to do." Jonathan hears his mother's feet scrape the floor and he gets ready to move quickly.

"Okay, okay, well, that's something anyway. But it doesn't pay a thing, does it? I just found out about it. He doesn't tell us anything anymore."

"Okay, I will. Goodbye." Jonathan's head jerks and he steps quickly toward his door, shuts it silently behind him and

sees Laura La Plante standing by his computer. She has clipped blonde hair and wears a long white layered dress which touches the floor. Her delicate face is clenched, almost angry, and she holds out an oblong box in front of her waist. The box is tied with a neat ribbon, bright red, and the whole package seems to pulsate, as if something were alive somewhere down inside it. Jonathan wonders what will happen next.

Jonathan walks into the gun shop and tries to look like he knows what he's doing. One thing is for sure, he will take care of business. Two clerks lounge behind a counter watching a television set mounted in a corner of the low ceiling. It's a situation comedy involving taxi drivers. A guy with wild hair has just tripped over a chair, canned laughter. Below the TV, glass cases filled with rifles and pistols surround a central island which houses the clerks and row after row of ammunition. Each gun case in locked with a tiny metal clasp which clings to the glass plate like a fat locust.

"You sell guns here?" Jonathan is standing by a rack of Playboy magazines but he doesn't look at them. Not even once. The clerks look at each other, then at Jonathan.

"Yeah. Lots. Take your pick." The clerks watch the television out of the corners of their eyes. Jonathan looks back toward the door as if someone might be waiting for him outside. But nobody, not even his mother, knows where he is right now. He is pretty sure of that. He tilts his head toward a tall glass case.

"That one, please."

"That's pretty expensive." The clerks watch Jonathan point at the glass case.

"That's the one."

"You want it gift wrapped?" Both clerks laugh. A commercial concerning toilet cleaner is on the TV screen and the clerks appear to relax a little. "It comes with a small box of ammunition," the first clerk says. He laughs again.

"No, don't bother," Jonathan says. He is not laughing. The clerks look at each other. Jonathan hands over his photo ID card. The first clerk takes out the shiny silver pistol and wraps it in newspaper, puts one rubber band around the newspaper, then several more. He drops the package into a paper sack along with a tiny box of bullets. The second clerk types into his computer and waits for the felon check to go through. Then he walks to the cash register.

"Okay, sign this release form right here. That'll be one hundred and ninety five bucks, mister." Jonathan pulls out two one hundred dollar bills from the shirt pocket under his coat. The first clerk hands over the package.

It isn't until Jonathan has walked halfway to the doorway that the second clerk sees the rat peek out of the floppy coat pocket. Rapid. Just a flash of the white head and the coal quick eyes. Then the street door slams.

Jonathan is sitting in the front row of the old vaudeville theater. He is waiting for Samantha Martin to appear. He can feel the warm rat in his coat pocket. This rat is very quiet and has caused Jonathan no trouble at all. It is quite content to burrow down into the pocket and sleep. It has been nibbling on soda crackers. The rat droppings are hard and don't smell as bad as Jonathan had thought they might. He has been flipping the pellets out of his pocket onto the floor by his seat.

Finally, the curtain is raised and Samantha appears. She is dressed like Esmeralda in *The Hunchback of Notre Dame*, thick fur ruffles on her sleeves, a Gypsy sash around her waist. Her face is radiant and tragic in the white blast of the stage lights. She waves her arms in a theatrical gesture to quiet the crowd. The theater falls silent, fifty people more or less, mostly kids and teenagers, a few mothers.

"Anyone who wants to be hypnotized should walk across the stage before we begin. I'll choose a few lucky folks to stay up here with me." Samantha has a large wicker basket by her side and Jonathan wonders if she has a new snake in there. Twenty or so people get up to walk toward the stage. They cross the platform from left to right and Samantha approaches them just as they are about to go down the steps on the far side.

Jonathan has been in competitive situations like this before and he is certain that he won't be chosen. He has never been chosen for anything. And the six chairs in the middle of the stage are already occupied by the time Jonathan gets to Samantha. She reaches out, touches his chin with the flat back of her hand, her forefinger almost touching his throat. A light upward pressure. Jonathan looks into Samantha's eyes and everything stops. The music over the speaker system stops. The line of supplicants stops moving. Whispers hover over the wavy lines of the auditorium.

"That's all. You can stay." Samantha Martin waves a commanding hand. "We'll have seven tonight. Set up an extra chair over there." A man pops through the curtain with a straight, hard backed wooden chair. "Over by the others." Samantha points her delicate finger, her cape hangs smoothly over her body down to the stage floor.

Jonathan can see his mother clearly, she is sitting in the last row, right in the middle. She does not look pleased to see her son sitting on the stage. He sees his father pass across the lobby doorway, as if going somewhere important, then pass again in the opposite direction. Samantha Martin is holding a gold watch on a long chain in front of the girl in the first chair.

"Chicken. I see you little chicken in there, hiding. Let's hear you cluck now, let's hear your true voice. Cluck, cluck now." The girl stands up and walks around the stage. She is clucking and crowing. The chicken noises are strange, off center, almost obscene.

"Let's see your chicken walk now. Your true chicken walk." The girl is walking with stiff legs, scratching at the floor with a pointed shoe. Samantha Martin sways gently in the lights and the audience is slumbering with silence when

Esmeralda points past Quasimodo's painted face toward something, the enemy approaching perhaps, danger. Her

face is loving enough, she would love him if she could, that is clear, but her eyes are clenched with fear and even the fur on her coat stands erect. Quasimodo's eyes bulge and he knows what he has to do. He looks past her pointing finger and his face firms with resolve.

"And who is home here tonight?" Jonathan jerks his head up. Samantha Martin is standing over him. Six chairs are empty and six figures are following each other around the stage, single file, making animal noises and odd gestures with their arms and legs. Samantha is swinging the gold watch, very slowly, back and forth in front of Jonathan's eyes. "Who is home right now? Who can we talk to?"

"I am here," says Jonathan.

"Who are you?" The gold watch settles into an angry vertical line.

"My name is Jonathan, I've told you that so many times. What more can I do? I've done everything you've ever told me. What can I do now?"

"Yes, yes you have, Jonathan." Samantha says and she reaches down and slips her hand into his coat pocket. She holds the white rat high up in the bright light. The brilliance of its white fur spreads like plumed feathers in her raised hand. The audience sways from side to side, as if blown by an invisible wind.

That's when Jonathan pulls out the silver gun. It is shiny and new and gleams in the fierce light of the theater. He is waiting for the right moment to start pulling the trigger. This time Jonathan Drewman knows exactly what his next step will be.

STORAGE

Noel has driven past the self storage lockers a hundred times. A grand opening banner has been stretched across the front gate for the past year—Henry's Shur-gard Storage. The corners flap in the wind, a long rip through the center, the letters "ry's" torn through. This time she will stop and look around.

Noel slows the red Volkswagen pickup and parks by the curb. It's nearly dark and she can see a light in the rental office. She wonders why it isn't closed, most storage yards are locked up tight at night. Noel walks up to the office door, then stops. She is looking through a dirty window, no curtain, a tight room with a large clock on the wall. A converted storage space, probably. A fat man stands inside, slightly bent, looking at a large diagram taped onto the wall. The man has made tiny notations on each square, some in different colors. His finger drags along the map, stops on a small green square. Then he looks toward the front door as if he hears something.

Noel steps to the side a little, then waits. The man's mouth moves, but Noel can't hear any words. His stomach wobbles as he picks up a newspaper clipping and pins it on the wall. Then the phone rings. Now she can hear him.

"Yeah, this is him." He kicks at the open office door, as if to close it, but his foot misses.

"Yeah, this is Henry's Shur-gard. We got spaces open. Sure. Sure. Listen, mister, that's what we do here, we rent spaces, okay?" Silence. Noel's body leans toward the lit doorway.

"Thirty nine a month. No ground floor access, no roll up door. It's along a long corridor with regular doors." Henry holds the phone away from his ear, moving his lips as he listens.

"That's gonna cost you seventy nine a month. Yeah, it rolls down. You can drive right up to it." Silence. "Okay, fine, see you then." Henry sets the receiver back on the hook. He looks at the open door.

Noel walks quickly back to her red pickup truck. She is not ready to talk to Henry quite yet. Her truck is full, though, and it's getting late. It will be better to just go home tonight. Maybe Fred will be in a good mood and help her unload in the morning. Noel pulls out onto the roadway, a thin white cloud of diesel smoke floats behind her. She knows the cloud is there but she never really sees it, except maybe at night in the rearview mirror, against someone's headlights.

It is morning and Fred is out on the driveway. As it turns out, he is not in such a good mood. "Look at this!" He has his face up against the windows of Noel's truck. "Where did you go? I thought you had a class to teach yesterday." Fred is short with a friendly brown beard. His hair is carefully combed up over a bald spot near the back of his head. Right now his right arm is straight in front of him and he is pointing one finger at Noel's white camper shell.

"Just calm down, Fred, it's no big deal. So I stopped at a garage sale after school. So what?" Noel pulls the tailgate down and stands in front of the opening, as if to block Fred's view. "So what's the big deal, anyway?"

"We don't have any more room, Noel, not one inch, anywhere." Fred shoves both arms in front of his waist, palms up.

"You really didn't have to run out here to tell me that, you know. It's my house. I know exactly how much room there is." Noel's arms are folded over her chest. Sometimes, when the furrows on her forehead are deep and angry, Fred will gently rub them flat. Sometimes Noel and Fred sit quietly in Berkeley coffee houses, drinking espresso and reading the East Bay Express. Sometimes, but not lately.

Fred's arms collapse at his sides. "Yes, it's your house. Right, I know that." He is silent, he looks at Noel leaning against the camper shell. "Okay, I'm sorry for all the fuss. Maybe you just need more space or something. Like I said before, why not rent a storage unit?"

Noel looks at Fred, then down at her dirty tennis shoes. The garage sale had been a little muddy. "Want to help me unload?"

"No!" Fred says but he walks to the back of the truck and looks in. Two old telephones, a dusty bookshelf, a baby's car seat, telephone wires in a snake's coil on the baby seat. Fred reaches out his arm toward the wire.

So Noel does rent a ground floor space at Henry's Shurgard Storage. She can back her truck right up to the roll up door. Henry is starting to seem almost like an old friend. His stomach bounces as he hands over the rental contract for Noel to sign. The good thing about Henry's is that it never closes, you can come anytime, day or night. And Henry is usually around, too. Noel figures he probably has no place else to go. She sees Henry watching from his doorway as she brings in her first load. The camper shell is filled so full that the bumper clangs against the concrete when the VW hits the dip where the driveway starts. Noel brings in load after load. But she takes her time. No hurry. She is thin but much stronger than she looks. She lifts and pushes and fills her space up. Finally there is barely room to walk.

Noel convinces Fred to take her to the flea market to sell stuff that won't fit into the storage unit. They pile up the red truck until it sinks to the curb and they go to the BART parking lot at Ashby and Adeline. Five cents here, a quarter there, thirty five cents for an old pair of men's pants, fifteen cents for a used toilet brush, a nickel for a partially burned plastic spatula. By the end of the day, she has almost a hundred dollars. As usual, Noel is the last person to leave the flea market parking lot. She walks around, casually looking over the stuff other sellers have left behind, picking up a few choice items. A perfectly good ironing board, a broken luggage rack. Just a few things here and there. After Fred finishes loading up the truck, it looks just as full as it had that morning.

That's when Noel gets a very good idea. She thinks why I'll build my own storage unit right in my own backyard. And a big one, too. I've got a lot of used boards and boxes and boxes of nails. But some of the nails are rusty and the boards are dry and cracked. The carpenter, a guy she met at the flea market, is reluctant. But he pitches in and pretty soon the pier blocks are in and the walls go up, then a skeletal roof. There is a minor tiff over getting paid and, next thing you know, the carpenter has disappeared. He has nailed up a note, to be sure, written with a broad, thick carpenter's pencil. He has apologized, sort of, but he has cleared out, nevertheless. The bones of the half built shed soak up rain and rotting leaves in Noel's backyard. Oh well, she says, hardly anyone goes back there anyway.

Noel is sitting tight behind the steering wheel of her red VW truck. She is at a stop sign a block away from Henry's Shur-gard, but her coffee mug has tipped, spilling espresso on her jeans. The truck is loaded with boxes and old furniture, a red and black bowling ball sits balanced on a box of paperbacks, an old sun lamp hangs like a question mark over the open tailgate. Noel is wiping her pants with a napkin from Denny's, pushing the spilled cup down into the crack between the front seats. She looks in the rearview mirror. A guy in a Toyota truck is waving his arms and his mouth is moving. She guns the engine and takes off in a cloud of smoke. She's taking no chances with the crazies around Berkeley, not since a few months ago when she flipped off a truck driver on the freeway. The truck driver had followed her off the freeway into a gas station, yelling all the way.

Noel stops in front of Henry's office to check her load. A few larger items cling to the top of the camper shell. She hadn't been able to find any rope at the garage sale and so everything is tied down with kite string. Strings run back and forth, through the legs of broken chairs, circling around an electric weed-whacker with no cord, fastening finally to a shovel with half a handle. It looks like a giant spider web. Noel is plucking at the strings, testing for tightness, when Henry walks up.

"Why Henry, you startled me. You walk so quietly." Noel's hair looks almost wet around her thin shoulders, her smooth face is focused in surprise. She is wearing short shorts and a bright yellow tank top and leans gently against the white camper shell.

"You need some help? That stuff looks like it's ready to fall off," Henry says. Henry is actually fatter than he looks at first glance. He waddles closer to the VW and examines the intricate web of strings. He pulls at a loose string. Noel is smiling at him.

"Well Henry, I guess I can get a few feet further, what do you think?" Silence. "You want to follow me back to my unit to make sure I get there okay?" Noel smiles again. Then she gets into her truck and moves slowly down the aisle. Henry follows her with his eyes but he doesn't move.

Noel realizes that she has too much junk and this morning she has vowed to turn over a new leaf. She is standing in back of her storage locker by a tall wire fence. Two fences come together in an irregular way, forming a sort of pocket. Kids have climbed over the fence here, the top wires are bent down and empty beer bottles are rolled against the chain links. Noel has brought out a brown paper sack full of old ads and flyers and is building a circle of broken bricks and rocks. She pulls out an old leaflet from ten years ago, looks at it, then lights it with a match and throws it into the fire circle. The papers come out, one by one, she reads, then lights them. A few she puts to the side, these are the ones she needs to keep. The papers flare bright, then shrink, flare again, then turn black. Some bits of burnt paper fly into the air and through the chain links out into the street. Noel is looking at an old photograph, herself in half a bathing suit posing topless on some rocks at an unknown beach. Not bad, she thinks, and places the photo carefully on the good pile. Then she sees a shadow on the wire.

"Hey, you can't have fires back here!" It's Henry and he has caught her red handed. Noel is squatting by her circle of bricks and looks up at him, arching her hand over her eyes, as if shielding them from the sun.

"Henry, it's me, Noel." She stands up and smiles. "There were some ashes here already, you know, I thought it would be okay to burn a few old flyers." Noel closes the top of the paper sack, folds it over. "I just thought it would be okay."

"Yeah, but you're burning stuff back here." Henry is pointing at the ashes on the pavement, small bits of ash swirl in the air around his head. "Item seventeen on your contract says no fires on the premises." Henry sticks one arm out in front of his body as if he is holding a copy of the contract. Noel stretches her arms over her head and yawns.

"Look, Henry, we're friends now, right?" Henry is watching her closely but he says nothing. "Well, anyway, we know each other now, so what's the problem, really?" She stops talking and he sort of nods his head. "Besides, Henry, I've been thinking about renting another unit. I've just got too much stuff." Noel looks down at her shirt, fingers a button, then picks up her paper sack and heads back to her storage unit. Henry watches her walk.

"Hey wait, I wanted to ask you something," Henry says and walks quickly forward. Noel turns to face him. "Have you seen the guy next to you lately?"

"What guy?"

"In number 109, you know, right next to you."

"Who?"

"A guy, he comes in on a bike, almost everyday. A black guy. You must have seen him." Noel sets the paper sack on the ground. She wrinkles her forehead.

"I haven't seen anyone around here, except you, Henry." She waves her hand toward her storage unit. "I'm busy here, all this is a lot of work, you know."

"Well, let me know if you do see him. He owes me rent money. If he doesn't pay up, I'll cut his lock off and sell his stuff." Henry steps toward Noel, then turns with surprising quickness and heads toward the manager's office.

Noel looks at number 109. Combination lock on the door. A splash of purple paint across the metal, as if the door had been damaged and repaired, maybe burned. An electrical wire runs out of a hole in the metal up by the roof, then goes back in another hole. She scratches her head and picks up her limp paper sack.

It is night and Noel is standing in front of her storage locker with a box full of old student essays in her arms. She needs to put these papers in a safe place. The door is rolled up into the ceiling and Noel is standing there with her possessions spread out uncomfortably in front of her. That's when she hears a noise from next door, the newly infamous number 109.

Noel sets her box down on the cement in front of her unit. She has stacked the largest boxes against the walls, then increasingly smaller ones on top of those boxes, on up to the ceiling. It's a good enough system but, finally, the boxes at the bottom can't stand the weight. They start to collapse and the whole room full of discouraged stacks starts to lean inward. Removing one box, if you could do it, would cause the whole enterprise to cave in. There simply is no place to put even one more box.

What Noel hears is a hum, a small appliance maybe, a fan, a low buzz. She puts her ear to the roll up door of number 109. The combination lock is gone and there is a faint light from under the door. He's in there, Noel thinks. She hesitates, looks back at her own storage area, then knocks. The buzz stops. She knocks again. Silence. Noel puts her hands on her hips, looks around. She knocks louder.

"All right, already." A voice from inside number 109. "There's someone in here."

"Well, come out then." Noel backs away from the door.

"Who are you?" The voice is male and strong, a little raspy. Noel imagines an old man, a worker in dirty overalls.

"I'm from next door. I'm your neighbor."

"Oh, okay." Noises from inside, then the door rolls up. Light pours out onto Noel's face. The man is not old and he is not wearing overalls. The area is crowded in front, piled boxes, old appliances, broken furniture, but Noel can see a trail and an open space at the back, almost hidden. "Well," the man says.

"Well, well nothing." Noel moves in a little closer. Now she can see where the light is coming from, a mattress, a chest of drawers, a mirror. "I was just wondering, that's all. I heard a noise." The man looks at her closely, notices the slim body, the precocious eyes, the loose shirt. Then he nods.

"I was reading," the man says.

"What?"

"A novel, I was reading a novel."

"Oh." Noel back up a few feet, looks over at her open door, the dim overhead light. She feels like she is losing momentum

"It's okay. I could hear you working over there sometimes. I even saw you through a crack," he says.

"What? A crack?" Noel moves quickly into the light of this man's storage locker. "What crack? Where?"

"Well, it's out front, actually, and that was a quite a while ago. Before you had so much stuff." The man is apologetic, his eyes are aimed at the floor. "You know, there's a crack where the door slides down."

"Where? I don't see any crack." Noel is stamping her feet on the pavement.

"Go shut your door from the inside, I'll show you." Noel walks back into her own unit, there is barely enough room to close the door. She rolls it down and puts her eye to the crack.

"I see your eye," Noel says. She is leaning, her forehead resting lightly on the door.

"I see your eye, too."

"Who are you?" Noel asks.

"George, who are you?"

"You saw me through this crack?"

"Just once, it was an accident really, a few weeks ago. I don't remember when."

"What did you see?"

"You were moving stuff around, then you were looking at something in a box. A photo maybe, or a letter."

"Well, George, you saw quite a bit, didn't you? Maybe you were watching me for a long time?"

"Not really, just a moment."

"This is a pretty small crack, what part of me did you see?"

"Just you. I don't remember."

"Oh well, it can't be helped now, can it?" Noel sighs. She rolls up the door and almost knocks George over. They walk back into George's unit. "I'm Noel," she says with finality.

"Would you like a cup of tea?" George asks.

"Tea? Here?"

"Why not here? I can make a cup of tea here."

Noel closes and locks her storage unit. She gets into her truck and just sits there for a moment. She feels dizzy. She has forgotten to unload. Two wooden oars are sticking through the window partition into the cab right next to her head. She reaches out to touch the oars. She had got them for free at a garage sale just as it was closing up that afternoon. She had hoped she would have room to stick the oars into the storage unit.

Noel decides to go home and talk to Fred. He always knows how to make sense of things. Fred is a sensible guy, not the kind of guy who would make tea in a storage unit.

That night Fred is a friendly ball of fur in the bed and Noel hangs onto his hairy back under the sheets and blankets.

"There's a guy living next door to me."

"At school? Boy, times are tough, I guess." Noel sits up in bed.

"No, Fred, at the storage unit."

"Oh," Fred is quiet for a moment. "You know I read about that in the Chronicle the other day. Unemployed guys are doing that nowadays, women and kids even." He turns toward Noel and puts his hand on her shoulder. "Have you talked to him?"

"No, not yet."

"How do you know he's in there?"

"I saw him through a crack in the door. I saw his bed. He has a comb by his mirror." Noel is kissing Fred. She wants to make love and she pushes his arms flat onto the bed.

Each storage unit has an electrical outlet. Her rent probably pays for the electricity. It's high enough, heaven knows. So Noel has jammed an old refrigerator against a wall and plugged it in. But now she can't open it anymore, even by climbing over boxes and pushing things out of the way. That's okay, sort of, she doesn't want anyone else to see it anyway. The fridge thumps and whirs and so Noel thinks it must still be working. But today she sees a brown fluid leaking from somewhere down by the bottom of the door. She remembers the not so fresh vegetables she had thrown in there a few weeks ago. Onions, tomatoes, a slightly crusty orange. What she sees now looks like brown slime from a monster snail. She had gotten the veggies cheap, free actually, and she had been intending to take them home to see if they were usable. It would be a shame to waste them, after all.

"Hi, you're here." The voice jumps down Noel's spine. She turns quickly. "It's just me, George." He backs up a step.

"Oh, it's you." Noel walks quickly toward him.

"Problems with the refrigerator?"

"What refrigerator?" Noel stops and gives George a penetrating look. "No, no problem."

"That's okay. Listen, I was just here for a while and I thought I'd see how you're doing." He pauses for a moment. "I mean I saw your red truck over there." George backs up a few more steps. He puts his hand to his nose but doesn't say anything.

Noel smiles, stretches her arms over her head. "It really is a nice day out, don't you think?" Noel is leaning toward George's door. She is naturally seductive, her legs flex where she stands, her arms a smooth dance when she walks.

"Yes, it is," George says, then stops. "Want to come over for a minute?" He points with his thumb toward his storage unit.

"Over there?" Noel looks at George carefully. "What are you up to over there, anyway?"

"I thought you said it was a nice day," George says. They look at each other for a moment as if trying to read each other's thoughts.

"Did you say you could make coffee in there?"

"No, I never said that."

Noel has her hands on her hips. "Well, can you?"

"Sure, why not?" They walk inside. She stops. He walks behind the crates, toward the rear. Noel hears the click of a microwave door. She runs her hand over an old French dressing table, the beautifully carved wood, the mirror worn through in spots.

"Where'd you get this?" she asks. George comes out from behind the crates.

"Here's your tea." Noel looks up in protest but takes the tea anyway. The truth is she likes this guy. In fact, they like each other.

Noel starts finding excuses to spend more time at her storage locker. She really is going to rent another unit but the only one available is three buildings away. Henry says wait, one will come open on her row. George is always there, anyway, even though he pretends to leave every day, riding fast by the manager's office on his bicycle. Noel starts bringing her students' papers there to grade, reading parts of them to George as he sits on his mattress or stands by the microwave. He tells her about the other people who live in these storage units, their names, what spaces they are in.

"Aren't you afraid he'll catch you?"

"Why?"

"Why? You owe him rent money and you just speed by his office window everyday? He's going to cut your lock off and sell all your things. He told me so." Noel's voice is high pitched, excited.

"No, he won't. And I don't owe him any rent money." George sits down on the mattress and sighs.

"You don't?"

"Look, it's the bribe that I owe. We all have to pay it but we're getting organized. We don't think we should have to pay a bribe." George and Noel look at each other. "How can he make us?"

"He can kick you out, that's what he can do." Noel feels dizzy. She huddles around her school papers. George is silent and standing up again.

"Come sit by me, George." He sits down next to her. "What's going to happen here?" She holds on to his arm and looks into his face. Then her eyes focus sharply. "Listen, I've been meaning to ask you something."

"What?"

"Do you think I could store a few things over here?"

"Over here?"

"Just until I get another unit, I'm really tight for space right now. I'm going to sell some stuff at the flea market this weekend."

It's a rainy day, one of those strange May rains, when you can see the sun but it pours anyway. George and Noel are sitting on his mattress. They leave the overhead door open so they can watch the rain hit the pavement. Noel has bought a bottle of Cold Duck. She has taken over almost half of George's storage area. Some of her stuff is mixed up with George's stuff. Noel and George are happy when they are together. They have things to talk about. Noel is holding the Cold Duck in her lap. Then Fred appears in the doorway.

"Fred!" Noel says, standing quickly. "What are you doing here?"

"Looking for you." He steps inside, sees George. "Why are you over here?"

"Talking to George. Fred, this is George. We're friends now. It's okay, Fred, don't worry." Fred stands clumsily inside the doorway, rain rattles down on the concrete behind him. He is wet. George stands up.

"Come on in, Fred, let's have some tea together," George says. Fred hesitates, rubs his hand over his wet hair.

"Are you sure it's okay?"

"It's okay," George says, "really." So they sit down on three corners of the bed, sipping tea. George gets up and down to fill the cups. Fred dries out. Noel knows she should feel uncomfortable but, somehow, she doesn't. It seems good to be all sitting on the same mattress. Then, all at once, Henry is in the doorway.

"What's going on in there?" Henry asks, "who's in there?" Henry is standing sideways in the doorway. He is fat and wet. Noel, George, and Fred look at each other.

Noel stands up and waves at Henry. "It's just us, Henry, it's Noel. I'm over here helping George move some things. Fred's here, too."

"Oh yeah?" Henry says. He peers into the room but acts like he can't see much. "Who's Fred?"

"He's my husband," Noel says. She smiles at George and Fred, then walks closer to the door so Henry can see her better.

"Henry, come on back here. Have a cup of tea," George says, then he stands up and waves his hands. "Come on back, get out of the rain." Henry shakes his head like a wet dog and walks around the crates and old furniture.

"Have a seat, Henry," George says. They sit on the four corners of the mattress. The rain falls outside, then the sun breaks the clouds apart and shines in the open doorway. Noel looks at the three men and smiles. She brings out her pocket knife and opens the bottle of Cold Duck. She pours four cups.

RESERVATIONS AT A SMALL CAFÉ

The white limousine is parked in the street outside the church but the driver is not visible. Music drifts down the steep brick steps, black men in tuxedos and black women in purple and red strapless gowns. Where is the bride and groom? Getting ready to emerge in triumph through the church doors? Tom sees a deli café on the opposite side of the street from the church. Perfect. We'll have lunch there, he thinks, why not there?

Tom walks into the Deli, a small bell jingles. Five empty tables. A sandwich menu, bagels, sprouts. A long row of cigarette cartons lined up behind a cash register. An old man with a newspaper is hunched up at a corner table, a half empty coffee cup in front of him. He is dressed in a suit and tie, an escapee, no doubt, from the wedding across the street. A man walks out from behind the counter.

"What'll it be?" he says. He is a short white guy in a Stanford sweatshirt that does not quite cover his bulging stomach. Clearly, this is his café. He is looking out the window while he waits for Tom to speak.

"I'll be back later with my dad," Tom says.

"Later?"

"He lives next door in the towers."

"Oh." The café owner looks at Tom with sleepy eyes. He walks back behind the counter, then turns, "What'ya want, reservations?" He laughs at his own joke. Tom looks at him for a minute.

"Yes, okay, reservations. Over by the windows there." Tom points to a table which looks out toward the church. "That will be fine."

"Okay, I'll put your name on it." The owner looks at the empty table, then back at Tom. He chuckles to himself but he is losing interest fast. Tom nods, then abruptly walks out the door. It jingles after him.

Down on the corner Tom sees what looks like the bride and groom, surrounded by people taking pictures. They are walking back from Lake Merritt, apparently, and they have stopped on the corner just before the church steps. She is like a black angel wrapped in a white cloud of lace and ribbons, he is tall, slender, almost invisible in her shadow. The bride turns to talk, then spins on her high heels. Tom cannot see her face clearly but he imagines it is full of radiance and expectation. She is looking toward the church steps as if she hears someone calling her.

Tom would like to go over there, stand near the bridal party. He could pretend he is waiting for a bus. He could listen to what they say. Feel some of their excitement. Tom has not attended many weddings lately. He is taking a break from a small house he is building up north. He turns the corner and walks toward his father's apartment tower.

"I'm Tom Eagle. I'm down from Oregon to see my father." The doorman sits behind a small, open window next to a massive glass door. He is suspicious, laugh lines around his eyes, but no smile.

"Do you mean the Mr. Eagle who lives on the seventh floor?"

"Yes, that one. Can I go up now?" The doorman reaches for his phone quickly, then looks back at Tom, studies his face.

"I'll call him. Who did you say you were?"

"I'm his son." The doorman mulls over this information, then pushes a button on a large board. "Mr. Eagle?" He waits. "Mr. Eagle, you have a visitor." No answer. The doorman looks at Tom with increased suspicion.

"Well, he's sleeping, it's his nap time. I'll go and wake him up," Tom says.

"Do you have some identification, something with a photo on it?" The doorman is up, standing by his chair now.

"Of course, I'm his son."

"We have to ask, you know. This is Oakland. Things happen here. Every night. Certain people would like to get in here." He taps on the huge glass door, as if testing it for cracks.

"I know. I want to get in here, too." Tom hands over his driver's license. For a moment it looks like the doorman might ask him to take it out of its plastic holder. He examines the photo, then looks closely at Tom. His face relaxes a little.

"Okay, Mr. Eagle. Room 222. Seventh floor. Go to the sixth floor, then walk up one flight of stairs." The glass door swings smoothly open, no squeak. Tom walks toward the elevator. He has been here many times. It is always like this. It's a good thing, probably, Tom thinks. This is Oakland, after all. The doorman calls after him.

"It's because we're remodeling." Tom turns around.

"Thanks. We'll be back down pretty soon, I suspect."

Tom is standing outside his father's door, listening. He thinks he hears voices, a voice. Maybe his father is on the phone. Eighty seven years old and on the phone talking. Tom knows that the door is always open and so he turns the knob, pushes. He stops. It's better to knock. He knocks loudly, then rings the doorbell. Nothing. So he goes in. But nobody is in the living room or the kitchen, no voices, no telephone. Silence. He pushes open the bedroom door. Edwin Eagle is sleeping in an old tee-shirt, naked from the waist down. No sheet in the dry October heat. The father's breath is heavy, filling the space between them, but it is not irregular. He's okay, Tom thinks, as okay as he can be.

Tom walks silently back into the other rooms and sits down at the kitchen table. A birthday card lies open by a vase of artificial flowers. It's the card Tom sent to his father a month earlier, a picture of Charlie Chaplin under a spotlight, his embarrassed smile, his sly posture. Tom imagines Charley Chaplin with no pants. It's difficult. Tom knows that his father will not want to go to the café. But the thought of eating in the tower dining room again is depressing. Tom realizes, suddenly, that his father is up, that he is standing in his bedroom door, half naked, watching him.

"It's just me, Dad." The father nods his head and goes back into his bedroom to put on his pants.

Tom and his father are sitting in the downstairs dining room. Tables are arranged in restaurant fashion, buffet tables form a large "T" in the center of the room. The walls are pastel, painted with scenes from the 1800s, old trains, picturesque barns, farmers and horses in their fields. Comforting images. Old people, women by and large, sit around and talk quietly. Mostly they watch—who comes in, who goes out, who eats what. They look at Tom and whisper to each other.

"Do we have to sit here?" the father asks, "I always sit here." His hair is not brushed and he is wearing a black shirt with a tiny antelope embroidered over his heart. He has lint and dandruff on the shoulders of his shirt.

"Well, I suggested the café around the corner, didn't I?" Tom pushes the prongs of his fork, the silver handle slaps up under his wrist. The father seems to hear this and tilts his head slightly.

"Eat is all they do. Look at them. They live to eat. And get fatter." He shakes his head. He is talking louder than anyone else, loud enough for four old ladies at a nearby table to overhear.

"But not me. I live to fuck." The father stares at Tom. But Tom just closes his eyes, says nothing. The father leans over, in a more intimate voice. "Have you met my girl yet?" The father is smiling now, his face red and flushed. He has a dimple on his chin, the white beard stubble looks longer inside the dimple.

"Yes, last time, remember." Tom has not met this woman but he is hoping his father doesn't remember.

"No, I want you to meet her. She's something all right. Three hundred bucks a shot, too, and that's something, I can tell you that. And only thirty years old. Can you beat that?" He looks at Tom the way Tom remembers him after little league baseball games, sixty years ago. Tom's team would win a game and the father would walk around the pizza parlor with that smile on his face.

"Let's eat," Tom says.

"Eat?" The father looks at the four women at the next table. They have their hands over their mouths, whispering to each other. "No, let's go to your café, then, let's go there." He stands up and heads for the lobby door. Tom looks back, as if to apologize for his father's behavior, then follows him. They stop in front of the elevator.

"Wait here a minute. I have to go to the room." The father is smiling.

"I'll come, too," Tom says.

"No, that's all right. Wait here. It's just the toilet. Be right back." The father steps into the elevator and pushes the button. He turns around to face Tom just as the door closes. Tom has taken off his glasses. His father looks white and strangely nimble as he stands behind the elevator door, like a stage clown about to bow to his audience. Like Charlie Chaplin. Then the elevator is gone. Tom sits down in an overstuffed chair and waits.

Tom is sitting at the café table which looks out at the church. His father sits across from him. Tom is looking out the window while his father scans the menu. The limousine has not moved, it is sparkling white and long in the middle of the street. Cars have to pull around it but traffic is fairly light on this end of the street. And, of course, limousines are entitled to a certain amount of leeway.

"Pastrami, I guess," the father says. He is still red in the face, flushed with some sort of pale energy. He looks at Tom. "Hey, are you there?"

"Huh. Oh yeah. Okay, pastrami sounds fine to me," Tom says and looks down at the newspaper that the last customer has left on the table. A man robbed at gunpoint at the Oakland Bart station. Interest rates drop. Record heat wave.

"So what's going on over there?" Now the father is looking out the window.

"A wedding," Tom says.

"Blacks?" Tom says nothing. "Well, it's a black church isn't it?" the father says loudly. Tom remembers his father barking over the family dinner table in Berkeley, crimes in the newspapers, crimes in the street. Soon nobody'll be safe, nobody, he'd say.

"So we'll have pastrami sandwiches, then?" Tom says quietly. The father gives Tom a quick look and jerks his head back toward the window. His neck is rigid, his hands trembling slightly. He looks like he wants to say something but no words come out.

"Yes," the father almost shouts, "Rueben sandwich, I want." The café owner in the Stanford sweatshirt walks up, no note pad, hands clasped behind his back.

"What'll it be, folks, what'll it be?" He has a broad smile on his face. That's when Tom realizes that a woman is now standing outside the window and Tom knows immediately that she's the one. That his father called her on the phone when he was supposed to be going to the bathroom. She has a round face, fleshy, smooth brown skin. Black hair to the shoulders and a plain red dress, the kind a young girl would wear, innocent, carefree. She is not fat but looks sturdy, the tops of her arms strong under the short sleeves. Through the window her eyes seem almost red, deep like jello in a bowl. Yes, she's quite attractive, balanced on one foot, trying to see whose sitting at the café tables. But the angle is wrong and Tom thinks that she can't really see him and his father sitting there. Or so it appears. Her eyes shut, then open again, as if she's just waking up from a brief sleep.

"Rueben sandwich," Tom says, "two of them." The café owner shifts on his feet.

"Something to drink?"

"Drink?" Tom says. "Dad what would you like to drink?"

"A beer," the father says.

"How about a Bud?" the owner says. "All's we got is Bud here." Tom can see by his face that he has just noticed the woman in the window. No reaction, though. Who cares?

"Yeah, a Bud. A Bud is great," the father says.

"Two Buds," Tom says. He wonders what will happen next. The woman does not move into the father's direct line of sight. Now she is looking out into the street, at the limousine, looking up at the people and the church. Maybe she's not the one, after all. Finally, she turns back toward the café door and walks forward. The front door is not visible from Tom's seat. He hears the jingle but does not see her pass the cash register.

Tom's father is drinking his beer. "What's it cost to rent one of those limos anyway?"

"A lot," Tom says, "a hundred a day, maybe." His eyes are resting on a point behind his father's head. She probably went to the restroom. Tom expects her to materialize any minute at just that point.

"Hundred an hour, you mean. Those things aren't cheap. White ones, especially." The father holds his beer mug up in front of his face, against the light, swirls the beer around. Two identical sandwiches arrive.

"Who gets what?" The café owner chortles way down deep in his throat. He plops the first Rueben down in front of the father who picks it up and begins to eat. He sets the other sandwich down in front of Tom but he doesn't leave. The café owner stands over the father and son, as if he has something more to say.

"Everything's fine here," Tom says.

"Good, good, want anything else?"

"Not right now, thanks."

"Okay." But the owner still does not move. He is looking out the window. Finally, he takes the empty tray and walks back behind the counter. The father eats quickly, neatly. No spills on his shirt or on the table.

"Son, I've got something to talk to you about. In a few minutes, maybe." He stuffs the last corner of rye bread into his mouth, swallows. His throat wrinkles in the shadowed light from the window.

"I know, Dad, that's all right." Probably she's waiting around the corner for his signal. A special cough, a raised syllable, a spoon tossed casually across the table. But nothing happens.

Tom and his father linger in the café for a while. Tom has nearly finished his sandwich. They look out the window. They talk. Tom waits. The café owner rolls up his sleeves, then rolls them back down. They order two more beers. The little bell on the end of the string jingles a few times. People come in, they go out. Tom realizes that the café owner is selling cigarettes and other household items from a shelf behind the cash register. This really is a neighborhood café.

A small black and white television is perched in a corner behind the counter. The sound is turned off but the images float like smoke over the still air. Beautiful girls on sandy beaches, happy wives standing in their spotless kitchens, smug men drinking beer on sailboats. The clock ticks a winding path around the chairs and tables of the small café.

Suddenly the door bangs open and there they are, standing in front of the cash register. The wedding couple. The little bell rings and rings as wedding guests crowd in after the newlyweds. They fill the front of the café.

"What'll it be, folks, what'll it be?" The owner is standing behind the cash register and the bride is looking at some cigarette packs lined up under the counter in a glass case.

"Pack of Salem lights," says the groom. His arm is around the bride, the flowing gown folds around his wrist, her face is hidden in white. The café owner looks down, narrows his eyes.

"I'm out of Salems, something else maybe."

"I see some down there," says the bride. The groom smiles and moves his hands apologetically.

"It's what she wants," he says.

"Nope, that's just a dummy. How about something else?" He points up at the cartons on the shelf, Camel, Marlboro, Winston, Hit Parade. "One of those okay?" The bride is not happy.

"What dummy? What does he mean, dummy? Give me the Salems. Know what I'm saying, just give me the Salems." Her tone is shrill and challenging. Everything slows down. The people jammed into the doorway back up a step or two. The owner pulls at his sleeves, looks down accusingly at his cigarette case.

"It's okay man, just sell me the smokes, okay, no harm done," the groom says. He is still smiling, the last thing he wants is trouble. The owner says nothing, runs his fingers over the letters on his sweatshirt.

Tom looks at his father, hoping that he will drink his beer and not notice what is going on. But he has noticed. His face is red. His breath is in quick sputters. Tom can see the limousine is ready to leave out in the street, the driver at long last behind the steering wheel. Tom feels the café expanding like a balloon full of gas. A corner of pastrami sandwich lies on Tom's plate. The father's neck is tight, his eyes focused, he is drawing himself up for some climactic moment of rectitude. He turns to face his audience.

"There aren't any cigarettes, young man, Can't you see that? No cigarettes, at all." The father turns back to his beer. He has said what he wants to say. The café owner backs up, putting distance between himself and his customers. He speaks quickly.

"No problems, folks, lots of brands here, just no Salems today." But all eyes are on the father now. He is sitting three or four feet from the wedding couple, who have turned to stare at the back of his head. The bride looks at her wedding guests and then back at Tom's father. Too late Tom sees the thin white umbrella that the bride is carrying under the folds of her gown. She swings it level with the father's head, not straight down as you might expect, but level like a baseball bat. It will be a direct hit. But, somehow, the umbrella misses, whirs like wind over the father's head. He cocks his ear to one side as if he has heard a sound he can't identify.

Then the bride and groom are out the door and down the sidewalk, the wedding party trailing behind, whispering, looking back at the café windows. Tom sees the newlyweds climb into the very back of the white limousine, sees the bride pull the umbrella in after her, tuck it away on the floor. The car door slams silently through the glass of the café window. Two guys push up and down on the trunk of the limousine and it rocks several times, then spins its tires and crawls uphill slowly, very slowly, past the church.

Then Tom sees the woman who had been standing in the café window. She is walking fast along the near side of the limousine, she is tapping on one of the windows. One of the middle doors opens and she climbs inside. The limousine picks up speed and turns the corner at the top of the hill. Tom is standing by the café table with his hands clasped together in front of his stomach. He looks down at his father and the fragment of sandwich. The father is tipping his glass, finishing the last drop of beer. The café owner has retreated to the back room. There is no sound and no movement in the small café.

Tom is standing in front of his father's TV set, watching the Oakland hills fire. The flames are giant mushrooms over the houses, the trees explode like bombs. The news reporters face the overheated cameras, flames reflected in their quickening eyes. The father sits deep in his chair.

"How close is it? It's getting closer all the time, isn't it?" the father asks. Tom holds up one hand, waves it, as if pushing air toward the TV set and his father. The reporter is saying that a certain house on a hill, a house of stucco and tile, has refused to burn. Nobody knows why. It stands alone on a street of ashes and smoking embers.

"It's close isn't it? What's really happening out there, Tom?" The father says this but he doesn't move. He seems strangely comfortable in his chair. Stuck there almost. Then the phone rings. Tom pushes the mute button on the TV remote, then picks up the phone.

"Eagle residence," Tom says. Tom backs away from the TV, then turns to his father.

"It's Max," Tom says and puts the flat of his hand up in the air, then claps it over the receiver. "It's Max in New

York. He's seen the fire on television. I guess it's on TV everywhere." The father does not respond.

"Yes, Max. He's here. He's fine. Right there in his chair." Silence.

"Well, what else can we do?" Tom holds the receiver away from his ear, balancing it on his palm. "We're not firefighters, are we?"

"Okay, sure. Actually, we did. We've been out for lunch at a neighborhood café. Rueben sandwiches. We got back home and here was the fire waiting for us on TV." Pause.

"No, no, the work turned out just fine. No problem. The roof is on. Thanks, Max, really. The house never could have happened without you." The father is staring at the TV but the sound is off. He holds the remote limply in two hands. "I really do appreciate all you've done up there, really, Max." Silence.

"Well, he's right here." Tom holds the receiver a little further away from his ear.

"Okay, well that's okay, I'm sure. He's doing fine. He's watching it on TV right now."

"Yeah, I know Max, we will. They'll announce it if we have to, right? Broadway Terrace is evacuated, I know that. That's why we're here watching it on TV, I guess." Tom looks at the TV screen. People are lined up inside a high school gym, army cots along the walls. First aid kits and canteens placed carefully on the cots.

"Right Max, we will. Okay, talk to you later."

"What's going on?" the father says. "I can't hear a thing." Tom walks up behind him, leans over. Tom pushes the mute button on the remote and the room fills with sound.

SISTERS

Xiaomei lays her hand on the telephone, then takes it off. She looks toward the kitchen. Her mother and father are sitting at the kitchen table. They are not speaking. The mother looks as if she might stand up to clear the dishes, she holds on to a thin cup of tea. The father looks toward the window. He is looking at the green grass in the backyard.

It is hard for Xiaomei to look at the father now, the sallow eyes, the thinness of his arms, the cinched belt. She picks up the phone again, then puts it down without dialing. She will call her sister after her father has turned up the television. That will be better. Xiaomei walks into the kitchen.

"We're going next Sunday, then?" Xiaomei asks. She stands behind her mother, facing her father. No one speaks. "I've made the appointment." The mother looks up at her daughter but does not stand.

"I am too tired to argue with him today. He does what he does, he goes where he goes," the mother says. She picks up the tea cup, then sets it down with a clatter. She does not look at her husband. "I have said all that I know how to say."

The father stands up slowly and walks over to his couch. Two television sets sit on a cabinet in front of the sofa, one shows a man talking but no sound, on the other the shrill flickering of a Chinese soap opera. There are two Chinese channels in the San Francisco Bay Area and he has a TV set for each one. He points the remote and the sound comes up on the first set—news from Taiwan.

"He doesn't work on his stamp collection now. He won't even work on a puzzle." The mother says this is a loud voice as she rinses dishes and puts them into the dishwasher. Finished puzzles hang on all the walls of the house, carefully varnished and mounted in wood frames. Puzzles containing tropical birds and ancient ships, mountain brooks and Roman ruins. Even the Golden Gate bridge. The father begins to speak but does not turn his head toward the kitchen.

"Pieces are missing from some of those puzzles, mother." He waves his hand at the walls of his house. "And what you say is not true, I am working on a new puzzle right now. Haven't you looked in the study room?" He keeps his eyes on the Chinese news.

"Ma, he's fine, let's just do the dishes." Xiaomei puts her hand on her mother's shoulder. The mother is thin under her fingers, frail with puzzlement and doubt. The mother has felt dizzy for weeks.

"Yes, the dishes," the mother says. A Chinese man speaks loudly on the television, he is talking about a recent election in Taiwan. The father sits rigid against the back of the sofa, eyes fixed forward on the screen. His face is thin and his lips have narrowed to a feminine grace, his skin has a yellow sheen and seems almost transparent, as if, looking closely, you might see the organs working underneath.

Xiaomei watches her father, sees his agitation. He does not like to hear of the Taiwanese Party winning elections. The father is from Shanghai, he brought his family to Taiwan after the revolution in 1949. Now things have changed. At least people acted civilized back then, the father likes to say, at least they were polite. Now they push and shout at the camera, they jump on tables and scream into microphones. The father holds up the remote and aims it carefully, as if shooting a gun. The politician's lips turn silent. Then he aims another remote at the second TV set and a woman's voice cries out, plaintive, sobbing. A man's voice, consoling, calm. Then silence. Dishes clack against the porcelain of the kitchen sink. Hot water plunges in the drain.

Xiaomei is standing in the office of the family doctor. He was a famous doctor once in Taiwan, now he is old and tired and is seeing patients in Fremont, California. Sometimes they are the same patients he saw in Taiwan. The doctor reaches behind his desk and pulls out a large x-ray photograph. He clips it on the wall. Then he clips up another, then another. The x-rays form a half circle at one end of the doctor's office. Xiaomei looks at the x-rays, then at the doctor. He has a stick in his hand, a round rod with a rubber stopper at one end. The doctor walks up the middle x-ray.

"This is his right kidney. Do you see the dark places here? And here?" He moves the stick gracefully over the smooth surface of the photograph. Xiaomei nods her head. She walks up to the x-ray, reaches out to touch the kidney with her forefinger. Then she touches her finger to her nose. Xiaomei can smell the faint heaviness of the photographic chemicals, the slickness of the paper.

"That's his kidney?"

"Yes. And his liver is there on the right." The doctor holds the stick at his side. "He has water in the chest area now, in his feet also." He stands back away from the x-rays, almost like an artist appraising his work. "The picture is pretty clear at this point."

"Yes," Xiaomei says. She feels like gathering up the x-rays, like taking them home. To study them. Maybe there's something in these pictures that the doctor hasn't seen. He is a very busy doctor and he doesn't appear to look closely at the x-rays. He doesn't stand close to them and bend his head over. "Is there anything else I should see in these pictures?"

"Why, no, I guess not." The doctor lays the pointer stick on his desk. Xiaomei is still standing among the x-ray photographs.

"I've made an appointment with a Chinese herb doctor in Chinatown," she says. The doctor is sitting at his desk now, tracing his finger over some charts. He does not look up.

"Which one?"

"The Black Toad specialist, just off Clement St."

"Why not?" the doctor says. "Who knows what might help? Or hurt? There is nothing a surgeon can do now, that's for sure." He lays the charts down and stands up behind his desk. "I have been your father's doctor for many, many years, since before you were born in Taiwan."

Xiaomei has reached out her hand again, as if to touch the fatal x-ray one last time, then she turns. She hears a slight tremor in the doctor's voice. She walks up to his desk and sticks out her hand.

"Thank you so much, Dr. Chiu, for helping our family all these years—for caring about us. It's been a long time." The doctor shrugs his shoulders and shakes her hand. Xiaomei walks quickly out the door.

Xiaomei has been living with her parents for more than ten years. She is the youngest daughter and she is not yet married. The other sisters have jobs and husbands and are living in far away places, two in the United States, one still in Taiwan. Xiaomei has her job and she has her mother and father. She had traveled to the San Francisco bay area to live with them right after graduating from college in Taiwan. She thought that living with her parents would be temporary, at first, but there were always good reasons not to get her own apartment. Now she goes to work every day at the hospital and she comes home at five thirty in the evening. Her parents sit at the dinner table at exactly 6:15 PM. Her father looks at the clock and then picks up his soup spoon. The chopsticks are always perfectly placed on the white tablecloth.

In Taiwan, Xiaomei used to stand with her mother in the kitchen. They could hear the father talking on the phone in his study room. He was an important man, an executive in the national oil company. A driver in a long black limousine stopped each morning to drive him to his office. Sometimes Xiaomei got to ride to her classes in the limousine. The women in this family really did not know too much about the father's life.

One day the father spoke to Xiaomei as she passed the door to his study. "Here are the new stamps I got in the mail." He was sitting at his desk. "Come here, look at this one." The father picked up a stamp with a pair of tweezers and held it in front of his daughter's face. She saw two brightly colored birds. Xiaomei did not know what to say.

"These are Puffin birds. They are extinct now."

"Why did they die?" Xiaomei had studied species extinction in her zoology class.

"They couldn't find the right food to eat," the father said. Then he looked at his youngest daughter. "These stamps are from many places in the world. Would you like to visit other countries someday?" Xiaomei was still standing in the doorway, she did not often enter her father's study. She couldn't answer his question.

"Do you ever get letters from your sisters living over there across the ocean?" The father was looking at the pale green Puffin stamp through a magnifying glass.

"Our mother has shown me some cards." Xiaomei stood on one foot, then on the other. "They don't write to me anymore. They have husbands now." She thought that her father must want to tell her something. Perhaps something that he had been meaning to say for a long time. Then the phone rang and the father was speaking quickly into the receiver. Xiaomei walked slowly back to her room.

A few years later, the father had a sudden heart attack and retired abruptly. Xiaomei's parents quickly sold their house and moved to California. The weather would be better there and two daughters were already settled in the United States. After finishing school the next summer, Xiaomei followed her parents to the Gold Mountain. What else could she do?

Xiaomei usually calls her sisters in the evening when her father is watching television. She uses the phone in the spare bedroom.

"Just tell me when to come," says the Iowa sister. "Is this the right time to come?"

"Should we tell him?" Xiaomei asks.

"No, of course not," the Iowa sister says. "You should never do that, anyway maybe he knows already." But the Los Angeles sister says that the father should be told. She says she will come up on the weekend and tell him herself, since no one else is up to the job. She does fly up but she doesn't tell him anything.

"It's not the right time yet," says the Los Angeles sister. "I'll do it later." Xiaomei and the Los Angeles sister are taking clothes out of the dryer and folding them into neat piles on the bed in the spare bedroom. Xiaomei is matching the socks and rolling them into tight balls. She piles her father's socks on one end of the bed.

"I saw him in here looking at his suitcases in the closet the other day," Xiaomei says, "he had them out here on the bed."

"That's how old people are, you know, sad and sentimental." Xiaomei looks at her sister.

"Maybe he wants to go somewhere, maybe he wants to visit someone." Xiaomei is folding her mother's blouses. "I asked him if he wanted to see Mr. Shu. I said we could fly down to Corona. He doesn't even answer when I ask him questions lately."

"It doesn't really matter, does it? He can't travel now anyway," the Los Angeles sister says. She folds a pair of pants. "When is our Taiwan sister coming?"

"Why don't you try calling her?" Xiaomei has loaded her arms with folded clothes and is about to walk out the bedroom door. "I called her yesterday. I told her it was time to come. They were on their way to Singapore on a business trip."

"Well, she'll have to come now, won't she?. Singapore will still be there afterwards, I'm sure."

The Iowa sister arrives during the week and now there are three daughters and the mother watching everything the father does. They sit at the dinner table eating and they watch him. They watch him when he sits on the couch in front of the television sets and when he gets up to go to the bathroom. Sometimes a sister bends over to listen at the bathroom door.

They follow him and they give each other meaningful looks. They take him out to eat at his favorite restaurants. They take him to Dim Sum in Foster City. The mother is still dizzy but she feels better now that her daughters are taking charge. The sisters hold conferences in the spare bedroom when the evening television is on loud.

"Will he go to the Black Toad doctor?"

"He had an appointment last Sunday but he refused at the last minute."

"I think he'll go now. We're all here."

"Almost all."

"She will come. Her husband still has a heart problem, you know."

"But what if…?"

"Why don't you call her? She listens to you."

"They were on their way to Singapore."

"Singapore? What's the big deal? There will be plenty of time to go there."

"Can you call the herb doctor again?"

"I did! This Sunday. One in the afternoon."

"Will he go?"

The three sisters are standing in the spare bedroom, one on each side of the bed, one at the end. They look at each other and Xiaomei can feel the years falling away between them, as if an elastic band connecting them were about to snap. The band stretches like rubber back through the past, back into their family house in Taipei.

Xiaomei was sitting in the swing in her backyard and two of her sisters were playing with wood blocks on a patch of grass by the back door. Her oldest sister walked through the door onto a short wood porch.

"Yahto," she called, "Xiaoyahto." Xiaomei dropped from the swing and ran to the back door.

"Can I ride on your back, Number One sister?"

"Not now. I'm helping our Ma. Were you playing with that cat again?" The oldest sister is holding a broom and she pushes the bristles toward Xiaomei as if to brush dirt from her shirt. The sisters look around the yard. A high brick wall, some patches of grass. No cat.

The cat lived somewhere nearby and it was very old. Its ears were bitten by battles with younger cats and the indentations were pitted with flies. Pink bald spots infested its dirty hair. This cat would cling to Xiaomei's shirt and push its face toward her mouth. She sometimes fed it milk in a blue and white rice bowl. Xiaomei was forbidden to play with this animal. Stray cats carry disease and have been poking their noses into gutters and garbage cans. But Xiaomei wanted always to hold this defiant cat and feel its stubborn life humming beneath the clotted fur.

Xiaomei is sitting alone in her bedroom, looking at a very long, stringed musical instrument. She has not played this gu-jun since her father got sick. She has not even been by herself for weeks. She and the Iowa sister have been sleeping in their mother's room because she does not want to be alone. The Los Angeles sister stays in Xiaomei's room. The father stays on the couch in the living room where the family can keep a careful eye on him. Today everyone else has gone out to eat. Going to Chinese restaurants is one of the only things that the father can do now. He walks so slowly. But Xiaomei has stayed home. She has announced that she doesn't feel well. It's true, she is tired and confused and needs to be alone. Everything is too complicated.

Xiaomei rubs her hand down the long strings of the gu-jun, then plucks one string. A finished puzzle hangs on the wall over her head. It is a Chinese painting of a man fishing from a boat on a large lake. A waterfall pours behind the boat and a single cypress tree rises above the man and flows out over the water. The man is playing a wooden flute and another fisherman listens. Xiaomei covers the instrument with a long red cloth. She will not play the gu-jun today.

It is early morning and Xiaomei hangs up the living room phone and walks toward the kitchen. She stops and looks at the rows of shoes by the front door. Her father's black leather shoes, her mother's pink and white tennis shoes, the shoes of her sisters, her own shoes. Today there will be a new pair of shoes—the Taiwan sister will arrive. Dirt has settled on the white tiles under the shoe rack, pieces of grass and soil from the front yard. Xiaomei walks toward the shoes as if she will straighten them up but then turns to the kitchen. She can hear her mother chopping vegetables on a wooden block.

"Who was that on the phone?" the mother asks.

"Dr. Mung."

"What does she say?" The mother looks up from the chopping board and scrapes chunks of asparagus into a plastic bowl.

"It's about the new appointment, a reminder."

"Oh, that." The mother is chopping chicken into tiny pieces.

"Will he go?" Both women look toward the sofa and the TV sets. The father is quiet, motionless. Eyes closed.

"Will he go?" the mother repeats, "Will he go?" She lowers her voice to a whisper. "Do you know what he said to me yesterday? When no one else could hear him." The mother has stopped chopping and scrapes the chicken into the bowl with the asparagus. She looks into the eyes of her youngest daughter. "He said I have not given him sons and that is why he is sick. That's what he said." She puts her hands flat down on the sink as if to push it away from her body. "How do I know what he will or won't do?"

Xiaomei knows that her mother is very close to crying. She can see the muscles loose in her face, the eye skin glisten.

"He is sleeping now?" Xiaomei asks. The mother does not speak for a few minutes.

"Yes," she says finally, "he is sleeping."

Today Xiaomei will take her father to the Chinese market. The mother will stay home with the other sisters. They all think that the mother and father need a break away from each other.

"Watch him carefully," the mother whispers in Xiaomei's ear as they walk out through the laundry room into the garage.

The father sits comfortably in the front seat of the white car. He is happy to go shopping with his number four daughter.

"And how do you feel today, father?" Xiaomei would like to speak clearly with the father? Confidentially perhaps.

"As with any day, daughter, no different."

"Your stomach?"

"As with any stomach at noon—empty. For this we are going to the Chinese Market, yes?"

"Yes." Xiaomei understands. Her father just wants to be a normal person on a normal shopping trip. That will be enough for him.

At the HoHo market, the father speaks rapid Mandarin and the shopping cart fills with cans and packages. Every aisle is piled high with boxes and people thread their carts narrowly through the tiny passageways between displays. Xiaomei and the father stop in front of the sea food counter. Live lobsters and crabs swim in long tanks. Fish lie in packed ice, intact, eyes forward as if still ready to swim. Fish of all types from all over the world. The father points to a medium sized catfish.

"We'll take that one." The clerk wraps the fish in a newspaper, seals it with masking tape. The odor of fresh fish is thick in the packed aisles of this jumbled market. It is because of this smell that non-Asians do not often come here to shop. For Xiaomei it is one of the smells of home. There are many Chinese in the market today. The aisles buzz with carts and voices.

Xiaomei is sitting in the herb doctor's waiting room with her mother and father. Her three sisters have come in the car but they have gone to speak with relatives who live in a nearby neighborhood. The mother sits on one side of the number four daughter and the father sits on the other side. Xiaomei can see directly into one of the herb rooms where a man weighs leaves and bark and roots on a small hand scale using tiny gold colored weights. These ingredients he spreads onto a wood block and chops them into small pieces with a large knife. The knife handle is wound with many colored strings tied in a careful pattern. Sacks and boxes are piled everywhere, leaves and dried plants, long roots in tall stacks, herbs tumbled upon each other, tucked into corners, piled on tall shelves, spilling over the sides of cabinets. Glass jars of musky powder, fiery liquids, all marked in loud red characters. The man with the knife reaches up to a high drawer and pulls out a small clump of bark, three pieces tied with three white strings. A palpable thickness flows through the air of the herb shop, as if Xiaomei is breathing the sum of all the herbs in China, granulated and pumped through the weight of silence.

Xiaomei is waiting for the doctor's door to open and for her to walk quickly up to her father and say "ni how, ni how." They have known this doctor, too, since the early years in Taiwan. But the father has not wanted to see her. Now the Black Toad doctor walks on quick feet through her door into the bright light of the waiting room.

Dr. Mung shakes the father's hand and waves them all into her office. They sit down. The doctor stands in front of the father. "How do you feel today?" Silence. All three women are waiting for the father to answer. He lowers his head and does not speak.

"He hardly eats at all," Xiaomei offers. The mother nods her head but doesn't move or say anything.

"May I look at your eyes?" The doctor touches the father's face. His eyes slowly turn up. She touches the skin under both eyes, feels the texture of the loose folds. "He is holding much water," the doctor says, "we can try reducing the salt he eats."

Dr. Mung sits down with the mother and Xiaomei. "We will prepare a special round of herbs today, to make him feel better and lower his salt."

The mother finally speaks. "I have prepared herb water before. He doesn't want to drink it anymore."

"These herbs are different. They just came in from China. He will drink these, I think. Cook them well."

"He won't eat anything I cook now." The mother says. She shakes her head and squints at the doctor as if she can't see her very well. "What can I do now?"

"Will your family be here soon?" the doctor asks.

"We are all here today," Xiaomei says.

"That is good. Stay close to him." The doctor stands up. Everyone stands up. The doctor opens a door and Xiaomei can see down a long hallway and into the herb rooms. A rush of men, chopping and scraping stems and leaves into small brown lunch sacks, each sack marked with bright red Chinese characters.

The doctor returns from the herb room with a large paper sack which says Safeway on the side. Xiaomei sees seven small sacks inside the big sack, one for each day of the week.

"Sheh Sheh," Xiaomei says and takes the large sack into her arms. She holds it gently almost as if she were holding a baby. "Well?" She is waiting for the doctor to speak.

"Well, then, cook the herbs carefully, let the smell of them fill your house." She pauses as if she wants to say something more. Xiaomei moves closer to the doctor and lowers her voice.

"How long does he have?"

"Who can say? A week or two, maybe less or more. Maybe more." Xiaomei and the doctor stand in the middle of the room, the father and mother are sitting in large chairs by the door.

"We haven't told him."

"Well, it's up to you, of course, but I'm sure he knows already. Let him drink the herbs. Let him eat good food. Let him hear music. What is the point of discussing it anyway? I could see it in his eyes." The doctor walks over to her desk and sits down. "Sometimes the old ways are better, I think. Not everything requires a conference and a confession. There is more dignity this way."

Three pots are boiling on the stove, a large gray pot in front with a short spout which is really a handle. Two smaller pots in back. Steams pours from the pots in long rushes, streaming and disappearing into the kitchen air. The sisters take turns adding water to the pots, carefully lifting each lid, pouring water from a long spouted pitcher. Xiaomei stands in the kitchen with her sisters, the Los Angeles sister, the Iowa sister, the Taiwan sister. The father lies on the couch watching a Chinese soap opera on one TV. The other set shows a traditional Chinese opera but the sound is turned off. A dragon drifts like a dream across an elevated, ebony stage. The odors from the pots have thickened the air to a pungent fullness, a kind of soft balloon against the nose and face. Xiaomei feels her skin glow from the moisture in the air. The family is waiting for some visitors from Taiwan to arrive.

The doorbell rings. The father gets up and moves very slowly toward the door, bent almost backwards, his upper body following reluctantly behind his legs. The mother and four sisters watch him but do not interfere. He opens the door.

There is a soft clamor of bodies as everyone arrives at the door at once. It is Mr. Fang and his wife. These families have not seen each other for more than twenty years. Shoes clack against the floor, voices fall like leaves through doors and windows. Then the father's voice, almost feminine, faint but clear.

"I'm so glad that you came today, I was afraid that you might miss me."

It is early morning and the sisters are gathered in the backyard, leaning over a red wok. Xiaomei is feeding Chinese money into a tiny fire in the bottom of the wok. The flames spin lightly over the colored paper, another sister stirs the charred papers with chopsticks to keep the fire going. Each sheet of money carries a gold or black splatch of color and some red characters. On the table near the wok sit three plates of fruit, three fruits on each plate. Mangoes, small papayas, Asian pears. Thin trails of smoke thread the air above a golden bowl filled with sand and incense sticks. No one speaks.

The sisters move quietly in a slow dance around the wok, their slippers scuffing lightly on the wood deck. The mother is watching through the kitchen window but does not come outside. Her face is pressed against the window, yet her body seems far away as if lost in an oblique reflection of light. The wind slips through the trees and flutters the dresses and sleeves of the gathered sisters. The fire spurts and skips in the red wok, then falls, finally, into a pile of black ash. The sisters look at each other. Xiaomei picks up the lid to the wok and carefully places it over the ashes. They walk together back into the house.

A SCARLET THREAD

Jake Dealman is a bus driver. He drives from San Francisco to Reno and back and sometimes he drives from Reno to a little town on the Utah/Nevada border named Wendover. But this trip he is getting overtime and will drive straight through to Salt Lake City. Good money and just two more hours. Wendover is a pretty strange place, anyway, half in one state, half in another
. Gambling casinos on one side of the street facing off against church steeples on the other side. Jake understands casinos well enough but churches are something he stays away from.

Jake used to drive school buses in Southern California. That was before he read in the newspapers about school buses being kidnapped, some even buried in sand out in the desert somewhere. School kids had been taken hostage. A bus had been set on fire. Drivers had been shot at. It's not that Jake Dealman was afraid, not that exactly. But why put up with that kind of treatment? Anyway, he had had enough of yellow buses that never got repaired until it was too late and you ended up stranded somewhere between Morningside Elementary and San Fernando Road with angry parents jamming up telephone lines all over town. And he had had enough of kids who would not sit still, who screamed and tossed food from their lunchboxes at each other.

Jake had always dreamed of the Greyhound buses he had seen cruising through small towns. They were sleek and in good repair—new tires, radios, air conditioners, even bathrooms in the back. What a sweet deal one of those would be! Some of them had dark tinted windows so that, when the bus passed, people on the sidewalk and in cars couldn't see inside. Like a limousine. So Jake quit the school buses and said goodbye to the little kids. He said goodbye to all of that hassle and moved to San Francisco. And why not? Jake was divorced, his kids were grown up and were impossible to get a hold of. All Jake ever got was an answering machine. So why waste his life driving a school bus?

Now Jake has swift Greyhounds to drive and, this week, he has the night run from Reno to Wendover with overtime to Salt Lake City. Jake likes the desolate stretches of Nevada. He has always felt a powerful connection to the desert, even in winter, the jagged outline of mountains, the flat and endless dry lakes, the puffed blue of sky. The desert is something true, unchanging, dignified in its rarified distances.

Jake is sitting in the driver's room at the Reno bus terminal. He's reading the newspaper and keeping a wary eye on the TV that hangs at a dangerous angle from the ceiling. He's wondering if his bus will be able to leave on time. Probably not. It's been snowing pretty hard, so the bus coming over the hill from Sacramento will probably have to put on chains to get through Donner Pass. Add a couple of hours for that. Jake likes to read the newspapers anyway, the San Francisco papers at least. Sometimes he gets the Chronicle in the morning and the Examiner in the evening, that way he has the news covered coming and going. He even reads the paper while sitting on the toilet. Of course, Jake realizes that a lot of people do that—in fact, a restroom is a good place to pick up an abandoned newspaper. He likes to think of himself as an educated person. An informed citizen, if you will. He thinks it pays to take note of what's happening in the world.

Jake folds his paper carefully and stands up. Time to look outside at this particular part of the world and see what's happening with the weather. Jake walks outside and looks down the long line of entry stalls. Nothing. It's cold and still snowing. He will call the dispatcher who will probably have a scheduling update. The door of the bus station pushes warmly against the snowflakes, melting them as they hit the glass and metal. Inside, puddles of water drip across the concrete. Truck drivers sit along the stools of the coffee shop. Today everything moves is slow motion. Jake walks past the slot machines, past the coffee shop and stands in front of the driver's lounge. Then he turns around and looks at the passengers in the waiting room.

Two kids slouch in the TV chairs, dropping in coins to watch a game show. A large woman overflows onto two seats, clutching boxes and plastic sacks around her lap. She twists her head in suspicious jerks, as if she expects someone to try to steal her merchandise. A young girl and a soldier walk up to one of the slot machines by the front door. The boy has very short hair and he reaches into his pants pocket for change, then he tries his coat, then his shirt. He looks at the girl. She does not seem to notice that they are standing in front of a slot machine. She leans her head against his shoulder and one foot tips gently off the floor. The soldier puts his arm around her and they walk across the room and into the coffee shop. Jake sees this and tries to remember when he was that young, when he was in the Army and walked with girls into coffee shops.

Then Jake sees a thin girl in blue jeans and long dirty blond hair step quickly through the door and shake snow from her coat. The Sacramento bus must have arrived. The girl is smiling and her mouth is like a triangle, red on the white curve of cheek. Other people are pushing through the door, stomping their shoes, lighting up cigarettes. But Jake sees nothing but the girl. She reminds him of a young pony in a snowy pasture, stretching her legs, walking with stiff steps through snow drifts. The girl takes off her coat and stands by a slot machine, looking around the room, brushing more snow off the back of her coat. Her smile is red and radiant, as if she has something to say and can't wait to say it.

Jake has been standing with his hand on the doorknob of the driver's lounge. A sign that says DRIVERS ONLY hangs over his head. Jake knows he still has half an hour until departure. Just enough time to call in to the dispatcher and finish reading the newspaper. But Jake is thinking about the girl, wondering where she is from, where she is going, what she is running away from. Everyone is running away from something. Jake opens the newspaper. Events, places, names. Faraway places and faraway names. Newspapers are like a warm bath. He feels peaceful and forgotten and private. As if he were covered with snow. Jake almost forgets to call the dispatcher.

Jake Dealman has driven halfway to Lovelock before he notices, really notices, where the girl is sitting. About five seats behind the driver's chair on the same side, next to the window. Bus drivers have mirrors that can see into all corners of the bus. You meet all kinds on a bus, so you can't be too careful. The main thing is to stay alert.

The girl with the bright red smile has been talking nonstop to the girl sitting next to her. Both voices are quick and loud, but Jake has not been listening to the words. Girl talk. Jake thinks that talking loud is a signal to other people that the talkers, at least, are normal. People do that. People want others to think they are smart and happy, that everything is okay. But Jake is not fooled by this subterfuge. Or by much else, for that matter. Jake notices the way this blond girl sits in her blue jeans, her poise, her straight posture. Her hands dart quickly when she talks. Her lips are easy and alert, intelligent. At three in the morning, the girls' voices are like sharp knives in the thick night. Jake does not like the other girl, too loud, a grating whine in her voice. Jake wonders if she will be getting off in Lovelock.

Jake looks out toward the mountains and thinks he sees water out there. Water on the other side of the dry lake. It's not snowing now. The clouds have parted and the moon lights a muted trail along the flat alkali floor of the desert. Jake knows that the station in Lovelock has no driver's room. He will have to use the public phone to call in to the dispatch office. But that's okay, he'll just add the buck and a half to his expense ledger.

Jake is standing in front of the pay phone. He is on hold. The blonde girl is dialing the phone right next to his. Jake can smell her, warm like a flower in a sunny garden. Damn dispatcher. What's the point of all these calls anyway? Nothing ever changes on this route. Jake notices that her white skin has a slight redness in spots, almost like a rash. A blush, he thinks. Her skin is like cream, smooth and soft. She shifts her feet, leaning into the telephone.

"Hi!" she says, "it's me." Silence.

"Heather, of course!"

"I'm calling you. You said I should, remember, even if it was late. Didn't you say that?" Pause.

"Well, anyway, I'm past Reno already. I tried to call you before I left but there was no answer."

"No, I didn't. You know I hate those machines. Look, I know it's late, it took four hours just to cross the mountains. It's snowing over here."

Jake is listening to every word, hoping the dispatcher doesn't pick up the phone right then. But she does.

"Four in the morning, maybe, I don't know."

Jake mumbles something into the phone, then pushes down on the hang-up lever but keeps the receiver up to his ear.

"Sorry, Dad. Are you with someone or something? I guess I'm interrupting. Sorry." Silence.

"I thought I heard something. Look, who cares about that anyway? I'm on my way to see you, right? How long has it been? Years maybe."

"Well, that's years to me, Dad. I just called to say not to worry. Everything's fine. The bus is fine. I thought you might have seen the snow on TV or something. I'll be a few hours late, that's all."

"Okay."

"Okay."

"Okay, Dad. Listen, I've gotta go. I think I see the bus driver coming. I'll call you from Salt Lake. In the morning, probably. Okay?"

"Okay, I will."

"Of course! What difference would that make?"

"Of course, I'm sure."

'Okay, bye."

Jake is still hanging on to his receiver. It feels like a loose straw in his hand. His head is turned toward the window and so he doesn't see Heather hang up the phone and walk over to the restroom. When he turns around, she's gone.

Jake hangs up his phone, stands there for a moment, as if he were thinking about dialing another number. Then he walks over to the snack bar. Jake always feels like his riders are watching him, as if they are waiting for him to head for the bus. He feels their eyes follow him as he walks through bus stations. It's true, of course, they are watching him. People want to stay off the bus as long as possible. So they watch the driver and follow him back onto the bus. Jake wants to read a newspaper but he knows he doesn't have time. All they have in Lovelock is the Reno paper anyway.

"Two Baby Ruth bars please."

"You want them in a sack?" The clerk's voice is a muted drone, like the sound of a truck heard from over a hill. He is holding up the two candy bars and looking off in the distance as if he would like to be someplace else. Someplace sunny and bright, no doubt.

"Don't bother," Jake says. "I'm just going to eat them, anyway." He stuffs the candy bars into his coat pocket and looks around the room. Time to go. Jake walks toward the door of the Good Truckin' All Night Café. He has a mad desire to buy a rose, a single solitary rose. But there are no flowers for sale in Lovelock. "A Rose and a Baby Ruth" is the song that's running through Jake's head. Jake Dealman knows that he has a whole lot of driving to do.

When Jake pulls the bus out on to Interstate 80, he notices right away that the girl sitting next to Heather is gone. Just as he had hoped. But the empty seat is like a missing tooth in the chilled night air. Jake flips the switch to get the heater going. Jake knows what will happen next, some guy will hit on her. He doesn't have long to wait. A young male leans over toward Heather from across the aisle and behind.

"Where you from?" His smile is comfortable and his voice soft. Heather looks at him for a quick moment, turns away, then back for another glance.

"I'm headed for Cheyenne…Wyoming," Heather says, a smile growing on her lips. "I'm from there too, I guess. And you?"

"Oh, a small place in Nevada, you wouldn't know it." He shrugs his shoulders.

"Maybe I would. Anyway I'm going to my parents for Christmas, my dad anyway. You?"

"Salt Lake. Time to hit the slopes. There's big snow this year." Now the boy is squatting in the aisle beside the empty seat. He leans toward Heather. "You ski?"

Heather doesn't answer right away. She looks out the window. Snow is falling again. "Yes, well I'm learning. Let's put it that way." She looks at the boy in the aisle as if she has just seen him for the first time. She smiles and the scarlet triangle of her mouth lights up the dark bus. "Do you know what the next town is?"

"I've got a map, I'll show you." He stands up and goes back to his seat, yanks at a backpack jammed into the narrow space between the ceiling and the luggage rack, finally pulling out a map. He leaves the flap open and a strap is now hanging down over an old lady's head. It hovers a few inches over her bluish grey hair.

He sits down in the empty seat. "My name's Joey, by the way. Since you didn't ask." He traces a line across the map with his finger. "Winnemucca."

"Winnemucca." Heather pauses for a moment. "What a funny name!"

"An old Indian name." Joey has a satisfied grin on his face. He passes a hand through the air and extends it toward the window. "This used to be Indian country around here."

"Really?"

"Yeah, you know that little town I said I was from? That's Goldfield, out in the middle of nowhere. A ghost town."

"There were gold mines there?"

"Yeah, I guess, there's no gold for anybody there now. There's nothing there. Just a few run down trailers and my Dad who thinks it will be a tourist trap someday." Joey folds the map carefully and sticks it in his coat pocket.

"Your dad?" Heather has a question in her eyes.

"Yeah, my dad."

"Oh."

Jake hears all of this. His ears are trained to separate voices from background noise. No one else on the bus is doing much talking anyway. Jake doesn't like the dude who has moved in next to Heather. He doesn't like his face. Not that he's ugly, he's good looking in a slack kind of way. Like Joe Camel on the big billboard outside Reno—it says "Smooth Character" and there's this guy with a camel's face, wearing a tuxedo and holding a jet pilot's helmet. A cigarette dangles from his mouth. Behind Joe Camel, you can see a slinky woman and two jets streaming across the sky, maroon exhaust billowing behind. He's a smooth character, all right, just slides right over there and sits by her as if nothing were out of order.

Jake would like to say something or do something to nip this guy in the bud. Like maybe slam on the brakes or announce an emergency over the loud speaker. Anything. But Jake isn't stupid. He keeps quiet and drives his bus through the lightly falling snow. Then the snow stops and the clouds shift, the moon comes out. It's an almost full moon surrounded by a bright halo. The snow along the sides of the highway kick up in windy flurries as the bus passes but the pavement is clear and dry. Jake consciously avoids looking in his mirrors. He does not want to see the moves that camel face makes. Jake doesn't like this game. It always turns out the same.

Jake would rather think about Thunder Mountain in Imlay, a little town a few miles up ahead. There an old Indian has built a crazy monument out of scraps of iron and tin, adobe and plaster. In a way, his place is like an ancient sandstone mural. He has painted horses and buffalo and ancient warriors standing on high cliffs. Perhaps, tourists stopped here in years past, but now the freeway just blows right through Imlay. The nearest exit is nearly a mile away.

But Jake did stop there once when his bus broke down. The bus was parked along the shoulder waiting for a replacement part to arrive from Winnemucca. Jake had walked over to the freeway fence and was looking vacantly at the plaster of Paris horses, the wild wall paintings of mounted Indians and buffalo. Then he saw an Indian girl, who looked to be about thirteen or fourteen, with a water hose drooping from one hand. An old Indian sat in a doorway watching her water a spindly cactus.

"I'm really from California," she said. "I'm just staying with my uncle for this summer." She squirted water onto a row of yellow flowers. Apparently, the uncle had been putting up barely legible signs and posters all around his property—signs making bizarre accusations concerning the Bureau of Land Management (BLM).

"They have killed his horses," the girl said. She set the hose down and let it run into the dirt under a stunted pine tree. Her hair was wild and uncombed, her clothes not recently washed. She looked at Jake meaningfully, then walked under the roof shade where the uncle sat. Jake took several photographs that day, of the girl and the signs and the ancient totems, and he was intending to mail them to her. But he didn't get around to it, then one day he did send them, in care of Thunder Mountain. But he never heard back from anyone.

Jake didn't stop in Imaly again but Thunder Mountain grew large in his memory. There was a wagon wheel he remembered, the spokes were carved into figures, gods and goddesses maybe. It seemed to Jake as if the wagon wheel might roll from its spot on an old water tower and take off through the cloudy sky. Rolling toward a happy hunting ground somewhere in the distant mountains. But he never again saw any people from his bus window, not the girl, not the uncle. Most of the protest signs fell down over time. The murals grew dim and streaked from rain and snow.

Jake Dealman has passed Winnemucca and Imlay. The mighty Greyhound is roaring down Nevada Interstate 80 toward Battle Mountain. His passengers are quiet and the sun is just coming up over the distant mountains. Jake loves the subtle changes of light just before the sudden burst of a desert sunrise. Today's sunrise will be thick with clouds. Jake is listening hard but he can't quite hear the words mumbling behind him. They are talking much more softly than before. He can see her mouth in the mirror, the tumble of tongue and lips, the falling out of syllables. He can see Joey's mouth moving, too, gently, earnestly. Then, suddenly, he can hear her words, like a quick waterfall around a corner of rocks, her voice splashing across the green plastic seats. Her smile slicing the transient air.

"You know, he wasn't even happy to hear my voice, like he was in a big hurry. How can you be in a hurry at four in the morning?" Heather asks.

She speaks quietly but with a certain angular texture in her voice. It's that extra edge that people adopt when they're speaking in public places, when they think somebody might be listening. As if all of humanity were their witness. Jake thinks that nobody listens to what anybody says on a bus, anyway, so why bother? But, of course, Jake always listens. He is like a benevolent spy. He is like the mother who listens to her fifth graders practice swear words with her ear pressed to a heater duct.

"What's the big deal, anyway?" she asks. "So he's got a girlfriend in bed with him. Who cares about that?" Heather trails her fingers across the window glass, shaping a design, making it fancier in wider and wider circles. Then she rubs it all out with the palm of her hand. Heather does not look directly at Joey. He slowly takes off his ski parka and places it carefully up in the storage rack. Jake sees him put his left arm across the back of the seat behind the girl. He moves closer to her and begins to speak but Jake cannot hear his voice.

"What's the big deal is all I want to know?" Heather says with finality. Then she raises her hand and touches her nose, almost experimentally, as if it might hurt. Jake sees Joey leaning in toward her ear, whispering. Jake doesn't want to look into his mirrors anymore. He has had enough. What the hell! It's the same old story every time, isn't it?

The next time Jake looks, Heather is bent over the empty seat in front of her, silently crying, her shoulders moving softly under her white sweater. Camelface is rubbing her back, ever so gently. You see, he cares so much about her. Jake is starting to feel sick. He wants to get to Elko where they will have a half hour break. He wants to read a Nevada newspaper, maybe, he just wants to be out of the bus.

But what Jake does is keep his eyes on the road and on the mirrors around him. He sees them hug each other tentatively, then wildly, kissing, cuddling under a blanket, then on top of the blanket, out in the open. Now they talk only in whispers. Of course, nobody on this bus pays any attention, nobody sees anything they are doing. They are alone in a bubble of time, sleeping at times, then talking, holding each other tightly, then loosely. They are locked together like two butterflies in midair. Delirious. Shameless. Five seats from the front of a Greyhound bus.

Jake has written off the bus and everybody in it by the time he gets to Elko. Sometimes the fiasco that is humanity is just not worth the effort you put into it. Of course, Jake is not surprised by anything after so many years driving busses. Heather and Joey are true lovebirds now. They walk everywhere together, to the snack bar, to the café, they stand in front of a small row of slot machines. He puts in nickels, she pulls the handle. Heather giggles when five nickels splat into the payoff tray. Two cherries. They would walk into the restroom together if they could. Full daylight has leeched all mystery from this busload of disreputable laggards. Jake watches them climb back on the bus and wonders where they all came from. That knot of military types in the far back, all smokers, fat guys, short hair, arrogant swaggers. Old men with wrinkled trousers. Old ladies with blue hair and K-Mart sacks clutched to their laps. Punks with green hair. Crying kids with drippy noses that never get wiped. A sorry bunch.

Jake watches a very pale boy with headphones on his ears. He's been sitting in the same position since Reno, looking out the same window. Never takes off the headset, never leaves the bus, never talks to anyone. Where is he going? Is somebody waiting for him somewhere?

Jake blows through Carlin and Wells without a side glance. He is really humming now. The Greyhound is fueled and flowing under him like a powerful river. Jake is the exploding yellow line that eats up mile after mile of blowing desert sand like a bellowing Chinese dragon. He has not looked into his mirrors, at least not lately. But, when he does, he sees that all is not well. They must be having a fight of some kind. Her eyes are red again with crying and he has a studied look of exasperation on his face. That smug frown that says, well that figures, I should have known she would turn out this way. The touch of redness on her skin has blotched into patches and she looks like she hasn't slept for days. Jake's stomach hurts. He had not imagined her looking so rough, so desperate. He listens.

"Well, what could I expect?" Heather says. Joey Camelface is patting her back. He doesn't say anything. His face is grizzled with morning after shadow. "So they will all be waiting for you in Salt Lake? And she'll be there, too?" Heather is looking out the window, one arm drooping over the seatback in front of her.

"Just a little skiing, that's all, just a little skiing." Joey says. "I haven't had a chance like this to ski for years." He continues to pat her back and then gives her shoulder a little squeeze. Heather is not consoled. She looks straight in front of her at the back of the bus driver's head.

"I guess I'll call again from Salt Lake," Heather says.

"Good idea, I'd say." They are not looking at each other now.

"Excuse me, I think I'll use the bathroom before we get to the next town." Heather begins to stand up.

"I'd wait, if I were you. It's pretty foul back there." Joey turns and scowls toward the seats behind him.

"I can't wait. I have to go now. I can't wait until…what town are we coming to?"

"Wendover."

"I can't wait 'till Wendover." She waits for Joey to slide back into his seat but he doesn't move.

"Excuse me then, can I get by?" Joey stands up and Heather squeezes by and walks to the back of the bus.

Jake will stop in Wendover for fifteen minutes. Once Jake had seen a clump of people around a crap table at a hotel in Wendover. He went over and saw that a little guy with glasses was throwing a hot run of dice and people were betting all over the table. Chips were flying. Jake threw a $20 bill on the pass line and in a few minutes he had eight $20 chips. He grabbed his chips, cashed them out, and got back on his bus. He hadn't wanted to see how many passes the guy with the glasses would make, hadn't wanted to see the dealer rake in the final bets. That guy's luck would run out, he knew that for sure. Jake will stop at this hotel again but this time he will not play at the dice table. It's against company rules to gamble while you're on duty.

Jake Dealman is driving the last leg, through the Bonneville salt flats. Miles and miles of cracked alkali. It's covered in snow right now but it looks about the same in the summer. White and flat. Jake is talking on the loud speaker. They are in Utah now and the back three rows will no longer be allowed to smoke. Jake takes great pleasure in this announcement, he hates cigarette smoke. But he wishes he had bet $20 in Wendover. The last chance to gamble. He has always been a sucker for that ploy—the last chance.

Jake looks in the mirror and sees that the lovebirds are exchanging addresses and phone numbers. All is well again, sort of. They have pulled out their wallets and are sorting through a handful of photographs. She writes something on the back of a photo and hands it to him. He looks at it and puts it carefully into his shirt pocket. They lean back into their seats. Time runs swiftly over the salt flats.

Jake sits in his driver's chair until everyone is off the bus in Salt Lake City. He watches carefully as the riders tend to their bags. Things have been stolen, he knows, and forgotten, too. It pays to be observant. Some of these folks will go on to Cheyenne but it's the end of the line for Jake. No more driving until after Christmas. Jake is wondering about Heather and Christmas, if she will make it to Cheyenne okay. He had hoped to talk to her for a moment but he thinks it's too late now. He steps off the bus into the icy air.

Jake sees her immediately as he walks into the white walled terminal. She is standing by the far wall in front of a bank of telephones. He can see only her back, the white sweater and narrow shoulders, the thin blue jeans, the blonde hair spreading over the angelic yarn. Jake starts toward the driver's room, then, abruptly, sits down on a bench, facing the telephones. He picks up a newspaper and stares at the print, turns a few pages. Heather hasn't moved. It's like she is waiting for a call or just looking at the phones in front of her. Maybe she's lost a phone number. Finally, she leans against a phone, but doesn't dial. Jake feels his blood melt. She's lost, she needs help. But he doesn't move. He can't.

Then Jake sees Joey Camelface, ski parka puffed up, standing at the other end of the waiting room. His back is turned and he is talking to another guy and a girl. They have come to meet him. So why don't they leave? Why just stand there talking? But they don't leave. They pick up pieces of luggage, then set them down again. Jake looks at Heather.

She is picking through her wallet. Looking for phone numbers, probably, looking for something to focus on, something to hold in her hand.

It's a sort of triangle, she at the phones, the boy at the far end, Jake watching. Jake feels very sad, depressed. He doesn't see any cure for what is wrong with this world. Then he spots the military guys, the smokers from the back of the bus. They are in a fat scrum, talking and gesturing. One of them turns quickly and heads straight for Heather. No! Not that. Jake jumps up and strides to the telephones. He is not thinking at all.

"Hi, I'm the bus driver." Heather looks up at him. No surprise. No recognition. Nothing. Jake sees the fat guy in the corner of his eye. He has pulled up short at a vending machine. Waiting.

"I mean, are you okay?"

"Of course," says Heather. She looks directly at Jake's face. "Why wouldn't I be?" Jake feels his air collapsing.

"Oh, nothing. I just….look, I get off here. You'll have a new driver."

"Oh, okay." Heather has turned back to look at the telephones.

"Well, good luck, then," Jake says. "I gotta go." He is hoping she will turn back toward him. She does. "Have a nice trip." His voice trails off.

"Okay, I will," she says. Now Jake sees the beginning of tears in her eyes but he is already half turned, walking away from her, and he can't stop. He hesitates, then walks forward toward the driver's room. Jake turns and sees two of the fat guys gearing up by the soda machine. Jake is in full retreat and he doesn't care anymore. Why should he? Then, suddenly, he sits down. He will watch this show to the end.

The two smokers are now talking to Heather by the phones. Jakes sees the brilliant and scarlet triangle of her smile. They are like a cluster of miniatures on top of a grand piano, trembling to a soundless music. Jake sees their mouths move, sees the words "McDonalds" and "walk" or thinks he does. The three figures huddle like pigeons in a hail of popcorn, then scatter toward the outer door. At the last minute, it seems to Jake that she turns to look back at him but he can't be sure. She is too far away now. He feels the cold rush as air and snow enter the building.

Jake Dealman buys a Salt Lake Tribune. He will read it word for word in the driver's room. There will be time enough to find a motel room later.

A NICE VIEW

Ed knows he's got a problem when he pulls up behind a highway patrol car and it just sits there going 45 miles per hour. Nobody on the road, just Ed and his wife in a rented Ford Festiva and a yellow line that stretches out like a vanishing ribbon in the direction of some red and black mountains. He knows better than to pass it but it's a real pain to mindlessly follow a smartass patrol car. All he can do is wait, creeping along in the stifling heat. The rental papers for the Festiva specify air conditioning but Ed has flipped every switch he can find and no cool air. He looks at his wife and sighs. She is tracing her fingers over the lines and arrows of a Montana map. First Montana, the blue sky state, then Idaho and Washington. Suddenly the cop turns off the highway and Ed thinks, great, he's gone. He's probably headed for some little jerk town with one gas station and a boarded up bar. But Ed doesn't speed up right away, he's too smart for that, he just plays it cool and stays at 45 mph. Then, all at once, the cop is back alongside the red Festiva, red light flashing, motioning toward the side of the road. The wife looks at Ed and points.

"Your seat belt!" She is almost shouting.

"Shit!" Ed yanks the belt down, it clicks into the slot. The patrol car slides over to the shoulder. Ed sees a male driving and a female cop in the shotgun seat. She gets out first and walks over to Ed's window. The male cop stands by his car door, hand on his hips, ready for trouble. The female cop stares at the seat belt and shakes her head. She has a sharp face and a round nose but seems friendly enough, in a way, almost confused. Ed's wife is fumbling through the glove box, tossing papers on the floor.

"I'll need to see your driver's license, your registration, your proof of insurance," the female cop says in a level voice.

The male cop walks up behind her, listens, watches. Ed hands it all over, the rental papers, everything. He looks at his wife. She's hugging a lap full of maps close to her stomach. The female cop holds the pile of papers while the male flips the driver's license over, sticks it on a clip board, stares at the registration. His face is getting red, his throat is swelling up with air. He jams his head up to the window.

"We have laws out here, too, you know." He breathes the words heavily, as if he's been running.

"I know that," Ed says, rolling his eyes.

"You guys just blast through here like it was nowhere, you think you can get away with anything." The cop's neck is bulging, wet rings sag under his armpits.

"We're just tourists," Ed says lamely. What else can he say? The cop is standing on one foot, leaning toward the Festiva.

"You weren't wearing that seat belt back there a few miles, were you?" His words come in short bursts. He looks at the female cop, she nods her head.

"We're not stupid, you know," the male cop says.

"Right," Ed says and he starts to get out of the car.

"Stay in the car, mister." The male cop slaps his gun holster, pushes the car door shut. "Listen to me, this is no joke, okay, we know you'll never show up in court."

Now what? They're a hundred miles from the nearest town. Anything could happen out here. Ed reaches for his wallet and pulls out a hundred dollar bill. He holds it between two fingers and waves it out the window. "Will this help?" he asks. The wife looks at the hundred dollar bill and shoves the maps back into the glove box. She slams the glove box shut and stares out the side window at nothing. The male cop's face gets even redder.

"Drive back to that gas station. We'll follow you," he says and the two cops get back in their patrol car. The stiff old man at the gas pumps reluctantly changes the hundred into five twenty dollar bills and writes out a receipt of some sort. He hands the piece of paper to Ed.

"You're posting bail, Mr. Tourist, that's all, just posting bail," the male cop says. The old man looks at Ed's license plate, writes down the number on the back of his receipt pad. Then he looks at Ed and shakes his head.

The Festiva is back on the highway and headed for the red and black mountains. The wife is still staring out the window. Ed is gripping the steering wheel. Nobody is talking. Then the wife speaks up.

"Boy, that sure looked sweet, a hundred dollar bill just hanging out the window." She gives Ed a disparaging look and rolls the window all the way down. "I need some fresh air." Ed's mouth fills up with words he will never say.

"So what else could I have done?" he says. "What did you want me to do? Go to jail, maybe?" The mountains go by, a thin slice of Idaho, then Washington, the Grand Coulee, tallest dam in the world, or at least it used to be. Who cares? Then a thin trailing of lakes beyond the dam, smooth and blue in the dying light. Ed pulls over to the side of the road and stops. The wife flips on the dash light and traces her fingers over a map. Below them stretches a long, metallic lake surrounded by black mountains. It looks different from the other lakes they have passed. The low sun is like fire skipping over the water.

"Soap Lake," she says, then pops the glove box shut.

"What?" Ed has his forehead down on the steering wheel.

"That's where we are. Soap Lake. It's the last of these lakes. No outlet, probably." Ed's wife has all the facts.

"It is beautiful, though, isn't it? All that salt. Look at it shine," Ed says. He does not move to start the engine.

"Well, at least we're somewhere," the wife says. "Finally, we're somewhere." She turns on the radio. They hear only static and strange squealing noises but she doesn't turn it off or look for a better station.

"Can we start over?" Ed says. He looks quickly at his wife. She looks back at him, then out the window.

"Start what over?" The wife does not appear angry, really, just tired. Ed steers the car out onto the highway and in a few minutes they pull up to a motel on the outskirts of a small town. The wife turns off the radio.

The motel sign is broken, the bottom half swinging free, like part of a clapboard from a movie set. The word "Soap" is painted on the upper half. Ed parks the car, looks at his wife, his hand on the door handle.

"Can we forget about it?" he says.

"Forget about what?

"Everything, the cops, the money, all of that."

"Okay," she says. It's as simple as that. The wife has nothing more to say. She looks at the motel sign, the bottom half swinging slightly in the wind. Ed gets out of the car and walks over to the sign. He turns back to his wife.

"It says mineral water on tap in the rooms. How about that?" She nods her head and rolls up her window.

A man with a limp white face is standing behind the motel desk. His eyes are coal black, sunk deep into fat cheek bones. His face reminds Ed of an unbaked pie. His name tag says manager. He brushes a hand at his slick black hair.

"Welcome to Soap Lake," the manager says. He's not looking at Ed but off to the side somewhere. "The home of the medicinal bath." He pauses and squints quickly out a window as if looking for Ed's car. "For the whole family."

"How much are the rooms?"

"Indians came here," the manager continues, "Nez Perce, from all over. There's hieroglyphics on the rocks down there." He points toward a window but it's dark out and the glass is cloudy with dirt and water spots.

"How much per night?"

"Well, it's pretty much off season right now. That's lucky for you. We're booked solid all through August." The motel manager is flipping through a book with big blank pages. "Everyone signs this book, you know, Herbert Hoover signed this book. That was before my time, though." The manager looks at Ed and his black eyes seem to bounce in their soft sockets. "Movie stars, too."

"How much?"

"Sixty five, seventy five with mineral water in the room." He closes the comment book with a clunk. "I'd recommend a room with mineral water. People come from all over the world to soak in this water."

"I'll take it. The one with the mineral water." Ed starts for the door, then turns around. "Can we test the bed? She needs a hard bed." The manager smiles knowingly and nods his head. Ed walks to the door and waves at his wife.

It is morning and the wife will sleep late. Ed is walking toward the lake, along the highway for a hundred yards or so. He passes a bar with three police cars clustered around it. Ten in the morning and there they are, knocking down donuts and cappuccinos. Ed thinks about writing down their license numbers, then shrugs his shoulders and turns toward the lake. He passes a restaurant with a large wood deck in front. A few cars are parked around a giant tree. He turns sharply walks slowly beside a long spur of water which connects to the larger part of the lake.

Ed's feet scuff black gravel and pale white dirt—salt, he thinks. A black and white sign sticks up out of the dark rock. NO SWIMMING. Okay, the lake is known worldwide for its medicinal qualities but nobody can swim. Maybe it just means this side of the lake. Spindly plants with corrugated leaves grow between the foot path and the water.

Far across the water Ed sees a long beach. Something is moving over there. Ed walks along the shore. Two seagulls spin over his head. He can barely make out the color of flesh across the water, someone is probably getting a quick start on a sun tan. It feels to Ed as if he is walking by the ocean, as if he is waiting for the surf to break and roll up to his feet. The morning wind blows soft and salty on his face.

Then, suddenly, the flesh color across the lake separates. He sees legs, maybe stretched in the air, the sense of nudity, then movement in between. Ed's hand reaches out toward the lake, his feet scuff across the rocks. He looks out over the water like a man waiting for a ship to come in. Now Ed can see it all, the round white orbs moving up and down, the feet high on either side. He takes off his cap and wipes his forehead with the back of his hand. He cannot move his head. His feet are stuck in black gravel. The sun is warm and climbing to hot in the somnambulant sky. The flesh colors move, then stop, then move again. Then suddenly they separate. Ed starts to walk. Maybe they noticed something. One shape sits up, white flashes on her chest. They are dressing. Black panties against the white sand. Blank pants.

Ed walks quickly around a cliff, but the side path he is on ends at a short bluff that juts out over the water. He sees a shape in the thin grass. He walks closer. It's the remains of a dead horse or donkey. Only a skull and some bones, tufts of hair and hide. Ed turns around and walks back the way he came. Now the bodies across the water are doing sit-ups, maybe, or stretching exercises. It looks like they are praying to the water, bowing, then standing up straight.

Ed sits down on a rock. He tries not to look at the couple across the water but he looks anyway. They are walking now, climbing up over a short ridge, toward a road. An old green car with the shape of a Volvo pulls slowly out, then disappears. Ed stands up. His feet move on the path. The sun

burns hot on his bare head. He looks down and sees he has
been walking around with his hat in his hand. He puts the hat
back on his head.

The green Volvo is parked under the giant tree in front of
the restaurant. Of course. Ed stops, touches the fender, looks
up the steps to the outdoor deck. There they are, sitting at the
first table by the screen door. Ed is sure that it's them. She's
wearing black pants and a black tank top. Ed walks up the
steps and he's certain that the woman is watching him all the
way. He doesn't look toward their table, the man is fuzzy at
the edges of his eyes. Ed walks quickly through the screen
door. Her eyes follow him. The lady behind the bar is large
and white and is wiping tall glasses with a big fluffy towel.
Ed does not look back toward the porch.

"Is it okay to swim in the lake?" Ed asks no one in
particular. The bar woman looks at Ed but keeps on wiping
glasses. She sets the dry glasses down on the bar.

"I mean I saw a sign down there that says no swimming. I
just wondered." Ed's hands collapse to his sides.

"Well," the barmaid says, "if you can swim, then go
ahead and swim." The white towel she is using flips back
and forth in the air in front of Ed's nose. She looks at Ed.
"That's what people come here for, isn't it? The water." Ed
turns so he can see the couple on the outdoor deck. He
wonders if they are listening. The girl has turned her face
toward the window.

"But the sign?" Ed says in a thin voice. The barmaid folds
the fluffy towel and places it carefully on the bar next to the
dry glasses. She just looks at Ed. She has said all that she has
to say.

"Okay then, thanks," Ed says and walks back out through
the screen door. He turns quickly toward the couple at the
first table and speaks as if they had been part of the
conversation.

"There really is a no swimming sign down there." He points in the direction of the spit of land where he had been walking earlier. The woman in the black tank top is watching him closely, he sees it, he feels it. She knows that he's the one. Of course, she does. Maybe it's his black cap. She smiles and raises her arms, stretching. She has hair like tufts of flowers in her armpits. She is brown and her face is smooth. The man has a red nose, a face like a fledgling hawk getting ready to fly.

"We swim there," she says. She has a foreign accent. The man nods.

"Anyway, we soak, the water is heavy and smooth. Like thick beer," he says and looks at the woman. Similar accent.

"You guys from around here?" Ed looks down the steps at the green Volvo.

"Actually, I'm from Spain," she says. "He's from Italy." The Italian picks up his bottle of mineral water, sets it down again. He looks at Ed.

"Are you looking for the Rainbow Family?"

"Who?" Ed takes a step backwards.

"Oh, sorry." The Italian waves his hand toward the highway. "They're way back over in Montana, anyway, by Flathead Lake." He looks across the table toward Soap Lake. "It's too crowded there, nothing but tents and dirty bathrooms. Not peaceful like here." He lights a cigarette, a brand that Ed has never seen. Ed sees the girl nudge him with her leg under the table. He looks up at the windows in the rooms above the restaurant.

"Is this a good place to stay?" Ed asks. The woman follows his eyes up to the windows.

"Well, it's cheap enough, but no view of the lake, really. The windows are too small." The Italian taps his fingers on the table top. He looks at the Spanish girl.

"But we didn't come here just for the view, did we?" he says. She doesn't answer. Another nudge under the table, a harder one. She looks back up at Ed.

"Where are you from?" she asks.

"Oh, we're staying just up the road a ways," he says. The girl looks like she's almost ready to start laughing. The corners of her mouth twitch. Her eyes are loose and watchful, like she is waiting for something. Ed turns toward the stairs.

"My wife is waiting for me."

But Ed does not want to go back to his wife. He walks in a circle and ends up back at the swimming prohibited sign. He can see the spot where the European couple had made love. An outcropping of black rock hangs above their resting place. The hills behind are black lava, curving up toward the road. A rim of salt rings the lake, broken up by a few black sand and gravel beaches. The water is like varnished steel, the sunlight bouncing sharply toward the shore. Ed stands there, looking at the water, then he reaches out to touch the sign, traces his fingers over the letters. Then he sees the bullet holes. Three of them. Funny, he hadn't noticed them before. Why would somebody come way out here to shoot holes in a swimming sign?

Ed walks back up the path to the restaurant. The table where the couple had sat has not been cleared yet. He sees a half full bottle of mineral water, an empty cigarette pack, a candy wrapper. Ed picks up the flattened cigarette pack and sticks it in his shirt pocket. He starts to sit down where the woman had been sitting, then straightens up and walks though the screen door. He buys a draft beer in a tall, cool glass and sits down at the table next to where the lovers had sat.

A group of elderly tourists sit around a third table, drinking Calistoga water from thin plastic bottles. They're talking about Soap Lake, the minerals in the water. It has iron, they say, and sulfur, all good for the joints. Also calcium for the bones. Someone mentions cadmium but they are not quite sure about the benefits of that mineral.

Ed looks up at the windows. They are small and circular, not much light could get in there. Such a nice view but not enough light. He wonders what room the couple is staying in. Could the Spanish woman see him sitting there, maybe, if she looked out her window? Well, she probably wouldn't do that, anyway. Ed thinks of his wife, asleep perhaps, in the motel up the road. Their room has a large double window that overlooks the lake. He had opened it wide when they checked in but his wife had closed it immediately. Mosquitoes. Wind. It didn't really matter, it would stay closed in any case. He knows that for sure.

Ed walks in the door to his motel and stops. The manager is on the far side of the lobby, explaining the medicinal qualities of Soap Lake water to an elderly couple. He moves his hands through the air.

"The healing waters come right out of the lake and into your very own tub. Imagine that!" He hands the woman a brochure with the picture of a young girl sitting in a bathtub on the cover. The girl has a towel over her bare shoulders. The woman holds the brochure at arms length and squints at the photograph. She looks at her husband.

Ed walks softly around the corner, out through the other glass door, and climbs the stairs. He opens the door and immediately smells something like sulfur, hears water running. He opens the bathroom door, expecting to see his wife. She is not there. Water is pouring from a single tap located above the normal water spigots. The water is a yellowish, almost copper, color and circles thickly in the tub. A pungent smell fills his nose like a balloon and reminds him, strangely, of a hospital. Where is she?

The tub is filling slowly but is getting near the top. Ed looks back at the bathroom door, takes a few steps toward the bedroom. He sees their suitcases closed and flat on the tidy bed. He notices with surprise that the double windows are wide open. Ed can see the gleam of the lake from where he is standing. Where is she? He goes back to the tub, sticks his finger in the water. Hot. The mirror is beginning to fog over. The water is about to reach the rim of the tub. There is no overflow drain. The water will spill onto the bathroom floor. Then he hears a door open, close.

"Oh, so you're here then," she says.

"It's overflowing. What's going on?"

"It's okay, Ed. It's for a mineral bath." The wife is somewhere behind him but Ed cannot see her. Too much steam in the air. He can't seem to turn around. He hears the muffle of clothing, a shoe hitting the floor. "Why not turn it off, then, Ed?"

Ed turns off the faucet. The handle is rusty, hard to move, creaking in his hand. He does not turn to look at his wife. He hears the click of a clothes hanger, bare feet on the tile floor. A bag zips. Ed looks at the water. The tub glows deep with color, as if oil has been stirred into the white porcelain. Steam rolls off the surface in quick puffs.

Ed thinks that this water has no bottom, that it opens into a black hole in the Earth. He can see Indians camped in the dark by the shore of a steaming lake. They have traveled for many days and some of them are sick. They rest their horses and they fill their skins and pots with water. They look up at the brilliant stars. They feed small fires with sticks and branches and pungent leaves. The Indians are waiting for the sun to rise over the mountains.

SHORT SHORTS

HOT WATER

"The hot tub doesn't work," Stewart yells into the phone. "I've been down there three times in the last three days and the damn thing still doesn't work. We pay a hundred bucks a month and this is what we get?" He slams the phone back on the hook.

Stewart picks up a lawn chair from behind the refrigerator and walks down two flights of stairs and out the back door of the apartment building. He unfolds the chair next to the red temperature switch and cracks open a can of Budweiser. He reaches over, tips the chair down, touches the water. Cold. Leaves float on top of the water. Several large leaves have sunk to the bottom of the tub. Stewart clicks the timer switch that controls the air bubbles. Nothing. He picks up a circular metal lid cut into the bricks next to the tub and sees a valve and some white pipes. He can hear something humming.

Stewart will wait for the repairman. Pickup trucks with lumber racks clunk down Calaveras Street. School buses sputter along, kids spilling out of windows. A convertible full of teenagers speeds by. Then six motorcycles. Stewart is still waiting. Finally a person with a tool bag in hand walks up and sticks a thermometer into the water.

"Hey, where's your truck?" Stewart demands.

"Around the corner, you can't see it from here," the repairman says and turns around to face Stewart. It's a woman. Stewart stands up and folds his lawn chair with a bang.

"I called for a repairman."

"That would be me." She shakes her bag of tools in Stewart's face. He steps backward, one foot tripping over the edge of the spa, rights himself, then stumbles past the telephones. He looks at the phones, shakes his head, then turns around and throws his crumpled beer can back toward a garbage barrel. The can misses and clinks loud on the echoing bricks and stones.

RED RED LIPS

The soap sprays in a flurry of bubbles, the huge brushes roll like thunder over the tops of the automobiles. So many cars, so much dirt, all washed away like the sins of the world. This car wash does not allow pickups trucks or campers. The customers get their gas, carefully pinching their receipt which contains the code number, and roll quietly up to the key code register. This is where they panic, punch in the wrong numbers, drop the receipt out the window into a puddle of water, park too far away from the register, open the car door and slip on the wet concrete. You name it, they've done it. I watch all this from inside the glass windows. I sit next to the drinks and potato chips in the spot where I used to slide the credit cards and enter the pump numbers. These days the gas pumps do all that but I still sell soda pop and cigarettes. Now I have plenty of time to keep an eye on the car wash. The boss said so.

One day the machinery breaks down, sort of, like it just won't quit. It keeps on going after it's supposed to stop. Eventually, the car owners get fed up and just drive out. Then the brushes stop. But the evil machine does it again to the next car.

So up drives this guy in a black CRX-SI, real cool, big sound, dark shades. The only thing is his girlfriend is yelling at him, see, and waving her hands in his face. I can hear the faint screech through the glass, that beautiful twisted mouth, the red, red lips. He's eating chips and pretending nothing is out of the ordinary. He punches in his number, cool as a cucumber. Zoop, in they go. All I can see is yellow bristle tails, soap, spray, flapping brushes. A tornado of steam and bubbles. Five minutes, still flapping. Ten minutes. The CRX must be clean by now. Fifteen minutes and I'm starting to wig out. What the hell's going on in there? I throw the main switch and the steam collapses into a wet puddle. I run out there.

She's the only one in the car, black hair pouring all over the seat. Pretty as a picture, too. Stereoo real loud. Lynyrd Skynyrd, "Gimme Three Steps." The metal arms and brushes hover like helicopter blades over the silence of the clean, clean car.

THE MAIL

Mail may be arriving today, very important mail. So Ali stays home from work, watching the windows. His 1975 Pontiac is parked comfortably along the curb in front of the house. At least today nobody can steal his parking space. The phone rings a few times. He doesn't answer. The television set is loud and familiar. Ali sees the neighbor's gray cat walk stiffly out of the shade and perch, eyes bright, under the tail pipe of the Pontiac. A neighbor's dog barks, it's the Vietnamese a few doors down.

Ali listens to the strange roommates downstairs eating their breakfast of fruit and cereal. They are like characters from American television, the advertisements where everyone is perfectly drawn, no extra flesh hanging out, no pain or strain. They go to work at exactly the same time every day. Ali hears the click and run of the icemaker in the refrigerator. The twist and squelch of faucets. Today the water pipes are bulging with pressure. Then the front door thumps, the wall mirrors trill. They're gone.

Ali can breathe now. He feels like he's bursting to the surface of deep water. Air sucks through his lifting throat and he walks into the bathroom. The ice cubes are already in the glass, his arm poised to pour the bottle. He drinks as a dying man drinks, slowly and with deep appreciation.

He does not see the Federal Express truck when it enters the cul-de-sac. It is headed back out when he walks over to the window. Then it stops. Ali is jumping down the stairs, flinging open the doors. His hand unknowingly brushes a delivery notice swinging from the front door knob. Then Ali is in the street and the mail truck is moving again. The cat jumps out from under the Pontiac and Ali almost trips. The neighbor's dog is chasing Ali, biting at his heels. The truck stops again. He almost slams into the back of the delivery truck.

Ali will get his mail today. The Earth will continue to spin in its orbit.

BOYS ON THE SIDE

The projectionist is winding the film onto the reels, adjusting the lens. The empty theater is black and the movie actors are wordless as they drive their bouncing car across the silver screen. Then people pop up like mushrooms in the tufted theater seats, whispers drift through the soundproofed walls. The projectionist's wife is collecting money and tickets. She counts out careful change and tucks the ticket stubs into a cigar box. Just then the ex-girlfriend knocks on the projection room door. Her hair is new blond and wild, her red lips set with purpose. She pulls a short, bald man by the hand. They will watch this movie. On the screen, Whoopi Goldberg sings Janis Joplin: "take another little piece of my heart now, baby."

"Is that her?"

"Who?"

"Your wife, who do you think I mean?"

"Yes."

"I want a good seat, one in the middle."

"Now? The movie's started."

The projectionist's penlight spears the rows of seats and the girlfriend trips, smiles red, coughs and sits. The projector grinds and clicks, the movie spins light through the thickening air. The woman in the movie has AIDS and her lover knows it. That's okay. She doesn't know he knows it. That's a problem. The projectionist sees the girlfriend slide out of her seat, head up the aisle. To the restroom? The projector bumps, the screen pops up, steadies, there is a funeral, someone sings. Then the lights fade up and the girlfriend touches the short man's shoulder, stands up in the transparent light of the credits. She folds her arms and glides like a reluctant ghost past the tiny square of clear glass through which the last frames click.

TOW JOB

The red Volkswagen pickup finally died that morning and now Nova is standing out in front of her house, looking at the bent tailgate. A pool of oil sits under the engine. The hood won't open. Ants have made a nest somewhere in the truck bed. They walk in meticulous lines down the side of the truck, circle the rearview mirror, then disappear into a crease under the windshield. A tow truck spins around the corner and Nova runs out into the street.

"It's there," she says, pointing, "right there." The truck driver tries to avoid her, speeds past, but he realizes that she's running too close to his truck and so he stops.

"I'm not here for you. I'm on another call down the street." He revs his engine.

"You have to be the one. I called over an hour ago." Nova has one leg up on his running board, yellow tank top, flowing hair, an insistent, yet inviting, smile.

"I'm the wrong guy," he says but he opens his door.

"Could you help me a little? I've got a problem." Nova spreads her arms wide, as if greeting an old friend.

The driver opens the red hood with a long crowbar. The wires and hoses are like a nest of snakes, out of control, venomous. They look at each other, his hand is on the hood, her fingers touching the rod that props it up.

"You should have seen the cloud of smoke it made. Like a bomb going off," she says and smoothes the sides of her jeans with the palms of her hands.

"Yes, I should have." He stops for a moment. "I've got to go now. There's a car I have to tow. Will you be here later?"

"Yes," she says. He puts the hood down gently but it won't close all the way. "Yes, I will." The ants are lined up by a leaky radiator hose. Some of the ants have their feet in a damp shadow of water.

A WIDE FLAT PIT

The old cat has died in the middle of the night. He was climbing out of his basket and collapsed onto the wood deck, half in, half out, tail stretched back to his carefully folded blanket. It is early morning and nobody has discovered the dead cat. In the kitchen that morning, the man appears first. He takes a sharp knife, cuts fresh fruit into small pieces, mango, papaya, watermelon, orange, Asian pear. The most difficult is the mango, the knife must be very sharp and must hit at just the right angle to avoid the wide, flat pit. He arranges strawberries on top, then a slice of kiwi. He walks to the stairway and looks up.

"Xiao Mei." Silence. "Xiao Shun." Silence. "Xiao Yatoh."

"Coming!" The man sits down and begins to read the morning paper.

"Is he out there?" The woman is standing by the table, looking out at the backyard, the water fountain, the stone Buddhas, one male, one female, the incense pot, the many flowers. She does not see the cat.

"He's probably out chasing female cats." The man does not look up from his cereal. The woman loves the white cat, the pink skin of his diseased ears, the red welts from fly bites, the strange eyes. This cat looks right through you, he sees something in the room that you can't see.

"Yes, probably that's where he is." The woman walks to the microwave, turns up the heat on a cold muffin. She looks out the window again, sees the bead curtain hanging silently in front of the sand pot, the sharp red incense sticks.

"I'll light them now," she says and she reaches for the sliding glass door.

CHRISTMAS CHOIR

The invitation had come in the mail early in December. Sheela was invited to a special after hours diamond sale. For valued customers only. She knew the name of this company, she had seen their ads on television. Elegant blonde women standing next to tall, rich men, long thin hands, glittering fingernails. She could easily imagine the people who would attend, clean purposeful people who smelled good and wore new clothes. They had good jobs. When the day came, Sheela looked carefully in her mirror and decided to wear her best white sweater, the one with the gold trim.

The room was very long and thin and the man at the door wore a black tuxedo and a neatly trimmed mustache. He looked like he had just come from a wedding. A group of high school girls gathered at the far end of two long aisles filled with rings and necklaces and pendants. The girls stood awkwardly behind fragile metal music stands and sang "Oh Holy Night." Sheela felt her heart spread inside her chest.

Then the music stopped and the men in tuxedos began to circulate among the valued female customers. The man who had been at the door walked up to Sheela. He remembered her from somewhere, he was sure of that. He said nice things about her white sweater. This man had the perfect ring for her. He brought it out and, very slowly, put it on her ring finger. It had one small diamond and three off center emeralds. It was not too expensive, really. It was patterned after a ring that a famous movie star had once worn. Sheela felt the ring flow onto her finger, felt it burn itself into place. She opened her mouth to speak and it was as if the air were suddenly filled with the tinkle of falling coins.

MOBILE HOME HEAVEN
TRAILER COURT HELL
(FINAL STORIES)

A RUSH TO ARRIVE

Hack Crowe is standing on his front porch looking up at the sky. Tonight is the night that the infamous comet will be most visible but all Hack can see is clouds. What a pain! He looks across the street and sees Francine's rose bushes bristling in the evening breeze. Her blinds are pulled tight. Hack hears a dog yowling in the distance.

Then he realizes it's not a dog at all, it's a siren, and it's getting louder and louder. Just great, somebody else has croaked. That's all we need around here. Now Hack can hear the lumbering engine making the turn into Thousand Flags, plunging past the mailboxes. Then it appears, red lights flashing, a huge fire truck, bearing down International Boulevard, blowing back darkness and eardrums in its rush to arrive. It stops right in front of Hack Crowe. The firemen are looking at Hack. Then they jump to the pavement, carrying a stretcher, and run around the truck, past the rose bushes, into the coach across the street. Spotlights from the fire engine illuminate the front door. Suddenly the firemen are out the front door, moving fast. It's Stan on the stretcher, he's covered in a white sheet, but Hack knows it's him—he sees his brown wingtip shoes sticking out from under the sheet. The fire truck speeds away. Silence.

Hack is still standing on his porch. The clouds have parted and the comet is visible—a blunted ball of fire, a shimmering tail. Hale-Bopp passes easily through the familiar light of the stars.

I'M YOUR DAUGHTER

Madge Sands is sitting by her big picture window, looking out at her persimmon tree. It's November and the strange fruit hangs orange and bulbous on the bare branches. Most folks don't like these soft persimmons. They are bitter until fully ripe and kids learn early not to steal them. But then, Madge thinks, there's not too many kids to worry about around this old trailer park, is there?

Just then an orange cat jumps up into the lower branches of the persimmon tree. It sits for a moment, perched on a branch, looking toward the sidewalk and the street beyond. Then the cat jumps fast, hits the ground and disappears, as if it's scared of something. That's when the doorbell rings. Oh, Madge thinks, it's probably the Jehovah's Witnesses again. Well, they're not so bad, really, they like to talk about the end of the world and Madge has been thinking about that lately anyway.

Madge peeks through the tiny hole in her front door and sees the fisheye view of a plump woman, kind of like a Mexican maybe, but she has a cell phone on her belt. Madge feels good when she sees a cell phone. Busy people are safe people, usually anyway. Maybe she's looking for some house cleaning business. Or maybe she just wants some persimmons. Some foreigners really like them. Madge leans against the door and turns the knob, pulling it slowly open. The woman at the door opens her mouth, hesitates for a moment with her lips half open.

"Hello there," she says finally, "are you Madge Sands?"
Silence. Madge, for some reason, can't manage to make a sound. Then she blurts out.

"I'm her." Madge takes a step backwards. "I'm Madge."

"Well, I'm your daughter." The plump lady lays her hand on her cell phone, as if she might pull it off her belt.

Madge's arms drop to her sides. "I mean I'm your husband's daughter, anyway, I'm Angela." Madge almost slams the door in Angela's face, then she slowly opens it back up again.

"What did you say?"

"I'm Angela, your husband's daughter and I thought I'd…"

"He's dead now." Madge starts to close the door again. "How can he have a daughter?"

"Well, his name was Fred and he married my mom and that's how he did it." Madge lets the door hang loose and it swings slowly open. The two women stand in the doorway and look at each other.

Madge is thin and rather small. Everyone says she is so nimble and spry for her age. Her face has hundreds of tiny wrinkles that move in oblique patterns when she talks. Right now Madge is talking on the phone with Francine.

"I suppose you're going to be out of town again. Down there with that niece of yours in… what's that town's name?" Francine says.

" No, that's not it at all."

"What's that town's called, anyway?" Francine's voice is pitched a shade higher than normal.

"Tiburon. Listen, Franny, something's come up. A woman named Angela popped up at my door yesterday."

"So?"

"So, she says she's Fred's daughter."

"What?"

"You knew we had a trailer down in Mexico near Ensenada, right. Well, she says she and her mom lived in a nearby trailer and Fred would come by and visit." Silence hangs heavy on the phone line. Then Francine speaks up.

"So that's what he was up to, no good is what I always thought. Something about that smile he had. I told you years and years ago you should go down to Mexico with him sometimes. Now look what he's gone and done." An exasperated sigh. Madge can imagine Francine leaning into the telephone like it was a stage microphone. Timely advice is her specialty.

"Okay, okay, so what am I supposed to do now? You know Fred and I never had any kids. I couldn't." Madge lowers her voice until Francine can hardly hear it.

"Whatever you do, don't let her move in," Francine barks into the phone. "Don't let her do that." Silence. Madge holds the phone pressed tightly to her ear but says nothing. Then Francine speaks in a coarse whisper, "she's already moved in, hasn't she?"

"Well, sort of, maybe." Madge waves the telephone back and forth through the air on the side of her head, then puts it back to her ear. "What else could I do? She says she's Fred's daughter."

"Find out, Madge, test her. See if she's for real." Francine is interested in Madge's dilemma but she has other phone calls to make. "I'll see if Mabel can play this week if you can't, okay, don't worry about it. It's just pinochle, it's not like we're playing bridge or something like that."

Madge hangs up the phone. The two green suitcases that had not been visible from the doorway have now been moved to the spare bedroom. Madge consoles herself. At least she's sleeping late and I can get a few things done. Then she looks out the window and sees fat Angela standing in front of the persimmon tree. She reaches out, touches the bright orange fruit, then draws her hand back. She does not pick the persimmon. She just stands there looking at it.

Madge has a big Mexican flower pot, more like a vase actually, sitting in the middle of her large kitchen table. It's a conversation piece and visitors to her coach always comment on the green jade finish and the embossed lily flower near the neck of the vase. Madge and Angela are sitting at the table, each eating a plate of scrambled eggs. Madge would like to have made a Mexican dish she remembers, involving tomatoes and sausage and tortilla chips, but she can't remember how. So scrambled eggs will have to do.

"How did you find out about me?" Madge blurts out. She had intended to beat around the bush a little bit, to lead up to the subject slowly. Angela lays her fork on her napkin and leans over her eggs as if she has been waiting for this question.

"My mom told me just a few months ago, just before she died." Angela's eyes are luminous and brown and looking straight at Madge, "she thought I needed to know."

"Oh, so she knew about me but I …" Madge's voice trails off into silence.

"It's just that hardly anybody had ever actually seen you. And he never said anything, so…" Angela picks up her fork and sticks it into the eggs. Then she looks up again. "I always suspected something though. When I was little, I used to sneak up to his trailer sometimes when he was gone and get the key that was under the rock. I found things. Woman things."

"Like what? I didn't have anything down there." Madge has finished her eggs and wants to clean up the dishes. She is standing by her chair, holding a small plate with a fork balanced on top.

"I don't know, a red sweater in the closet, some kind of a medicine bottle for women. Maybe I was just over sensitive or something. But I did have a strange feeling about it." Angela stands up with her plate and her fork in one hand.

She reaches out and softly touches the flower on the neck of the green vase.

"A red sweater?" Madge turns toward the sink. She remembers the red sweater, all right, she can almost see it hanging in the cramped closet alongside her bed. So that's where it went. She had looked all over for it years and years ago. Then she forgot about it.

Madge and Angela stand by the sink. Madge washes and Angela dries the dishes and the frying pan with a thin coarse towel. Angela opens a cupboard and puts the dishes away. Her touch is gentle and the dishes settle into place without a sound.

Madge is up a lot in the night. Sometimes she just can't sleep. She thinks too much—that's what the ladies tell her at pinochle anyway. She can almost see Naomi with a slight curl in the side of her lips, saying: "Oh Madge, dear, it's just that your mind is always turning things around and inside out." She would pause and look into Madge's eyes. Then Naomi would look at Blanche for corroboration. Blanche would just stare at her cards.

She thinks about the past, of course, the dead relatives, the real estate company where she used to work, even about the houses that she had sold long ago. But right now Madge is thinking about the trailer at San Miguel beach. The brick wall built by Winceslao Coparubias and the iron gates welded by that funny looking guy in Sausal. This was back when she and Fred had both been excited to have a trailer on a beach in Mexico—thirty years ago when staying by a beach anywhere seemed like a fantastic luxury.

Madge starts out for her bathroom, stops, then opens the bedroom door and heads for the hall bathroom. She sees a light on in the den. That's where Fred used to sit sometimes with the light on late at night. She feels her veins pumping in her wrists and her toes pressing down into the thin carpet. Madge pads silently up to the bathroom door, thinks about flushing the toilet, but doesn't. Then she's standing by the den, leaning ever so slightly into the light of the half open door.

Angela is on the floor with photo albums arranged around her. She has her face down by the photos and her butt up in the air. Maybe she doesn't see so well, Madge thinks. She's looking at pictures Madge and Fred had taken in Hawaii. Madge can see the palm trees and the huge plane tree in Lahaina. Madge imagines herself on the floor with Angela, explaining the photographs, telling her about the old days. Madge imagines herself speaking up, walking into the room, putting a hand on Angela's shoulder. But she doesn't do any of that. Madge walks quietly back to her room.

Madge is getting a picture in her mind. She can see a day coming when Angela will walk up to her, in the kitchen at breakfast probably, with a determined look in her eye. She will have something special to say, a special favor to ask. It will involve money, of course, and, most likely, Angela's plans and hopes for a certain future. Madge is no fool, she has been around the track a few times herself. This picture is not entirely unpleasant, however, it feels warm in a certain way, like an old wound that has healed but still hurts, familiar and somehow comfortable. To tell the truth, this breakfast scene almost feels like it has already happened.

She turns on the light in her own bathroom and looks into the mirror. This wrinkled face does not seem like it's hers. Madge is particularly concerned by the network of furrows and creases on her neck—her skin is like a topographical map. She puts one hand on her throat and stretches the skin tight. Then she puts a little lotion on her hands, rubs them together, touches her neck and turns out the light.

Madge and Angela are walking along the sidewalk at the town square. Madge would like to show Angela around, to show her the ropes, so to speak. In the middle of Sonoma sits a large park with a city building off center on one side. It says Bear Republic at the entrance. Two fire engines are parked along the north side of the grass. School kids are lined up alongside the fire engines and a fireman is standing high up on the bright red chassis, showing the children how the water hoses work.

The two women stop and watch the children. Then Madge turns quickly to Angela. "I was just thinking of that ancient fire engine that used to sit next to the restaurant in San Miguel," Madge says in an offhand way. "Do you remember that old fire engine, Angela?" Angela just nods her head. "Fred told me once that it had been hauled away to the dump." Madge looks closely at Angela. "But then that was long after I quit going down there, I guess." Madge sighs.

"Look, Mrs. Sands, one of those kids is climbing up." A skinny boy with red hair and a face full of freckles has broken from the line and is scrambling over the wheel well of the smaller fire engine. The fireman hasn't seen him yet.

"Well, all that was way before your time, probably." Madge is wondering if Angela should start calling her Mom. Mrs. Sands sounds kind of odd and formal. But she doesn't say anything, nothing at all. Finally she speaks up. "Let's get ice cream over on the corner. Those kids will be over there any minute and the line will be a mile long."

Angela and Madge walk past the school kids and the drone of the fireman's voice. "There is a right way and a wrong way to do everything," he says, "everything depends on our doing things the right way." The line of children leans forward then backward like a string of seaweed waving in a tide pool. Madge cannot see the redheaded boy but she feels pretty good about the rest of these children, very orderly, very obedient, just the way things ought to be.

Madge is on the phone with Francine. "She's moved in and now you're buying her ice cream at Frapachinos?" Francine's voice is shrill and impatient.

"Yes, but…" Madge shakes her head as if she has water in one ear and can't get it out. She is talking ever so softly, barely moving her mouth.

"Listen, Madge dearest, just put it to her bluntly. Ask her who she really is. That's it! Who does she think she's fooling here, anyway?" Francine sounds like she is ready to hang up the phone. Madge holds her palm over the receiver and looks down the hallway toward Angela's door.

"Okay, okay, I understand, but she seems so innocent, so kind and, well, so generous in a certain way. I don't know." Madge is looking at the clock, waiting for nine o'clock to strike. It's a cuckoo clock and a tiny wooden bird really does come out of a small door every hour, on the hour. Suddenly the cuckoo does pop out, dips down as if pecking a sunflower seed, then snaps back inside with a loud metallic click.

"Generous. Oh sure, I'll bet," Francine says, "I heard that, by the way, it's that crazy cuckoo clock of yours, isn't it?"

"Listen Franny, I've got to go. I'll let you know what I find out, okay?" Madge puts the phone back on the table. It's time to knock on Angela's door. They are going shopping at the big mall in Santa Rosa. That should be fun. Madge walks down the hall and stands in front of Angela's door. She hears music, Mexican music. And a DJ talking fast about a "gran venta" at a store in Petaluma. Madge has a splattering of Spanish still left in her, maybe, but she is scared to try it on Angela. Oh, well. She knocks on the door.

Madge has pulled her old Volvo into the Shell gas station on Arnold Drive. She has been intending to get gas for almost a week. Now the gas gauge is bouncing on empty. Angela is sitting in the front seat with her wallet in her lap. She has taken it out of her purse because she wants to buy some chips or nuts, something to eat in the car.

"Okay, then, it will take a few minutes to fill it up." Madge opens her door and stands in front of the gas hose. She hears Angela's door shut, then she sticks the nozzle into the gas tank and the gasoline flows cold through the hose. Madge returns to her car door and looks in the window. Angela's wallet is sitting on the passenger's seat alongside her purse. She opens the door and grabs the wallet and starts for the gas station door, then she stops and sits back down behind the wheel. She is looking at a driver's license photo for Angela Morena Tapia and the address is 169 Sabado Tarde in San Ysidro, California. Birth date, October 18, 1980. And the pictures, photographs of an older woman, Angela's mother, perhaps, a very old woman, a grandmother, and kids, lots of little kids. No men. Madge flips through the photos but no picture of Fred. She looks up, thinks she sees Angela in line at the checkout stand and quickly shuffles the wallet over onto the seat where she found it. She hops out the door and grabs the gas hose. Just in time. Angela is walking toward the car. She might need her wallet to pay for the bag of chips in her hand, Madge thinks. But maybe not, maybe she took a few dollars with her. She sticks the gas hose back in the slot, puts her credit card away and sits down in the driver's seat. She looks over but Angela is already eating chips. She's ready to go. The wallet is nowhere to be seen.

"Have some chips," Angela says, "guacamole and sea salt." Angela holds the bag in front of Madge's nose while she snaps her seatbelt into the slot. "These are really good." Madge takes a few chips.

"What's the deal with the sea salt, I wonder?" Madge says and puts the car in gear.

"It's healthier when it comes from the ocean," Angela says with a smile and a nudge of complicity. "It's more natural." The two women pull out onto the highway and head for the big mall in Santa Rosa.

"I'd like something Italian, I think." Angela is looking at the signs surrounding the Food Court. "Or maybe Chinese." Madge eyes the rows of pizza slices behind the glass.

"Let's sit down for a minute." Madge bends over and rubs the calf of her left leg. They sit at a flat plastic table next to a jungle gym swarming with kids. Shouts and screams fill the air. They look at each other for a moment and neither woman speaks. Then Madge starts, "You know, Angela, I've been thinking…"

"I know. I know. We need to talk, right?" Angela's hands are resting on top of her purse which is sitting in front of her on the table. She looks up at Madge. "It's about time, I guess."

"Well, yes, it is, sort of."

"Okay. My mom never told me too much about anything, really. At first she told me he was Uncle Fred. When I was little, he came over to our trailer a lot. He used to bring big sacks of fruit and vegetables from Ensenada or Sausal. He liked to play around with us kids, my cousins and me. We even played hide and seek and we'd throw the ball over the trailer and shout 'Ally Ally Otson, all home free.' Then he'd disappear for a few months. Maybe even longer. It seems like such a long time ago." Angela pauses and looks at Madge. "I just don't want to hurt your feelings or anything."

"I guess you were born pretty soon after we moved the trailer there." Madge scratches her head, as if trying to remember some incident long ago.

"When was that?"

"Oh, mid seventies, I guess, 1975 maybe."

"I don't know. Your trailer was always there, behind the red bricks, through the black iron gate. I loved the little brick arch over the gate. So fancy, like a fairy tale." Angela holds her head tipped to one side, remembering.

Madge seems to be holding her breath, then she asks, "When is your birthday, Angela?"

"Oh, December 28th, right between Christmas and New Years Day." Then she closes her lips tightly and squeezes her purse. She looks up at Madge. "You've never asked me what I want to do, have you? About my future, I mean."

"Oh that. Well, I…" Madge feels dizzy, like after drinking too much champagne. Or like the day after a sleepless night. You turn your head suddenly and your world starts to spin.

"A nurse, I want to be a nurse and work in a hospital."

Madge puts her hands flat on the table and pushes up. "Let's have pizza then." She walks over to the glass and points at a fat slice with pepperoni and mushrooms. "How about that one?" Angela is by her side.

"Vegetarian maybe?" Angela says. Madge turns.

"What about San Ysidro?"

"Huh? San Ysidro?" Angela's hand is stuck in the air, pointing at a pizza with green peppers and pineapple. Her hand drops. "It's a town on the border. The American side. My auntie lives there and my cousins. Why ask me that? Who cares about that dumb little town?"

"Oh, nothing really, I just remember passing through there with Fred. There was a McDonalds there." The boy behind the glass hands over two extra large slices and points to a bottle full of hot pepper and a bottle with grated cheese.

"Help yourself," he says. The women sit down to eat.

Madge slams the phone back on the hook. Francine has just said, "Listen, Madge, she's either Fred's daughter or some kind of cheap crook. Don't you think it's time to find out which it is?" Madge had felt heat moving up her neck, into her face and scalp. She doesn't think Francine should be talking this way. It's none of her business, really. So she had hung up on her.

But Madge really does want to get serious about Angela. How can things go on as they are—a big question mark? Sure there's the red sweater and the "Olly Olly Otson, All Home Free." Only Fred would still be singing that odd children's ditty. But what does it prove? Then there's the driver's license! Was it all some illegal way of getting across the border, maybe? And the birth date? And how come Angela doesn't have a Mexican accent if she's lived in Mexico all her life? Well, sometimes it does sound like an accent but then it goes away.

Madge decides to do some research. She goes to the library and sees stacks and stacks of books, lining the walls, filling the shelves, the dark, ominous colors of the dust jackets, the nosy librarian who says quite loudly that she'll need more information about any people Madge might be wanting to locate. Madge thinks about going to the police department but, when she sees all the dark blue squad cars parked out in front, she forgets about that idea. She has heard about the internet but nobody she knows even has a computer. What about the telephone? Call people. Ask questions. But you have to have phone numbers first, don't you?

So Madge decides to go to the travel agency up by the Sonoma Market. That's what she needs to do all right, go to Mexico or San Ysidro maybe. When Fred died and quit paying the space rent, the management down in San Miguel wrote her a letter about the trailer. Move it or lose it or pay up is what they said. But Madge didn't do any of those things. So now she guesses that the trailer probably isn't hers anymore, anyway. Everyone had said, why Madge, just go and get it, bring it back up here and sell it. Put an ad in the paper, Madge. Sure, sounds easy if you don't have to do it yourself. But an airplane ticket to San Diego would be easy enough and Madge knows you can easily rent a car in an airport.

Her legs are shaking as she walks into the Wurlitzer Travel Store. The four agents watch her from behind their desks. They've seen too many old folks from the trailer park who just drop by to pass the time. Madge occupies herself collecting flyers, pretty full color photographs of Acapulco, Guadalajara and Mazatlan. A beautiful girl and boy run hand in hand on a white sparkling beach under waving palm trees. The water is so blue that it's almost green. Finally, an older woman gets up and walks over to Madge.

"Can I help you with something?" Madge's arm jumps and the brochures skitter across the tile floor. She bends slowly to pick them up.

"Well, I think you can," Madge says.

Madge tells all her friends she's going to Los Angeles to see her sister. Actually, she does have a sister there, in La Habre in an old people's convalescent home. Madge doesn't want to see her though. On the last morning, Madge sits down with Angela at the kitchen table to say goodbye.

"Don't forget to water the plants, okay, and bring in the newspaper everyday," Madge says, "you know what people think if they see a pile of papers out front." Angela agrees and says nothing, just looks at Madge with pendulous eyes. Then her cheeks puff out.

"You know, when I walked up to your door, the first thing I saw was your persimmon tree." Angela fingers her teacup and looks toward the window in the living room. "It reminded me, somehow, of our loquat tree in San Miguel. It was right in front of the house on the front row by the parking lot and people used to pick the loquats when they walked by." Angela sticks her hand out in the air as if she is holding a piece of fruit. "Loquats are so round, so tart, the fat shiny seeds, always three, black and slippery against your tongue."

Madge doesn't know much about loquats but she remembers eating them in Ensenada. And that Fred liked them a lot. Angela looks at Madge and her face shines in the morning sun from the kitchen window. "People would pick them sometimes and, if they were tourists, gringos, my mom would open the window and yell out at them. But nobody ever listened to her. They just kept on walking."

Madge nods her head and imagines herself on the airplane. The pretty stewardess is handing her a cup of tea and a biscuit. The pilot is talking on a loudspeaker and his voice is calm and soothing. There is a peaceful humming in the air as if the world were waiting for some important moment to pass. But there is no hurry and the ticking of Madge's tiny gold wristwatch slows, hesitates, and almost crawls to a stop.

"You know what she told me just before she died?" Madge thinks she sees tears in Angela's eyes. "That's how she met my dad, she yelled at him for eating one of her loquats. And he came back to talk to her." A long silence hangs over the kitchen table. Madge rubs her thumb over the glass on her wristwatch. Angela lowers her eyes to the table, finally straightens her back and neck.

"You know, there is something I've been wanting to ask you about," Angela says. Madge turns her head to listen.

The first thing Madge sees when she walks in the front door of the tiny brown house at the end of Sabado Tarde street in San Ysidro is a picture of Angela on the mantelpiece over the fireplace. The woman who answers the door is talking in Madge's ear but she doesn't hear it all at first.

"¡Válgame Dios! You're from San Miguel, I mean you're Fred's wife. ¡Qué una sorpresa! Sientate. I'll get you a cup of tea." She heads off toward the kitchen, then turns around. "I'm Victoria, Esperanza's sister." Esperanza is Angela's mother, Madge knows that, and that she died recently. Madge walks sidewise to the mantelpiece and what she sees makes her reach out, then grab her hand back in shock. In back of a group picture of five women is a smaller frame— it's Fred in fishing gear, sitting in a landlocked boat. Grinning a mile wide. A Mexican woman stands beside the boat. Madge moves quickly away from the fireplace just as Victoria walks back into the room.

Victoria hands a steaming cup to Madge and motions for her to sit on the couch. Madge sits. "It was such a shock when my sister died. All the way down there in Ensenada and nobody to take care of her. I couldn't go down at all, I had to work." Madge nods her head. She understands what grief is and that people have to work. Then her head jerks up.

"Her daughter?"

Victoria gives Madge a strange look. "She never had any kids, my sister, it was her sadness to bear." Victoria lowers her head. "My girls did the best they could for her, the twins both went down the last couple of weeks." Madge feels dizzy and pushes herself further back into the couch.

"Fred?" Madge says, almost under her breath, her lips moving slightly.

"Your husband, he helped us out a lot. One time our car broke down while we were visiting my sister, Esperanza. I couldn't believe it. He got out his tools, took the engine apart and, a day later, it ran. I couldn't believe it. He was a good man, he was." Victoria is looking carefully at Madge, perhaps wondering what to say next. "You were lucky to have such a husband."

"I guess so," Madge says finally. She doesn't know what to say or what to do. "He did like to fish but that old boat of his never ran half the time." Madge tries to laugh but it comes out like a cough. Victoria looks over toward the mantel on the fireplace.

"Oh. Yes." Victoria smiles in a tolerant sort of way. "All the men around that trailer park like to fish."

"But they all just sat around our trailer and drank tequila, didn't they?" Madge is finally finding her voice. "That's one of the reasons I stopped going down there, all that drinking and pointless talk."

Victoria and Madge are silent for a few minutes. Victoria gets up and walks into the kitchen. She pours more hot water into Madge's cup. "My sister is buried in the little cemetery up above the houses on the other side of the highway. Did you ever go up there?"

"No, but I heard about it. Fred always said it was where he wanted to be buried. But he died a thousand miles away in his sitting chair in Thousand Flags. Just like that. One day he just stopped breathing after breakfast. I didn't even know he was gone until half way through the morning." Madge has her breath back now and feels like she can stand up okay. "I guess I'd better be going." Victoria stands up. She moves forward like she wants to touch Madge, to hold her somehow. But Madge's feet edge backwards just a little bit.

"Are you going down to San Miguel?"

"I thought I was," Madge says, "but I don't know."

"I'd go with you if I could," Victoria says, waving her hand at a fly that's buzzing around their heads. "I've got to go flip burgers in about an hour. It's a job. I'm just glad I've got one, I guess." She moves toward Madge again, this time Madge holds her ground and they touch hands.

"We heard a lot about you, you know, my sister and I. Fred talked about you all the time." Victoria stops, grips Madge's hand. "He loved you, I know."

"Your daughters?"

"Oh, one is off at school, you know how kids are, the other one's working up above San Francisco somewhere. Or so she says, anyway. I think there's a boy involved. Whatever, they don't have time for me or San Ysidro. Too busy."

"Yes, too busy." Madge echoes. The two women walk to the front door.

From the airplane Madge can see for miles. She looks toward the south and imagines she can see the border where the neat suburban tracts give way to barren desert and then the shacks and littered gullies of Tijuana. She imagines Fred driving comfortably down those dusty, bumpy roads with his infernal pickup truck and his God damned proficiency in Spanish. Madge sucks in her breath and lets it out slowly. She is a little taken back by the words she has just said to herself. Well, he had been happy down there and she hadn't and that was that. Might as well say it like it was. Madge can almost see the multitudes of men and women who used to linger around the border fence down toward Las Playas. Waiting for the sun to go down, for their chance to bolt through the dark into a different life. So many people, so many stories to tell. Madge can feel the airplane beginning to vibrate, turning in the towering clouds, leaving the border behind. The sun is setting in the west and in a little more than an hour Madge will land in San Francisco.

Madge and Angela are standing in front of a cage at the Petaluma SPCA animal shelter. A shelter employee is pointing at two small puppies in a cage. Dogs are barking everywhere. It is hard to think clearly. Madge is scratching her head.

"You know Mrs. Blue says dogs have to be under twenty pounds," Madge says and looks at Angela with a question on her face.

"These two little guys are way under that," Angela says, "and so cute, too." The employee straightens up his shoulders. He's getting ready to speak.

"They're half Weimaraner and half Vizsla." His lips linger slowly over the words. "Dropped off just yesterday, the mother got hit by a car."

"Killed?" Madge gulps air and then sighs. "Such cute puppies...they look exactly alike, like twins." Angela looks quickly at Madge as if she is about to say something, then stops.

"Well, puppies usually do look alike, don't they?" Angela says. She is down on her knees, calling the puppies forward. They romp toward her, heads down, tails pumping. The employee steps up to the wire cage.

"Actually, half breeds like these two usually don't look alike, you can have eight of them, all different colors, shapes even," he says with a smart smile, then he turns and walks back to the office door. The constant barking ebbs and flows according to some inscrutable rhythm—louder, almost ecstatic, then softer, then louder again.

Madge looks down at Angela, reaches her hand halfway to her shoulder, then pulls it back slowly. Angela stands up. The puppies are a light reddish brown and they are playing now, tumbling over each other in the antiseptic sawdust of the dusty cage.

Angela looks off into the distance for a moment and then says, "You know, if we got both of them, I could take one with me when I go."

"When you go?" Madge keeps her voice steady.

"Well, you know, when I … when I start looking for…" Angela stops and turns toward Madge, as if she has heard something in her voice. She reaches out and touches Madge's sleeve. "You know what I mean, don't you?"

Madge doesn't know, really, but she has felt the twitch on her sleeve and her arm feels warm under her sweater. "Let's get them both then, Angela, and Mrs. Blue be damned." The two women giggle. "Can you imagine what she'd say if she could see them now? These guys are going to get pretty big, I think, way over twenty pounds, anyway." Madge wrinkles up her eyes and puckers her mouth. Angela laughs at the face that Madge makes.

"She'd have a heart attack!" Angela says and then, absently sliding her hand over the cage door handle, she notices it is unlocked. She looks over toward the office door and then at Madge. She winks one eye and opens the cage door. The puppies run out into the hallway, then around the corner into the exercise yard. They dash this way, then that way, biting at each other's ears, tripping each other, tumbling and rolling in the dirt. They skid, trip and fall, then they're up again, spinning toward the brick wall, bouncing off, collapsing in the dirt for a split second. Resting. Then they're running again, peeing on the bricks, tipping over a trashcan, they spin wildly through the cups and paper plates, sending refuse in all directions. The women try to catch the dogs. They try and try. Finally Angela catches one, then Madge the other. They all stop, all four of them, out of breath, panting, waiting for the next moment to occur.

THE POSTWOMAN ALWAYS THINKS TWICE

Delivering the mail to Thousand Flags looks easy but for some reason it's not a favored route at the Sonoma Post Office. A huge silver box opens up with a key at the back and you just fill the slots, over a hundred of them. The old folks are the problem. Some of them like to wait for the mail, like curious crows, perched on a bench provided for just that purpose. Others stand in the cool shade of the clubhouse.

Today is a good day, however. As Denise pulls the mail truck into the turnout in front of the big mail box, she sees only one figure under the shade. A large figure, one that she recognizes. Mrs. Hardy, it is, Mrs. Myrtle Hardy. As it turns out, there is a substantial package addressed to a Mrs. Hardy this day. From a medical clearinghouse back East. Denise pulls hard on the hand brake and grabs her mail sack. She looks inside. All the mail bundles are neatly sorted and ready to slide into the slots.

Denise usually starts at the right and moves left down the line of boxes. She can see Mrs. Hardy fidgeting under the sun canopy at the end of the clubhouse.

Denise picks a bundle and slides it in, picks and slides, picks and slides. She is watching for a tell tale shadow, the giveaway that someone is standing behind her. It's only a little after one thirty. No shadows yet. But before long Denise feels something moving close behind. Finally, the hard working postal employee stands up straight and turns to face her shadow.

"Oh," Mrs. Hardy says "I didn't mean to intrude or anything." Denise doesn't smile. "I'm just waiting, you see, just waiting." Denise starts to turn back to her work, then shrugs her shoulders.

"I've got a package for you."

"You do?"

"Just a second."

Denise hands over the brown, drab parcel and Mrs. Hardy pulls it in close to her wide body, rocking slightly on her feet. She looks down at the address label and her lips move. Then, holding the box gently in her arms, she walks quietly away.

NO PERSONS UNDER FIFTY FIVE ALLOWED

Leroy Crowe is going to throw a New Year's Eve party. His dad is headed for Roswell, New Mexico for a big UFO conference and Leroy is making plans. Of course, he knows that his Dad will find out eventually. How could he not? They live in a lame trailer park, after all. These old folks watch everything you do around here. The biggest event of the week is when a fire truck comes to haul an old lady off to the hospital with the rest of the geriatric crowd watching the whole show from the safety of a hundred kitchen windows. What a gas! But Leroy doesn't care. He's been a good boy long enough. Why did he come out to California to live with his Dad anyway? He could have played Grand Theft Auto all day back living with his mom in South Dakota.

So Leroy is sending text messages to all his friends. Which amounts to exactly two other teenagers living secretly in the over fifty-five Thousand Flags Mobile Home Retirement Village. One of them is a girl who is living with her grandmother. And rumor has it that this grandmother was one of the skinny dipping girls on the inside cover of the original Woodstock album. Of course, Anastasia is probably the one who started that rumor. Being a little bizarre comes with the territory if you expect to be on Leroy's speed dial. As for the party, it's going to be different. Leroy is not sure how different but he's sure it's not going to be the kind of sedated costume party that the old geezers throw every Halloween down at the clubhouse. This party will be for real.

Leroy's cell phone vibrates in his pants pocket. He pulls it out. A picture of Anastasia dressed in black pops up on his cell phone screen. She looks kind of like one of those tortured prisoners in Iraq. The one that's standing up on a pedestal, arms stretched straight out from his sides.

"Is he gone yet?" she whispers. Leroy walks quickly into the bathroom and shuts the door.

"No, not yet." Leroy clicks the lock on the door. "He leaves tonight from San Francisco."

"He's leaving the car, right?"

"Yeah, sure, but how's that help. He's got the keys." Leroy leans over and flushes the toilet, then runs hot water into the sink.

"Oh sure, well I know how to get that old Nova going, don't worry about that."

"Right, sure you can, you can do anything, can't you?" Silence. Nobody speaks for a few moments.

"Am I getting a little too much in your face, Leroy?"

"Whatever." Leroy sticks his hand in the hot water stream and jerks it back quickly, then rubs his thumb against his wrist. It hurts. "Listen, Ana, gotta go. I can hear him out in the kitchen." Leroy clicks the phone together and sticks it in his pants.

He walks out the bathroom door and sees his dad over by the sink eating a leftover burger. The door to the microwave is hanging open. Hack Crowe looks at Leroy Crowe, shifts his oversized body and waves the half eaten burger in the air.

"They charge for meals on airplanes now, you know," Hack says. He stuffs some damp fries in his mouth and looks out the kitchen window. He is waiting for the airport shuttle to pull up out front.

The abandoned cemetery five streets down Arnold Drive is the only place Leroy can ever think of to hang out with Anastasia and Harold. They don't dare do a thing around the trailer park. What if someone started asking questions? It's really great fun being an illegal! But the cemetery is just right, they can sit around all day, drinking beer or smoking joints. That is if they can get a hold of anything worth drinking or smoking. Nobody, absolutely nobody, ever goes there. Most of these old geez bags don't even know this cemetery is here. You see, the truth is that most of these grey beards aren't even from around here, they don't even know the history of this place. Their families move them in here because it's cheap. Of course, Leroy hasn't been here long either, only a few months, but he keeps his eyes open. And he has read an article about old cemeteries in the Sonoma Times.

The tombstones are totally overgrown with sticker bushes and climbing vines. Even the biggest ones are barely visible. But it's a very peaceful place and there's a special spot right in the middle where an old fountain used to splash. You can sit around the rough concrete rim of the fountain and not even hear the highway a few hundred yards away. Anastasia and Harold are already there, perched like lazy birds on the fountain ledge.

"Nothing like being on time, Leroy." Ana says She leans back as if bending into a spray of falling water. Then she pushes forward quickly. "Out of breath, Leroy? Huffing and puffing again? Better watch those calories."

"Yeah" Harold glares at Leroy. "Like we really like hanging out in cemeteries, you know." Ana gives Harold an odd look. Leroy drops his day pack heavily on the ground, puts one foot up on the green canvas bag.

"Okay, so you probably wonder why I called this meeting, right?"

"Meeting?" Ana pins Leroy with her eyes. Nobody speaks for a moment.

"I mean, it's about the New Year's Eve party. That's all." Leroy has his arms up in the air, shrugging off blame for whatever might happen next. "We have to make some plans here don't we?" Ana looks at him and raises her right hand like she's sitting in a classroom and she's playing the part of the studious little girl with the wire rimmed glasses.

"Can I speak now?" Ana shakes her black hair around her shoulders and waits until she's sure she has everyone's attention. "It's your party, Leroy, maybe you should figure it out. You're a bright boy." Actually, the boys are kind of scared of Anastasia, but they have to act like they're not. Now they just look at her, the coal black skirt, the white, white face, the red lips and the fuzzy shirt that isn't buttoned very high up. Then her face brightens a bit. "Okay, I know, let's just steal stuff, like trick or treat, you know, but this time we just trick people and to hell with the candy."

The two guys just stare at her. They can almost smell the spray of the ancient fountain cascading over Ana's black, black hair.

"What?"

"Steal stuff? What stuff?"

"Like backyard statues, maybe?"

"Like clothes off clotheslines?"

"Nobody hangs out clothes around here!"

"How about garbage cans?"

"Like wheel chairs?"

"Yeah, like wheelchairs and canes and walkers, all that kind of junk."

"Wait a minute, it's not even Halloween. It's New Years." Leroy holds his hands out flat in front of his wide chest, as if he has just made a major discovery. Nobody speaks. "Anyway, where would we put all this stuff?" Ana and Hal look at Leroy, then nod their heads up and down.

As if by signal, all three get out their cell phones and check for messages. Nobody has any but it looks like the meeting is over. They push bushes out of the way and start walking toward the street.

"Like lawn chairs, maybe." Harold stops for a moment. "We could put a few out here and then we wouldn't have to sit on that hard concrete." Harold says this and looks down at his shoes. He doesn't speak up much and he has the feeling nobody listens when he does.

Leroy and Ana are standing by a white picket fence at two in the morning. They are looking at a stone Buddha in the middle of a garden of rose bushes and neat gravel paths. Leroy whispers in Ana's ear.

"Is that it?" He leans slightly on Ana's shoulder. She bumps him away.

"Shh. It's so peaceful out here at night. Like everything's dead almost," she says. Leroy looks at her. He can hardly see her face in the dark but he sees what looks like a red light reflected in her eyes.

"Well, are we going to get it or not?" Leroy says and pushes impatiently at the white pickets. "Come on, I see a curtain moving. That old witch will see us." Ana jumps quickly over the fence, like a boy, and walks up to the Buddha. She turns and waves at Leroy, pumping her arm silently. Leroy looks at the fence, shakes his head and walks around to the gate, carrying a red kiddie wagon. They have decided to carry the wagon so the wheels won't squeak.

It's a Guan Yin Buddha, a female, not the fat garden male that you usually see. Leroy and Ana carry the loaded wagon through the gate and out into the street. When they are far enough away, they speak softly.

"See" Ana says. "That wasn't so hard."

"Yeah, that was cool." Actually Leroy's arms hurt from carrying the heavy wagon but he won't say so. "Let's do some more."

They set the wagon down and Leroy starts pulling it through the moist night air. The wheels squeak as they turn into Hack Crowe's driveway on International Boulevard.

Ana and Leroy and Harold get busy. School is out and so they have all day, every day, to hang out in the cemetery and make plans for that night's thievery. The fruits of their labor begin to accumulate in Hack Crowe's mobile home. The stone Buddha relaxes like a queen on the dining room table. A pot full of dead roses rests in a corner by the TV. Pool balls and a couple of ping pong paddles are scattered across the kitchen counter. A life buoy from the swimming pool sits indignant in the bathtub.

They have crept into backyards at midnight, crawled under trailers, eased themselves into unlocked storage sheds. An electric lawn mower appears on the living room carpet, pruning shears squat on the washer in the laundry room, a red five gallon plastic jug of gasoline waits patiently under the wheelchair ramp. Slowly the riches are piling up. Finally, the really good stuff. The rusty old wheelchairs, the abandoned walking canes, the depleted oxygen tanks. Now the trailer's starting to feel a little cramped. There isn't a whole lot of room to walk around. And only one more day left in the year 2005. What can they possibly liberate next?

"I know" Ana says, "let's steal your dad's car!" Leroy had a feeling she was going to suggest this. And now she has.

"How?" Leroy says. He shakes his pudgy neck back and forth. He thinks the old rattletrap Nova isn't worth the hassle. Leroy doesn't even like to ride in it on days when his dad has to drive him to school after he's missed the school bus.

"We'll hot wire it. I've got the wire right here in my bag." Ana pulls her hefty daypack off of the back of her chair and shoves her hand inside the open flap.

"It's not that easy." Harold speaks up, then looks at Ana as if he wishes he hadn't said anything at all.

"I've done it before guys, okay?" Ana digs a pair of pliers out of a pocket in her black trench coat. She holds the wire in one hand, the pliers in the other. "Let's go."

"Why?" Leroy stares at the pliers in Ana's hand.

"So we can go shopping for the party, silly." Ana grabs a pen and starts writing on a pad of paper. "We need to get supplies, don't we?" And they do. They hot wire the Nova. They drive down Arnold Drive all the way to Highway 12. They march through the Safeway store and collect everything they will need. Five giant bags of potato chips. A jumbo pack of granola bars. Three six packs of Mountain Dew. A package of hotdogs. A sack of buns. Marshmallows. Who knows? They might light a fire somewhere. No need to try and buy beer or wine though. Hack Crowe has plenty of champagne hidden on the top shelf of the hall closet. The plan is to drink that right away.

It is almost midnight and the illegal teenagers are making final preparations for the big moment. The large screen TV is focused on the big shiny ball ready to drop as the new year descends on New York City. Dick Clark has his arms held high in the air, a sort of invocation in honor of all the impatient residents here on planet Earth. Ana is seated in a wheel chair by the dining room table right next to the female Buddha. She has a glass of champagne in her left hand. The television is muted and Hack Crowe's sound system is playing Pink Floyd, *Dark Side of the Moon.* Ana has chosen the music. She feels that her real roots lie in the 1970s, certainly not the hip hop twenty first century. Leroy and Harold just think it's cool to be spending New Years Eve with such a clever and sexy female. And the music, well it's pretty spaced out, that's for sure. Anna reaches into her daypack and pulls out a long thin joint. Both boys shout out at once.

"All right, now things are cooking!"

They pass the joint around and Harold starts coughing. He tries to hold his breath but he can't. He just coughs.

"Did you roll this yourself?" Leroy is wondering what else Anna has inside her Grandma's trailer. She has never allowed Leroy or Harold inside her room. Not yet anyway.

"What do you think, big guy?" Anna takes a quick drag and hand the joint to Leroy. She raises her arms into the air and starts to sway back and forth. Pink Floyd is singing "Us or Them."

And that's the exact moment when Ana starts to take off her shirt. The boys are transfixed from the first unbelievable moment. The blouse has buttons, but she doesn't unbutton them. She just pulls one arm out, then the other. Leroy holds his breath, he won't let the least bit of air squeeze out. Harold is afraid to move his hands or feet. She pulls the cloth up over her head, catching her long black hair like a jet trail through a cascading sky. When the shirt is off, Ana carefully unbuttons all the buttons. Then off come her Levi jeans and she tosses the whole pile into a corner of the room. The blouse catches on the handle bars of a lawn mower and hangs there, suspended from the throttle lever. Of course, she's still wearing a skimpy white bra. Of course, she's still wearing stringed triangular panties. Black ones. Nobody moves. Leroy and Harold are waiting to see what happens next. But minutes pass and nothing does.

"Leroy," she says, "would you mind turning up the thermostat just a little bit. Don't you think it's getting cold in here?" Ana is oblivious. She is sitting with crossed legs, like the Buddha, and she has an oak cane across her knees. The champagne glass is tipping this way and that on the palm of her almost open hand. She is swaying to "The Great Gig in the Sky" and now the boys are getting ready to light another joint that has turned up, this one is soaked in hash oil. That should get things right on track. Leroy has been saving this very special item in an old match box since last summer.

"Leroy, I'm cold." Ana speaks loudly now. Leroy can see goose bumps on Ana's arms and so he jumps up and heads for the hallway. He dodges a rusty wheelchair and a red wagon loaded with potted plants. He flicks the thermostat up to eighty degrees.

Then the telephone rings. It's Hack Crowe. He wants to know how things are going back in good old Thousand Flags. Leroy talks to his dad.

"Everything's fine, Dad, we're just watching Dick Clark and the big ball on Times Square." Leroy hands the joint to Harold who lights it, puffs, holds his breath in, then starts coughing. He passes it to Ana. "Just Anastasia and Harold, that's all." Ana takes a deep drag.

"No, no, Dad, nothing's happening here at all." Leroy waves frantically at Harold to turn the stereo down.

"Just a little music from the TV." Leroy puts the phone on his other ear. "Yeah, sure, I've been eating just fine. Have you ever known me to starve?" Leroy pats his stomach and stares at Harold and Ana. Ana is passing the joint to Harold in a slow, sensuous movement, like in a dream.

"Listen Dad, I hope you guys find a flying saucer or something real soon but everything's perfectly normal back here in mobile home heaven." Silence. "When? Okay, fine, I'll see you then, okay?" It looks to Leroy like Harold is getting ready to put his arm around Ana's bare shoulders. "No, I wasn't trying to be a wise guy, no not at all. Okay, then. Bye."

The high, wailing cry of Pink Floyd swings like a serpent through the air of the littered Crowe's nest. The female voice is tremulous and penetrating, like the keening edge of a universe gone wild. Leroy is on one side of Ana's wheel chair, Harold is on the other side. They are like supplicants bending and twisting in a winding, cumulous wind. The clock is one minute from twelve midnight. On TV the ball is starting its long drop.

At first Leroy can barely hear a sound in the far distance, then it's louder. It's a siren, a cop car, or a fire engine, an ambulance. Probably a cop. Ana reaches for her clothes. Leroy lurches toward the stereo. Harold runs to the bathroom and throws the roach in the toilet bowl, hits the flush handle. Nothing happens. He rattles the handle, then runs out of the bathroom. The siren is deafening now, like it's next door. The teenagers run to the kitchen window and look out.

It is not next door. It's way down the street. A fire engine, no two fire engines, no an emergency vehicle and a fire engine squatting in the middle of the roadway. Then a cop car sails by fast. The kids duck down. When they look out again, they see the emergency vehicle take off in a screech of tires. The fire engine sets up a howl and follows it down the street. Only the police car remains, its red light winking and spinning shadows down the suddenly silent street. The sirens fade into the distance.

Leroy and Ana and Harold are huddled together by the kitchen window. Somehow the water in the sink has turned on. Hot water and steam are pouring down the drain. The teenagers stare at the water. Ana waves her hand in the steam. They look at each other. Ana has her shirt back on, almost. She is pushing the buttons through the button holes. Leroy turns off the water. The New Year has arrived.

WALKING THE DOG

Madge is looking out her front window just as the sun is setting behind her persimmon tree. The fruits hang pendulous from the leafless branches, like bright orange bulbs. She is wondering when it will be safe to walk the dog. Fudgeboy is a big guy—eighty-five pounds and counting. Thousand Flags allows only dogs under twenty pounds. Madge's daughter has left the dog while she is away at college, learning to be a nurse. Madge looks again, the sun is gone, the sidewalk darkening. She taps Fudgeboy on the shoulder. Now is the time.

Woman and dog walk slowly along the quiet pavement. Fudgeboy lifts his rear leg in decorous curves toward the trees and bushes. He sniffs a light pole and looks curiously up into the bright yellow ball. Then Mrs. Blue walks up.

"Out walking with the dog, I see, Mrs. Sands." Mrs. Blue has her hand on her hips, a "your-rent-is-due" look on her broad, plaintive face.

"Yes, it's so nice out tonight, isn't it? Not even cold yet, not even like winter." Madge stutters a little and pulls hard on the dog leash. Fudgeboy sits down on his haunches and waits.

Mrs. Blue pats Fudgeboy on the back, as if estimating his length, then she continues down the sidewalk. It is Sunday night. Mrs. Blue is checking to see if the white garbage sacks are placed properly by the curb for Monday morning pickup.

Madge Sands leans down and holds the dog close to her leg, feeling his warmth.

CLOSE OF ESCROW

Lala is stacking one dollar bills in a small pile on her kitchen table. These are not the bills you see sliding efficiently from ATM machines or lying in docile slots in the supermarket cash register. These are the crumpled dollars shoved into shirt pockets, the stretched bills yanked from the bottom of an overloaded purse. Lala presses them flat against the tabletop, one by one, rubbing them back and forth with the heel of her left hand. She has maybe twenty loose bills scattered across the table. Albert walks in the kitchen door. Lala doesn't look up.

"Now what?" Albert waits for Lala to raise her head. "Getting ready to go shopping, I guess." Albert looks at his wristwatch. Lala presses a dollar bill against the flat, hard table. "Isn't it a little late for shopping, Lalita?"

"Eight o'clock is late now, is it?" Lala still doesn't look up. She has seen enough of her husband for one day. Then, quickly, she jerks her head up. "What do you care? You're headed for La Alcachofa, anyway, am I right?" Lala and Albert look at each other for a few seconds, as if considering their options. Albert speaks first.

"So what passes with the dollar bills? Been playing poker or what?" He grins big at his own joke. Albert wears a Mexican hat, a Sahuayo from Michoacán. It has a rawhide chinstrap and a little tuft of string hanging at the back. Albert has been in Los Estados Unidos for fifteen years and he knows his way around.

"Okay, Albert, look, I got a phone call today from Francine's son—remember, I used to work for her?"

"Yeah, so?" He pauses for a moment. "Which one is that? You clean house for all the old viudas over there at Thousand Flags, don't you?" Lala gives Albert a stare, shakes her head, finally, and pats the top of the pile of dollars.

"You know, Francine is the one that got sent away to the nursing home down south."

"Yeah, yeah."

"Never mind, hombre, just go on down to the Alcachofa with your borracho buddies. I've got work to do." Lala slaps a dollar bill onto the table with a bang.

"Okay, okay, so what did he want, anyway? For you to clean his house down in Santa Cruz or what?" Albert waits for a reply, then turns and heads for the door. Lala shouts at his back.

"He's sold the place." Albert stops short. "He wants to give us all the furniture, everything in the whole house, that's all." Lala waits for Albert to turn around. He does and he looks at Lala with blank eyes. "Oh, that got your attention, did it, Alberto boy?" Lala stands up and rests her hand lightly on the top of her pile of dollar bills.

"It's a trailer, Lalita, a pinche trailer, not a house. And it's all junk, probably." But Albert does not go out the door. He stands there, watching Lala. "Okay then, so what are you doing with the dollar bills?" He walks over to Lala and they both sit down at the table. Pretty soon, all the bills are pressed into the short stack.

Lala looks at the pile and measures it with her fingers. Fifty bills, a few inches. A hundred bills would be twice that. You could hide that stack almost anywhere. Lala looks at Albert.

"We've got to get all the big stuff out in one day just before the end of the month. That's when escrow closes. He said it twice to be sure that I understood." Albert sits up a little straighter, his hand reaches out to touch the pile. He knocks off the top bill and carefully places it back on top.

Lala is standing in Hack Crow's kitchen, looking across the street at the deserted mobile home where Francine and

Stan used to live. A For Sale sign is stabbed into the not-so-green grass. The sign contains a photo of the real estate agent and her phone number. Lala has a quick picture of new people moving into the mobile home she knows so well. Their furniture is strange and their clothes look out of place. She coughs at the thought, maybe too loudly, because pretty soon she hears Hack pushing his chair behind her. She turns around.

"Mr. Hack, what are all those garbage sacks doing over there across the street? It's not even close to Monday yet." Lala holds her hand in a horizontal line over her eyes, as if she were avoiding the sun.

Hack edges his desk chair up onto the kitchen linoleum. "So what'ya want to know for, anyway?" His voice is quick and mildly excited.

"I used to work for her, remember? I liked her a lot." Lala's face suddenly gets hot and her eyes feel tight and damp.

Hack looks at Lala and pauses for a moment. "Well, they took her away didn't they? Where to, that's the question, isn't it?" He pushes his chair back a few feet onto the carpet again.

"But why all the white sacks, Mr. Hack, if nobody's living there? What's in all those sacks? So many of them." Lala's voice trails off into silence. She has been talking faster and at a higher pitch than she intended. Hack is looking puffed up and sure of himself. He always thinks he has special knowledge to contribute in cases like these.

"Junk, that's what! The son and his wife threw it all out there. I saw them." Hack raises two arms into the air like he is leading an orchestra, then lets them fall to his sides.

"How do you know it's junk?"

"I looked."

"At all the bags?"

"Maybe, maybe not." A pause. Hack is looking at Lala's face, trying to figure her out. "Some of them anyway." Hack wants to get back to his computer. Who cares about a pile of garbage sacks, anyway, when big things are about to happen all over the world?

Lala is at the stove, chopping onions, greasing a frying pan. She feels a little bit dizzy. Hack Crowe has pushed his chair back to his desk and his fat fingers are darting around the internet. He has been following the pictures coming back from the Spirit Rover as it crawls slowly across the red dust of a Martian crater. He prints all the photos out in color and hangs them on his living room wall. Then he takes a pool stick that he bought at a garage sale and points to this rock or that sand formation and mutters to himself, "I knew it, I knew it, it was just a matter of time." Lala looks at him out of the corner of her eye, then back at the kitchen window and the trailer across the street. She knows that very night she will call her sister. Something has to be done.

Lala is sitting at her kitchen table staring at a blank piece of paper. Her sister Socorro is leaning over her shoulder.

"So here is where the halls starts and this is the kitchen, okay?" Lala makes a few lines on the paper, then looks sideways at her sister.

"I can't even remember, La." Socorro shakes her head and her long black hair dances around her ears. "It's been years since I helped you clean that place."

"Mija, we need a map or we'll get lost in the dark and bump into things." Lala is the oldest of the six Montoya sisters and she feels like she is their mother most of the time.

"This is crazy, anyway, breaking into an abandoned trailer. You want to go to the carcel, La, because that's what will happen when we get caught doing this. They'll put us on the police blotter in the Sonoma News Bulletin." Socorro backs away from the table and pushes her hands out in front of her chest.

"Socorro." Lala's voice is sharp but low. "I have a key. It's not breaking in. They gave me the key, remember?"

"Sure, tell that to the cops. I can see it all now. Two Mexicans caught inside a little old lady's trailer while she's away at an old people's home waiting to die." Socorro's face is serious but the corners of her mouth are starting to turn.

"It's not funny, mija, she did die."

"Neither is searching around inside a dark trailer for a stack of dollar bills. That's not even close to funny."

"It's $10,000, not a stack of ones." Lala looks at her sister. "Who told you anything about a stack of dollar bills anyway?" Socorro smiles lightly.

"Who do you think?"

"You listen to that borracho instead of me?"

"No, no, listen. How do you know they hid the money? Did you ever see it?"

"Maybe not. But I heard them talking about it. Anyway, Franny told me about it once but her Spanish was so bad I couldn't understand it all." Lala pauses. "She wanted me to have it, you know, I could tell that's what she wanted."

"And what about your English, La? I guess it's so good you could understand them perfectly, right?"

"My English is better than you think."

"Okay then, since you know so much, where did they hide the money?" Socorro sits down hard in a chair at the end of the table. "That map of yours isn't going to help us find that pendejo dinero, is it?"

"Socorro! I never heard you talk like that before. Qué tienes?" Lala's voice sounds like it's on the rough edge of a crack. The sisters stop talking and look at each other for a moment.

"Nothing's wrong with me. It's just that... Look, okay, let's make the map if that's what you want to do," Socorro says. "You're my big sister, aren't you?"

Lala and Socorro bend over the piece of paper and add lines here, draw in furniture there, mark the bathroom doors. They even sketch in the stove and refrigerator. Then the beds. Lala takes Socorro's hand and puts the pencil on her palm.

"Okay, now mark where you think they hid it. It takes up this much space." She spreads her fingers to a span of inches. "Just this much."

"La, the son has probably found it or thrown it out by accident by now. How long has it been, six months or what?" Socorro stands on the kitchen floor with the pencil poised in her fingers like she might start to write on the walls.

"Don't say that, mija." Lala thinks of the white garbage bags she saw from Hack Crowe's window. She tucks the finished map into her purse. "Listen, don't tell anyone, okay, not a word. Especially not Alberto. He's got a big mouth." Socorro nods. They walk slowly to the front door. Socorro has her hand on the doorknob. Lala bends forward.

"Have you seen all the garbage sacks in front of that trailer lately?" Lala says. Socorro turns.

"I don't know, maybe. You know, I don't come over here that much anymore." Lala is still leaning in conspiracy toward her sister. Socorro waits a moment and rubs her forefinger behind her ear. "Well, I can't really remember." Then Socorro walks out the door.

Lala and Socorro are standing in the dark by a pile of white trash bags near the corner of International Boulevard. One of the sacks is broken open and old newspapers and assorted knickknacks have spilled into the street. An ashtray from a Reno casino, a cup with its handle broken off, a small pile of clothespins, a scattered deck of playing cards.

"It's junk, La, look at those cards, all bent and cracked. What good is this stuff? No wonder he threw it out here." Socorro leans down and picks up the Queen of Spades, holds it up in the air against the streetlight. "La Reina" she says, then sails the card out into the street.

"Socorro. Don't make a mess, okay?" Lala looks up and down the street. No cars are coming. "This stuff has been out here all week, I'll bet. Look at these sacks, all torn up and leaning over." Lala bends down and picks up the Jack of Diamonds. She looks into the shiny surface of the card and sees Francine on the back of her eyelids. She is walking to the pinochle cupboard to get another deck of cards. The card slot is narrow and thin and, from the right position, you can see scoring pads, decks of cards and something thin and flat way far in the back.

Francine had always wanted to sit at the end of the table. She used to fan the cards backwards when she shuffled. The ladies, all four of them, had kept an eye on Lala while she was cleaning the kitchen, the bathrooms, then the bedrooms. Lala could tell that they wanted her to bring food to the card table, drinks and chips probably. But they would never ask. Two of these ladies used walkers. Madge was talking about the ripe persimmons on her tree. Naomi mentioned that Safeway didn't carry persimmons. Then it was time to play pinochle.

Blanche picked up her cards. "Franny, these cards look a bit worse for wear, don't you think, kind of old and bent over." Blanche flipped a tired card out onto the center of the table. A red Jack.

Francine thumbed the cards in her hand. She gave Blanche a sour look but Blanche was looking down at her lap as if she hadn't said a word. Silence. Francine tried to shuffle the double deck but some of the cards stuck together and spat out onto the table.

"Why, yes dear, why didn't I notice? They are sort of roughed up, aren't they? I'll get some better ones." Francine stood up and started to walk around to the other side of the table.

"Hey, I can get them. No need to bother," Madge said and she reached toward a small drawer in the dining room cabinet under the big mirror.

"No, no, Madge, I'll get it. They're in a certain place." Francine bumped her hip on the end of the table as she hurried to get in front of Madge.

"But it's easier for me, dear, I know where you keep them, after all." Francine brushed Madge's arm to the side and then her wide body covered the expanse of drawers. She opened a drawer, reached inside and pulled out two brand new decks.

Lala had seen all this as she stood drying dishes at the sink. The ladies had to get rid of the small numbered cards since pinochle didn't use them. They sifted and stacked and pretty soon they had a fat pile to get rid of. They looked at Lala and so she walked over and took the extra cards.

"Would you ladies like a soda maybe?" Lala said. She stood on one leg and watched the ladies fidget.

Finally, Naomi trilled. "Oh, yes, but it's so much trouble for you."

"Not at all, not at all." Lala had said and she walked directly to the refrigerator.

Now Lala is standing by the white garbage bags, holding the Jack of Diamonds in her hand. She shakes the card at her sister.

"See this is how they spent their time, playing their silly card games." Lala starts to throw the card on the ground, then tucks it into her purse. Socorro stares at her in silence.

"Well, we can't stand here all night. What are we going to do?" Socorro whispers this in a low, irritated murmur. She kicks one of the sacks and it falls into a limp heap.

Lala sighs out loud, then walks over to the nearest, smallest sack, picks it up and looks at her sister. "I am not leaving here with an empty hand, I'll tell you that." And she marches over to the Dodge van and toss the sack in the back.

Days pass before Lala thinks about the hidden money. The theft of the garbage sack had frightened her. What if someone had seen them? What if a cop car had driven by? Of course, cops hardly ever drive through the Thousand Flags Mobile Home Retirement Village, do they? But you never know! The white sack turned out to be filled with old clothes and kitchen stuff, stained potholders, used plastic cups, decomposed sink sponges. What a ridiculous mess! But, to tell the truth, Lala had saved a few items to sell at the flea market, a perfectly good plastic spatula and a silver tea strainer. Nearly every Sunday you could find the Montoya sisters at the Petaluma flea market. They would arrive at six o'clock in the morning at the old drive-in theater on Washington Street and set up a big table under a shade canopy. By two in the afternoon they would sell almost everything they had managed to cram into the Dodge van. Then they would say to themselves, we'll just shop around for a few minutes, maybe find a real late-in-the-day bargain or two. These were fun days and profitable ones, too.

Lala keeps herself busy cleaning mobile homes, tending her invalid old ladies, cooking dinner for her old widowers. She is trying not to think about the ten grand. But she can't help imagining her three kids with new shoes for the first day of school, new jeans, new bicycles. The smell of newness is an intoxication for Lala.

She watches Armando Peréz drive the old flatbed truck through the trailer park, picking up the garbage sacks, spinning off toward the dump in a spray of gravel and cigarette smoke. Lala had thought, at first, that she might talk

to Armando about the white sacks, after all he was her
husband's cuñado, wasn't he? But, in the end, she doesn't
want to tell anything to anybody. Why give people ideas?

Lala would hear rumors, of course, people dying, mobile
homes for sale cheap, relatives snooping around. They say
that prison guy, you know the ladron that stole his father's
car, well, he's back in Soledad again. Now there's crook to
watch out for. And those kids who live here, running around
at night stealing things. But that's the way things are, Lala
would think, that's just how things are nowadays. And that
lazy son of Hack Crowe's, who would believe it? Going to
college in Berkeley! It's that sort of thing that pushes Lala
toward her decision. She's going in after the money—and
the sooner the better. The very thought of the dark
doublewide with the blinds pulled tight puffs Lala up with
excess air. Her shirt feels full and her tight pants pull at her
legs. The next morning Lala is sitting down to breakfast
when Socorro pops in the door. Lala almost shouts.

"Tomorrow night, Socorro, we're doing it Sunday night
when there's no moon." Socorro holds up her hands in mock
defense.

"What?"

"I know where it is, Mija. I figured it out." Lala waits for
her sister to ask where but Socorro hurries past the kitchen
table.

"I'm late for work, La, I just dropped by to borrow the
vacuum cleaner, okay, the one I was using at work broke
down." Socorro yanks open the closet door.

Lala pushes up from the table and stands in front of her
sister. "It's in the pinochle hole!" The sentence blows out of
Lala's mouth in a sudden gust. "Can you imagine that, the
pinochle hole?"

"Oh, really?" Socorro picks the vacuum up by the neck
and drags it around Lala to the front door. "I'll bring this

back around five, okay Sis, sorry but I'm in a big hurry, we'll talk then."

Lala swallows a slice of orange and crunches a piece of hard toast. Then she opens her purse and pulls out the map. She looks it over quickly, nodding her head, then she draws a tiny square on the paper. She makes an "x" inside the square.

Lala decides to try out her key before the big night. That would be smart, wouldn't it? What if the son has changed the locks? He's the type that might. Not that he's not a nice guy or anything, Lala thinks, remembering the phone call. He even knows some Spanish. But you never know. So Saturday night, as usual, she cooks for Hack Crowe, then about eight o'clock, just as it's getting dark, she walks down his steps and looks over at the dark trailer. Her blood jumps in her veins. Is that a light moving around inside the kitchen window? Lala looks up the street, sees a car with its headlights on, turning into a driveway. She looks back at the trailer. Just a reflection, probably. But Lala is scared again and fumbles with the keys in her pocket. There it is, the one with the triangle shape at the top, she knows how it feels even without looking.

Lala takes a breath, walks over to the dark mobile home. She stops to look at a rose bush. Francine had loved roses. During her later years, she used to come out on the porch in her walker just to water this particular bush. She would hold a large Windex bottle in one hand and shoot a steam of water at the dirt under the bush. Then she'd stand there, leaning over the front of her walker, looking at the roses. Lala touches the thorns with her thumb but is careful not to draw blood. No roses on the bush now, not enough water probably.

Lala walks up the green wheelchair ramp and pulls the screen door open. She slips the key into the lock. It turns. All right, all is good! As an afterthought, she pushes the door slightly. It moves, then stops. Of course, the chain. Now what? She could reach inside with her fingers and try to dislodge the chain. No, too obvious, that would take time. Lala pulls the door shut and pulls out the key. She sees headlights far down the street and walks quickly down the ramp. What will Socorro say about this? No, don't tell her, she'll just fuss, like always. Think! Lala opens the door to the Dodge van and climbs in.

Lala has written down an attack plan and she carries it inside her purse alongside the map. She and Socorro will enter the mobile home by the back door in the darkest hour of the night, three in the morning, probably, Sunday for sure. Lala has realized that only one door can have its security chain locked and so the back door should be no problem. They will wear soft shoes and use tiny little penlights. They will be quick and decisive. They will speak only in whispers and they will use expressive sign language. They will get the money and get out fast. At first Lala thinks that they might wear wigs or some sort of disguise but she ends up deciding that plan is too complicated, too much like the soap operas on the Spanish language channel. Nevertheless, they will be as swift as cats and nobody will see them.

But none of that ever happens because Lala can't wait. At noon on Sunday Lala sighs heavily, jumps in her van, drives over to International Boulevard, grabs a broom and a mop, steps up to the backdoor of Francine and Stan's trailer, slips in her key and opens the door. She is standing in the entry room in front of the washer and dryer. Right where she has stood so many times before, loading clothes into the washer, folding clothes from the dryer, hanging damp rags on the short clothesline stretched from wall to wall. Lala looks around quickly. Everything looks just as it has always looked. She starts to walk through the door into the hall and kitchen, then stops and turns around. She opens the dryer. Still clothes in there, a couple of towels, a pair of pants. Lala recognizes Francine's black slacks. She pulls out the pants and hold them to her nose, they still smell like Francine. She folds them neatly and sets them on top of the washer.

Lala walks out to the front room and looks out the big picture window. The real estate sign has the words "SOLD" nailed over the top half. Of course, that's what agents do to advertise. But Lala feels odd and detached seeing the word there in such bold letters. She walks down the hall into the main bedroom, then into the bathroom. Francine spent a lot of time in here, she used to play Hawaiian music and stand in front of the mirror in her Hawaiian costume. She would practice the hula moves she had learned years ago when they had a dance teacher who came to the clubhouse once a month. Lala looks at the chair under the mirror, sitting up on a plywood platform. Francine's son had built that platform so his mother could get in and out of the chair more easily. Lala looks under the sink and sees the cleanser and the washing towels. One more cleaning certainly wouldn't hurt this trailer, she thinks, just a few extra minutes, nothing more. Lala begins to wash the sink, then moves over to the toilet with its extended seat, then the shower. Nobody's been in here for months, look at all the dust.

Lala is dusting the tables out in the front room, then the television set. She can see the depressions in the lounge chair where Francine used to sit. The big dictionary with the red jacket that Stan used to look up words. Lala can remember his scale flecked face behind that book, staring at the same pages for hours. She picks up the remote and clicks on the TV, quickly pushes the "mute" button. Lala's English is pretty good, good enough to clean houses, that's for sure. But TV, that's another story, especially the news. The commentators talk too fast and use too many big words. You miss one word and the whole idea is lost. It's impossible. So she just watches the pictures flash by.

Pictures of American soldiers in Iraq, houses exploding, car bombs going off. These soldiers carry loads of equipment on their backs and walk slowly through the streets of Baghdad. Lala can see their eyes. Frightened, puzzled, almost innocent, yet aggressive. Like the soldiers she had seen years ago near the army base in Zacatecas. Mexican soldiers. Lala loves America, she loves the clean streets, the new cars, and, most of all, the water. Her hometown, La Boquita, was always dusty, always short on water. There the water ran to a faucet in the yard and you filled a bucket to make the toilet flush. In Los Estados Unidos water is everywhere, in every room, underneath the grass in straight white pipes. The grass grows green and has lines in it after you mow it with the electric mower. Lala loves the grass and the water. She turns her face away from the soldiers and clicks the remote. The television winks and dies.

Lala has not thought too much about the stack of bills hiding in the dining room cabinet. She has not walked anywhere near the pinochle cubbyhole. But, after mopping the kitchen floor and cleaning the sink, she stands in the dining room and looks at the table where the ladies played pinochle. She can almost hear their scratchy voices, their shrill cries of delight and consternation. Lala reaches out, touches the cabinet under the mirror, slides her hand over to the pinochle slot. Her fingers rest lightly on the drawer knob. Time flows slow through the midday air.

An extra large U-haul trailer is parked along the curb in front of the coach on the corner of International Boulevard and United Nations Way. This trailer has an open roof and the stacks of furniture and boxes shoot up high above the metal sidebars. The Montoya sisters swarm over the U-haul, threading ropes through the legs of chairs and the handles of suitcases. They have a number of short ropes, not a single long rope. So the pieces of rope are tied and stretched at odd, impromptu angles and the resulting web is like the creation of a mad and impulsive spider.

Lala is standing on the curb with a large oriental throw rug in her arms. The son, Dan, and his wife have just finished loading a few items into the camper shell of their pickup truck. Dan walks up to Lala.

"Well, that's about it, I guess." He looks at Lala. "I can squeeze that in for you. I see a good spot." He takes the rug from Lala's arms and shoves it in between a mattress and a dresser mirror. The wife moves her arms back and forth as if to warn Dan that he might break something.

"Thanks, that's a good fit." Lala is watching her sisters tie off the ropes. She is hoping that it all stays together when the truck gets moving fast. Dan looks at Lala in a quizzical way.

"You know what's weird. I thought I would ask you guys to clean the coach one more time. But now I don't think it needs it. After being vacant for six months you'd think there would be tons of dust and spider webs."

"Oh, we can clean it tomorrow, no problem, just give us a call Mr. Dan, probably a lot of hidden dirt you can't see." Lala rubs her hands together as if she's brushing dirt off her palms. "It's the hidden dirt that really gets into things, you know."

"It is?" Dan replies. His eyebrows wrinkle up as if he has just encountered a new and challenging idea. Lala stretches out her hand and touches an embroidered trunk. Dan's eyes follow her fingers.

"That was something my Aunt Helen gave my mom before she died." Dan's throat looks stretched and full.

"I know," Lala says, "I dropped it once when I was cleaning under it and it broke." She has tears in her eyes. Dan looks at her and touches her hand.

"Well, it's okay now, I guess." He has known Lala for over fifteen years. They have spoken Spanish together. His voice is thick. "I guess someone will use it for something." Lala and Dan stand close to each other without speaking. He is still touching her hand.

Suddenly the U-haul truck's engine fires up and the exhaust pipe starts to vibrate. A thin trail of white smoke threads a curve through Dan's and Lala's legs. Albert, Lala's husband, is driving the truck and he sticks his head out the window and waves at the people standing on the curb. "Ready?"

No one speaks for a long moment. Then, finally, Lala waves to Albert and climbs onto the back of the truck. "Someone has to watch that all this stuff doesn't fly out on the highway," she says. Socorro jumps into the cab with Albert and the other sisters pile into the Dodge van. The U-haul pulls slowly away from the curb. Lala looks at the man and woman standing on the sidewalk, then looks over at the abandoned mobile home. The silver skin of the roof flashes bright in the strong afternoon sun. The mobile home glows green and waves of visible heat seem to lift it ever so slightly up into the warm hovering air. Then Lala looks into the corner of mirror still showing around the end of the oriental rug. She sees the slight beginning of a smile.

POEMS

FALL

It's Autumn now, isn't it? I thought so.
A mellow light
A slight effervescence across the trees
A certain dust of air.
The dogs run in tight circles
The wind rushes the clouds.
No one's ready but it's time.
Put on a heavy shirt
Toss dirt into the breeze.
Rest assured. These days are passing.

12/05

PAY PHONE

They were standing by the payphone in the rain. He was opening and closing his raincoat, fingering the buttons, she was looking down at her shoes. His mouth moved silently and he looked over at the phone, then picked up the receiver and banged it up and down a couple of times. She reached up and touched his arm and he seemed to brush her hand away. "Will he call?" she said, hopefully. Her voice echoed between the concrete buildings on either side of the phone. Rain fell in torrents down the metal gutters onto the pavement around their feet. "How do I know? How do I know?" he said and kicked at something invisible in the dark. Two women and a child walked by the phone booth. The man and the woman watched the little girl run through a puddle, kicking her feet through leaves and water. "Let's get out of here," he said, "this is awful. I can't stand it." She started to open her umbrella. Then the phone rang. Loud. A noisy van drove by and the bells of the school rang five times. A light bulb flicked on in the wall under the woman's umbrella.

12/05

PAY PHONE

The sun is vacant behind urgent clouds
The black telephone hangs like a pendulum
In the rain between them
The man fingering the buttons on his raincoat
The woman squeezing her wet umbrella.
They lean toward the receiver
Which balances comfortably in its slot
Her arm caught in midair
Toward him
His mouth moving silently
Brushing her back
Between the blank buildings
The concrete gutters gushing
Past their feet
The light from a far window
A faint rim in the enveloping mist.

Suddenly two women and a child
Walk briskly by and
The little girl kicks her feet
High through leaves and puddles.
The man swings his shoe at
Something small
Invisible in the dark.
He rattles his keys.
Then the phone rings
Loud and jumping
On its hook and a fat van growls
Past as the school bell gongs five
Times tripping a bulb that burns
Dim spark under her slow umbrella spreading.

THERE'S A BOMB IN STARBUCKS

On TV the rattled cappuccino guy
bursts through the glass door into the street
a rusted flashlight held
high in his waving hand
as police close off the block
stretch yellow tape between the walls
and tie a rope to hold
the surging crowd of curious onlookers.

It seems a disheveled man has walked
blithely into Starbucks
past the startled surveillance cameras
and asked for coffee grounds
to fertilize his garden.
then he disappears like dust
dropped on a thick brown carpet.

But he has fooled no one
apparently
as a vigilant employee
sees the insurgent device crouched
explosive under the toilet rim
a bomb big enough
to kill and maim
the police will claim
he was large, this man
two hundred pounds
long hair, a black backpack
and a bad smell.

For days his grainy shape
is televised
he slouches through our living rooms
the heavy coat, the backpack
the digital number stitched
across his sleeve
the raised and rusty
flashlight flashing fear
like a lighthouse
across the restless, weary nation.

1/06

ZACH

Attacks the puddles
after rain
chasing grubs and worms
burrows under rocks
to hold a squirming
Salamander high
above his tilting chin

His brain's in love with everything
that moves
each wriggle
each twisting leg
and hairy eye reveals

A newer secret
a glimpse behind the screen
the thin green glass
that splits the light
and glints at every breath.

1/06

CAT IN THE RAIN

It's been a thousand years
But I still hear
Her skinned cry
Under the blundering murmur of rain
Calling
Over the thin grass of winter
Louder now softer
Calling as a bird would call
Circling through the trees
Softer now louder
Calling
Minick are you there?
Minick Minick
Are you here?

2/06

GERMANY 1946 (photograph by Otto Hagel)

The shattered buildings are
Staggered ligaments
Empty squares that stare
Across rubble and scattered stone.
Behind a groaning trestle
A church leans into the photograph
It is alone
In a motionless landscape.
But wait!
A boy in the foreground
Neat stockings
And a carefully balanced
Backpack trots
Down the wide granite steps
Picking his way
Over rocks and vines.
His head follows his feet
As if he sees behind the page
The scientist holding an
Incandescent filament
Up to his eyes
The exact point of ignition
The boiling point of rage
The fuel that fed
The bombs that fell
And blew apart
The pesky questions
The smug remark
The sage reply.

2/06

TWO WOMEN IN A BAR (Pablo Picasso, 1902)

The women's backs glow blue
Tilting toward the absent glass
Perched fat on the flat counter
Their heads are humped coral
Hair trailing like spilled wine
Down bare shoulders.

What tremor vibrates the unseen space
Between them?

Legs lean to one side
The corner of a careful eye tilts down
Their stools are swung
Below a pale swath of patched blue
Their arms invisible
Reaching somewhere inside the frame.

What sound clamors through
This lumped flesh?

The glass is a white mirror
Of memory
Half full of shadows
Its emptiness spills
Diamonds and pearls
A sifting of color which
Pushes up to the surface
And splashes the flat walls
With the sleepy flush of
Dream and disrepair.

2/06

SUNDAY DRAG RACE

The road out of Boulder City slides smoothly
Past the church parking lots
The holy Mercurys and Chevy coupes
Growling slowly by the Arctic Circle
And the lonely Railroad Pass
Where we comb the desert
For the missing link in a fence
Cut at midnight the week before
Just past the abandoned shack.

The race track is long
Straight like a tempting snake
Lines of joyful faces
Behind the leaning fence
Girls glistening in the hallelujah sun
We hold cans of cold Ham's
In our eager hands while
A race car roars at
The starting line
Thin motor mounted on rails
Like a mantis bending down to pray.

Then the green flag drops
The squall of tires
The billowed smoke
The wheels weaving and straightening out
And suddenly a kid is out there
Alone on the track
In front of the blinding rush
And the scene freezes
Like a still photograph in your

Grandmother's black and white album
Inevitable, fixed forever,
The smoke, the flag, the swerving
Exploding dragster
The kid
A sudden flash of blonde hair
Gone under the tires
Wheels flying like spun moons
Around a sun gone dim with dust
The air humming
The splintered voices
All screaming at once.

2/06

BLUE VELVET

The green hose shudders
Swells
Water bursts from
Rubber seams
Screams
And the camera dives
Under the lawn
The blades of grass
Tower like trees
Twigs are roaring logs
Banging up against a deep blue sky.
And beyond our ken
Pounding shadows are moving closer
Bulging mouths
Pincer arms flailing
Squirming in an old and frightened wind.

Two beetles thrashing
Huge against the lens
Desperate claws
Dragging us closer
To the end
The dissolution
The lost nucleus
The tip over the edge
of a flattened and
raging Earth.

1/99

EXPECTATION
(Night Café by Vincent Van Gogh, 1888)

People come here for the light
Scattered at reckless tables
They sip drinks
Blow smoke
Elbows planted on solid glass
The yellow floor tiles spread
Limpid conversation
Toward the door
Which waits patiently like
An old woman in a shawl
Half open
Hope is on the way.

It is ten minutes after midnight
The pool table lies flat
Its shadow eating a brown
Stain into the golden floor
Three balls crouch and
The stick is a bony finger
Pointing south
Along the fuzzy green felt.

The chairs lean forward
As if listening
A man stares
His legs gone under his knees.
The light chases itself
Nervous circles around a flame.
The junction of color
Gathers
Then pulses a wave

Of raw desire into
The long strides of the
Mouth moving night.

1/99

GUNPOWDER 1954

I walk with stiff legs
Past the boys lagging
Nickels in front of the New Drug store
The forged note a slow fuse
In my pants
Past the 45 records
The cherry coke counter
To the smiling druggist
His nose sniffling
Behind the rows of toothpaste
And denture cream.
My voice is a thin trill
As I ask for potassium nitrate
A small box please
He looks through my still raised hand
As if he can see fire burst
Like stars from my fingers
Held in the high air
Before his face.
Then he slides it round
Over the short glass
Hard cardboard in my fist
And I'm out the door swinging
Down the singing street
Two boys running hard behind me
Touching my shoes
You forgot the sulfur
You fool
Now what will we do?

1/99

LEON HEADS WEST

FATHERS GRAB YOUR DAUGHTERS
Screaming out of Tulsa
In a '57 Chevrolet
A new valve pulsing in his brain
The preacher man bellows down
Route 66 where hamburgers
Dream in the surly sun
The waitress takes a long look
Pencil in her hair
The jukebox croons a lazy tune
He eats his cherry pie
Looks deep into her careless eyes.
PLEASE
Somewhere past Kingman Arizona
The Chevy pulls up
Close to the Colorado
As if it were an A&W at midnight
Headlights curl over the water
Standing on the hood
He swings his arms
High over the world
As baby trees and reeds
Stretch tall and dance
The hairy breeze.
PLEASE
FATHERS GRAB YOUR DAUGHTERS
WIVES BEWARE
Born at the seventh minute
Of the seventh hour
Look in the sky
Touch long the flower
See when a woman's

Got the need of power
He is the one
The one they call
The seventh son.

2/99

EL PILAR
Cuba

Hemingway's boat sits safely
On wood stilts
The books in his library
Are closed and stacked
The horns of wild animals
Tilt as the tourists
Tiptoe through the rooms
Step up to the old Remington
Touch the coal black keys.

At the museum down the street
You can see a mute
Delivery truck punctured
By a hundred
Bullets
A mother leaning to touch
Each round red hole
Her daughter's hesitant hand
Hanging in the slow pointing air.

The fastest packages in Havana
The large letters say
Then you feel movement somewhere
A whistle in the breeze
Hats wave in a distant window
Footsteps drop
Pockmarks popping
In a grey white wall.

2/99

FORTY MILES OF BAD ROAD

The demon jukebox moans
Softly in Harry's New China Café
Inertia drifts like scattered parsley
Rice and gravy
French fries
A ten cent donut forked over the
Counter like a flipped coin.

It's Forty Miles of Bad Road
When loud Larry walks in
A forfeiture of rebels lagging
Black pant legs behind his
Homegrown back.
He looks at each booth
The lame duck burger
The slow suck of cherry coke.
He's come a long way
After all
Constipated with the need
To parry blows
Punch through restroom walls
His eyes a lactic prayer
For plenitude.

He cries "I want a furburger"
And throws his topless patty
Up
Palm hard above his head
It sticks
Ground meat to the spackled
Ceiling tiles
A suction of fat and fascination.

We all look up
The burger hangs
Holy over our tables
In contempt of air
A hapless hologram
Of wisdom
Hanging there.

3/99

HOMELESS

He stands fat
In the long space between the lockers
Of his old school gym
His big duffle droops shirts
And underwear onto the
Low wood bench
His arms dart
Here and there in shallow
Rapid arcs
The shower is contemplative
And hot
Soap slipping into the creases
Of his skin
Water draining away
Leaving no trace
This man can hear
The swimmers shout in the pool
Far away
Hear shoes clip hard tile
Cleats tick an old
Rhythm round the room
He will be here tomorrow
And the next day too
There is a softness in the air
A locker door swings loose
On a squeaking hinge
Voices ring and fade
His ears are flat
In a warm circle
Of noise.

3/99

PHOTOGRAPHS
San Francisco 1906

You see them in the hallways
Of public buildings
Silent along the walls:
The Palace Hotel is in flames
Skeletal as a Hollywood set
Smoke billows like fresh light
From incandescent windows
City Hall
Its dome crushed by
The weight of fire
Weighs into the rubble
Of brick and ash
The sun is a blank white
Circle at noon.

You see the dark figures in the foreground
Standing in the wide streets
Thin suits and ties
Derby hats on their heads
Feet flat on the hot earth
Two men stroll measured steps
To the lower left
Other men stand on the cobblestones
Gesturing in clumps
As if waving down the smoke
Pushing the flames away.

You see these photographs
In the lobbies of the plush hotels
And you look past the

Rich black and white where
The new thick walls are phosphorus
The pale paint shiny
And slick with
Smoldering.

3/99